I0677819

CABIN

in the

COVE

THE MADISON MCKENZIE FILES
(BOOK 4)

BEV FREEMAN

Jan-Carol
Publishing, Inc

"every story needs a book"

Cabin in the Cove
The Madison McKenzie Files
Book 4
Bev Freeman

Published October 2024
Little Creek Books
Imprint of Jan-Carol Publishing, Inc
Copyright © 2024 by Bev Freeman
Front Cover Painting: Bev Freeman

ISBN: 978-1-962561-49-5
Library of Congress Control Number: 2024947945

You may contact the publisher:
Jan-Carol Publishing, Inc
PO Box 701
Johnson City, TN 37605
publisher@jancarolpublishing.com
www.jancarolpublishing.com

In Memory of Betty Meade Clay

(Definition of the word MOM)

11-02-31 – 02-19-23

Mom, you were a natural mother.

You were the best!

DEAR READER

Some of you expressed that you missed my stories during the last three years. Well, I missed writing. However, I had a calling I could not ignore. Mom was blessed with a good, long life. She never asked for help and even resisted accepting it. Due to the effects of dementia, I was forced to take charge and became her caregiver. She finally relinquished her car keys and accepted the situation.

In November of 2022, she got the last laugh on me. I put 92 on her birthday cake. She was 91. That 92nd birthday never came. We lost the sweetest lady I ever loved on February 19, 2023.

I'm grateful for all returning readers and hope we add many more new friends to the *Madison McKenzie Files* club. Please help me spread the word: "I'm back." Thanks for waiting.

With humble appreciation,
Bev Freeman

1

Residents of Cold Creek, Tennessee gathered for breakfast at Shirley's Restaurant, watching the big screen TV.

Meanwhile, in Pennsylvania, the groundhog squinted in the light of early February. Men in tall hats and black coats announced, "Having not seen his shadow, Punxsutawney Phil predicts spring is coming early here in the East."

The restaurant erupted into cheers and applause. Ben let out a sigh of relief.

Rick Malone patted him on the back. "You escaped again this year, Ben. Everyone pays for their own breakfast," Rick said and slapped a $100 bill onto the bar next to the cash register. "Coffee is on me?"

The town's people all laughed as they filed out onto Main Street in the quaint little mountain town.

Rick, having been forced into retirement after a critical injury to his arm, was now sheriff of Cold Creek. Maddie boosted her husband's spirit, insisting she had his back as deputy. Rick expressed his objection, saying flattery did not make the job any more attractive. However, he reluctantly accepted the responsibility.

Madison McKenzie Malone, better known as Maddie, and Rick enjoyed a peaceful life for nearly three years. Accepting her role in the arrangement put Maddie in third position, as Bud is honorary Deputy Dawg. She spent most of her time at the desk in the sheriff's office across the street from the Restaurant. Seeing the smiles on faces of her neighbors and friends, she said to herself, "Right answer, Mr. Phil Groundhog."

Rick approached his wife. "Could you tell by the reaction what Ole Phil predicted?"

She leaned into his embrace. "Who could miss it?" She paused to receive a sweet kiss. "There is a message for you on the answer machine—the ranger at Rocky Fork?

"I listened to it last night."

"This one came in early this morning. Better call him." Maddie turned, walking into the office.

"No, that was late last—"

"Yes, 10:56 p.m. The second one is 6:43 a.m." Maddie stared, stone-faced.

"Remind me not to argue with you," Rick said and kissed his wife on her forehead. "I'm going to check out the complaint of vandalism. I'll be back soon. Probably won't have a good signal up there on the trails, but I'll check my messages whenever I can." He kissed her lips and said, "Bye, sweetie, I love you."

Maddie snuggled into his broad chest. "I love you, Sheriff Malone." She punctuated her statement with a seductive kiss.

"I can go in a while..." Rick couldn't pull away from the love of his life.

"Are you taking Bud?" she asked, slipping from under his grasp.

"Aw, okay, okay, I'm going," he laughed, then walked onto the patio. "I wouldn't go into the woods without my Deputy Dawg! Come on, Bud. We've got a complaint to investigate."

Maddie watched Bud take his seat next to the sheriff in the new Subaru Ascent, largest of the Subaru line. The all-wheel drive provided the accessibility necessary for offroad and winter driving conditions coming with mountainous territory of rural law enforcement. Bud settled into the soft leather interior.

Maddie walked to the passenger side of the vehicle. "You keep Rick in line, won't you, Bud?" She noticed the dog's nails didn't snag like the fabric of the last cruiser. She clicked the halter seat belt to secure Bud.

"You ready, Buddy?" Rick ruffled the hair between Bud's ears.

Bud's tongue lulled out. He stared at the windshield, giving a low, "Woof."

"You two be careful," Maddie's voice followed as her sheriff and deputy drove out of sight.

Maddie returned to her kitchen, washing a couple plates and cups from the sink. She checked to see everything was put away or turned off. She strolled to the sheriff's office, starting her day opening mail. She filed the newsworthy pieces in the records drawer and placed "personal" on the larger desk across the room. It was her habit to never open any of Rick's mail. He continued getting updates from the FBI and TBI, much of which are marked "personal." She wanted nothing to do with those. Rick recognized without even opening them which to toss and which to take seriously.

Today, one of those marked "personal" reminded her of the serious category. Even though she was the former sheriff, nosy was not in her character. She placed the oversized envelope on Rick's desk with the smaller envelopes.

The sun finally shined on the porch of Shirley's, and Maddie heard Margie call out to someone. *Must be Doc returning from his early walk.* She didn't look to see.

A couple minutes passed, and the door opened. "Hey, Maddie," Margie said, sticking her head inside the office. "You want some grits and sausage? Ben expected a big crowd for the ground hog prognostication."

"I probably should. I'll starve before Rick is back." Maddie picked up her personal phone, punched in a few numbers on the office phone, and joined Margie on the walkway.

"Leftover grits just don't taste good to me, so I don't save them," Margie said. "I know Henry's boy's hog loves the slop I send home with Henry. He says his will be the biggest one at the County Fair in Gray this year. I hope that boy wins something. He tries hard to make it each year but gets beat out by the Tilson Boys. No telling what they feed their hogs!"

"I know, it makes you wonder, doesn't it?"

They both laughed.

Margie and her husband, Ben, were the owner/operators after leasing the establishment from Maddie's parents for a year. They chose to leave the name "Shirley's Restaurant" because it had been the first business in Cold Creek and built by Shirley's grandmother, also named Shirley. The name came with a fine reputation of over more than a century of good country cooking.

Ben had told his wife, "Why mess with a good name? She started out as Shirley's, and she'll continue as Shirley's."

Some of the items on the menu changed, but basically, they still served the best biscuit and gravy breakfast in East Tennessee. Shirley's was also famous for pinto beans and a "secret recipe" cornbread for lunch and dinner. Ben added fresh seafood; only fresh was good enough, in his opinion. So, Shirley's was always packed on Thursday through Saturday. People drove from Asheville, Kingsport, Johnson City, and all around the Tri-Cities, as far away as Abingdon, Virginia, for their famous cooking.

Margie was known for her delicious cakes and pies even before they bought Shirley's. She served homemade cobblers in season, chocolate cobbler year-round, strawberry in spring when Scott's were in, peach from South Carolina in summer, along with local blueberries and blackberries, and, of course, autumn supplies a variety of apples from Coffee Ridge.

There were never any frozen vegetables served at Shirley's. Tourists from all over the country who had visited before I-26 opened continued going the necessary six miles out of their way to get a meal as they passed through East Tennessee. Word of mouth proved to be great advertisement for the restaurant and kept them busy besides the local customers. It was nothing to find a forty-five-minute wait for lunch or dinner.

Ben hoped adding additional dining space on the south side of the original structure would prove to be a good investment. He had a vision, and Henry Jacobs, a hometown resident, not only approved of the expansion, but Henry designed it from old photos of the original Shirley's, which burned in the late 1800s.

In the meantime, Ben, provided a cleared space under the old shade trees behind the restaurant on the banks of Cold Creek. He placed comfortable seating, tables, and porch swings suspended from large oak branches for guests waiting their turn to order. In fact, so many folks preferred eating picnic style that Ben added an additional waitress just for outside during those busy times.

The Jacobs brothers employed a small army of construction workers with the best reputation within three counties. Demand was high, and Ben was patient, silently hoping to be ready for Autumn Festivities.

Henry and his brother Ross's team consisted of a dozen carpenters, three stone masons, two electricians, and two plumbers. They rarely had to go out of the county for additional work. Henry did new and old hardwood floors himself. Ross, a licensed electrician, also did ceramic tile and stone masonry.

After her big breakfast, Maddie surveyed the main street. Doc waved from down the street as he entered his office. Mr. Olsen called out from the porch of his Hardware Store, "Mornin', Maddie. Where's Bud? He usually comes to meet me when I sweep."

"He's on official business with Rick," Maddie said as she pushed the door open. "I'll come and visit in his place in a few minutes."

She ducked inside to answer the phone.

"No, I'm sorry, the sheriff is out on a call. Can I take a message for him?" She looked at the CID. "Blocked. Hmm, and they hung up."

She noted the time, 8:42 a.m., then replaced the phone on its cradle.

Meanwhile, Rick rode with a ranger on his ATV to the vandalism of signs. Bud preferred to run ahead of them on the trail, sometimes following a scent up the hillside or down to the creek always, keeping the vehicle in sight. This was the fun part of official business for the honorary deputy.

"There's the first one we found," Ranger Scott laughed. "As you can see, not a good family friendly addition to the bear. We do get a lot of kids up here with their parents, you know."

Rick slid off the seat. Pulling his cell phone out, he photographed the graffiti. "Do you need to take the sign off to fix it?"

"Luckily, they used water-based paint," Scott said. "Ray already checked, and it will come off with a little elbow grease."

"Good, have him get at it. I'll photograph them all. Graffiti has a real signature to it. I'll run it through files and see if we get any matches elsewhere." Rick loaded back onto the ATV. "You had enough running yet, Bud?" He slapped the side of his leg to summon his deputy.

Bud responded by running ahead of them up the trail.

Ranger Scott drove after Bud when he turned left and crossed a shallow place in the creek. They raced up to the fork where two creeks came together. Bud waited for a signal from the ranger. The ATV forded the creek on the left side, so Bud followed. In only a few yards, they stopped, getting out to examine the bear sign.

Rick laughed aloud while trying to photograph the comical depiction of a momma bear feeding two cubs. "I gotta hand it to this guy," Rick said, "he's a good artist."

The men and their scout dog had to backtrack to White Cliffs Trail. Bud disappeared up the snake-like switchbacks, panting to cool down when they reached the top of the ridge. Rick reached for a pack behind his seat. He poured water into a collapsible bowl and offered it to Bud.

"You ready for the rough part of the trail now?" Ranger Scott asked, drinking from his water bottle. "We get ticks in these high weeds; you might want Bud to ride on your lap from here on."

"Up, Bud," Rick said.

Bud jumped up onto his lap with no backtalk. The threesome covered the remainder of the signs and returned to the parking lot just after noon.

"I'll get on this as soon as I get back to town," Rick said, opening the door for Bud. "Call me if you don't hear from me in a couple days, will you?"

He waved to Ranger Scott and drove out the gravel lot and onto the paved road.

Back at the sheriff's office, Rick and Maddie laughed at the humor the artist portrayed in their graffiti.

"I might know who did this," Maddie said. "Once, when I spoke to the middle school classes, I noticed some unique art on the walls of some of the rooms. The teacher said she wished there was more art available to the children. The young lady who'd painted the pictures is very talented but is from a broken home and received no encouragement except at school. She stayed in trouble more than most girls her age." Maddie tilted her head and studied the pictures. "I'd like to take these to Miss Powers to look at. Are you okay with that?"

"Sure," Rick said. "If we can figure out the culprit without running them through TBI, we might be able to help her, instead of punishing her." Rick placed his hand on his wife's shoulder. "I love the way you always want to approach youngsters differently than adult criminals. Like Holly's adopted boys. Where would their lives be, had you not intervened?"

"Come on, Rick. Just look where I came from. A kind TBI agent pulled me up by my boot strings and helped me look at life differently. If I can pass your approach on, who knows what benefit could take hold?" Maddie leaned in and kissed her Mentor. "I love you so much, Rick Malone."

"You are way kinder than me. As I recall, you didn't take my advice often."

"I just made you think it was my own idea, the way to handle my aunt," Maddie smiled. "But it was actually yours."

2

Early the next morning, Maddie drove to Temple Hill Middle School. Stopping by the office, she asked directions to Ms. Powers's class. Ms. Powers was observing students involved in testing. TCAPs were being administered to a class. Ms. Powers stepped out into the hall so they could whisper and not disturb the kids.

"Aw, yes, this does look like Brooklyn's drawings," the teacher said, shaking her head slowly. "She's evolved on her own. Why would she do such a thing?"

"Attention? Maybe? Her art might be her only outreach," Maddie suggested. "Do you know where she goes to school now?"

"She should be in high school, in Erwin, I'd guess. If she's in school at all. She's sixteen now. I haven't heard anything of her whereabouts or situation, except that her mom was in prison for distribution of a controlled substance."

"Ms. Powers, will you call me if you hear anything about her?" Maddie asked and handed her one of her cards.

"Please, call me Marcie," the teacher said. "Sure, I'll even ask some of her other teachers to see what they might know."

"Great. I'd like to talk to her as soon as I can."

Maddie drove to Erwin. If Brooklyn was in school, she hoped to talk to her before Rick got deeper involved.

The lady in the office, Jennifer, told her that Brooklyn was not in class today. She'd been given OSD—out of school detention—for her involvement in vandalizing the cafeteria wall.

"She's so talented, but she doesn't put her gift to the right application," Jennifer said.

"I know," Maddie said. "Too bad. God-given talent needs guidance. I hope to head her in the right direction before it's too late." Maddie smiled as Jennifer handed her the home phone number and address where she might locate Brooklyn. "Thank you, I'll be in touch."

Maddie programmed the address into her Garmin. It looked to be only a mile or two toward Unicoi. She drove out the old highway to Fishery Park, where she took Lockwood Drive, angling off to the right and straight up a hill. On top, she saw Blankenship Circle, where the Garmin told her to turn right. Finally, she saw Ridgecrest Drive on the right. She turned again, feeling like she must be nearly on top of the mountain. Sure enough, one more curve and she could see I-26 across the valley. The only higher elevation was where the Fire Tower stood on the opposite mountain. She'd not been on these roads before.

Maddie spotted house number 332 and turned onto the concrete drive. There were no other cars, but the garage door was closed; there could be one in there.

Maddie walked to the door and rang a doorbell. She heard a lovely melody chime in the house. The door opened in a couple minutes, and she looked at a stringy-haired teenager wearing a sloppy T-shirt and a pair of yoga pants.

"Hi, are you Brooklyn Mills? I'm Madison Malone." She shoved her hand toward the teen.

"Yeah, I'm Brooklyn," the girl said, a hesitant hand moving forward. "I'm on detention from school; I'm not skipping," she quickly added.

"I spoke with Ms. Jennifer at the high school, and she told me where to find you." Maddie leaned to look past her. "Is your mom home?"

"No."

"I'd like to talk to you. This is a wondrous view. Can we sit out here?" Maddie walked toward a porch swing and sat.

Brooklyn followed, sitting in a rocking chair.

"Oh, please sit here, I have something to show you on my phone."

The cautious teen stood but didn't move toward Maddie. "Am I in trouble?"

"Should you be?" Maddie waited for a moment, but there was no answer, so she continued, "I need you to identify some photos."

Brooklyn walked closer and finally sat, sliding as far from Maddie as possible. "What photos?"

"Do you recognize this artwork?" Maddie turned her phone screen to face Brooklyn.

"Artwork? That's graffiti," the girl chuckled.

"It's very good art, in a graffiti display." Maddie turned to look her in the eyes. "So, you do recognize this?"

Brooklyn nodded slightly.

"Why would someone do that to the signs viewed by families with young children?"

Brooklyn shrugged her shoulders.

"Brooklyn, I think you have wonderful potential as an artist. Why are you throwing away your talent on something that can send you to jail?" Maddie's forehead formed a deep crease between her brawls. "At least you used water-based paint; that's easily washed off. Trouble is, I feel like you need to be the one to wash them. What do you think? You're out of school. Can you reach your mother by phone?"

Brooklyn took in a deep breath. "No, she doesn't like me to call her at work. I'll go and clean the signs. Can you drive me up there?"

"What if my husband calls your mom? He's the sheriff, you know?"

"She won't care if I go. I just cannot call her." Brooklyn stood up. "Let me put some different clothes on. You wanna come in the house?"

"Sure." Maddie got up and followed the teen into the house.

While Maddie waited, she snooped around the kitchen. There was very little food in the fridge. The cabinets were sparse as well. She noticed a door going toward where the garage should be, so she opened it to look. No car. She returned to the living room, looking at photos on the fireplace mantel. In all the family shots, Brooklyn was much younger. The adults appeared to be her folks, and no other people.

"Do you have any brothers or sisters?" Maddie called out.

"No, just Mom and me," Brooklyn answered as she walked in from the bedroom.

"And your dad?"

"He, um, he died in a construction accident when we lived in Alabama." Brooklyn looked at the photo on the mantel. "He was my world; I miss him something awful."

"How long has he been gone?"

"Ten years." Brooklyn walked to the front door. "I'm ready."

"Don't you want to leave a note for your mom? What time does she get home?"

"Late. I'll be back before she comes in."

Maddie didn't ask a lot of questions on the way up to Rocky Fork. She hoped Brooklyn might start talking. She didn't.

By the time they reached the parking lot, Ranger Scott was waiting with a four-wheeler to take Brooklyn around to all the signs.

"Scott, this is Brooklyn. She wants to wash the signs she defaced. If you can call me when she's done, I'll come for her. Okay?"

"Sure, deputy, I'll be glad to," Scott said. "I've got all the supplies. Ray got a few of them yesterday, but he cut his hand pretty bad, so I was glad to hear that you were bringing Brooklyn to finish the job. It will be a couple hours or more."

Maddie drove back to the office finding Rick sweating and covered in smudges of black smoke. "Rick, what's happened?"

"I'm glad you're back," he said. "I need to clean up and change. You stick by the phone..."

"What are you not telling me?" Maddie grabbed his arm. "Tell me!"

"Honey, Jess and Shirley's house burned this morning, right after you left. They were not in it, but I don't know where they are. It's obviously arson. Erwin FD is still investigating. There's a clear trail from an accelerant leading from the front and back doors."

"And you're sure they got out?" Maddie's voice edged on hysteria.

"Yes!" Rick pulled her into his arms. "I'm anticipating a call. Doc says he saw a truck in front of their house before daylight, and he's sure Jess was helping Shirley get into the back seat."

"Oh, no, but who, why? I don't understand." Maddie dropped into the swivel chair in front of the large oak desk. "You still are not telling me all you know."

"Yes, I am," Rick said. "But think about this—your folks are my in-laws. It must have something to do with me. Me and the TBI." Rick walked to the door. "The recorder is on; if you get a call, keep them on the line if you can. Fake hysteria, whatever it takes to keep them on that line."

"Fake? I won't need to fake anything!" Maddie's tears burst like a dam. "Who could do this?"

Rick didn't say anything. He just shook his head and left the building. Bud followed him.

"No, Bud, stay with Maddie."

The dog sat on the wooden sidewalk, which ran across the front of the sheriff's office. He whined, watching Rick walk toward the cottage.

"Come here, Bud," Maddie called. "I need your strength." She gave the dog a long hug. "Maybe you can help. You can sniff around the property—"

The phone rang. Maddie's gut wrenched.

"Hello?" she said slowly.

"Hey, Maddie. What's going on? Henry said Jess's house burned." It was Holly's voice, high-pitched and shaky.

"I can't talk right now and tie up this line. Let me call you back on my cell. Okay?"

"Yeah, sure, but right away, while little Mattie is sleeping," Holly said.

Holly answered on the first ring. "Sorry, I just wish I could come to you, but Mattie is teething, and it's so hard to get her to sleep. I've rubbed Orajel on her gums, but it's not helping."

"Oh, don't use that," Maddie said. "Not even baby Orajel; it burns the tissue. Freeze her pacifier or feed her popsicles, but stay away from the meds. They only make the situation worse!"

Maddie's years dental assisting with her Aunt Denny taught her plenty about the oral world of soft tissue.

"Gee, I wish I had known. Poor baby. I made her worse."

"Give her baby aspirin or what your pediatrician recommends, and she'll be fine," Maddie said. For just a moment, little Mattie took her mind off the tragedy in her own life.

"So, what's going on?" Holly insisted.

"My folks' house was set on fire, completely destroyed, and they are missing, no bodies in the ruble. Doc saw them getting into a truck early this morning as he was doing his run." Maddie drew in a long breath, blowing it out slowly. "Rick went to our house to shower, and I'm minding the phone. Someone will surely call. For whatever reason, he thinks this is because of his connection to the TBI."

"Oh, no. I'm so sorry," Holly said. Her voice felt soothing to Maddie. "I wish I could help."

"You can, Holly. Do what you do best—pray!"

Maddie was quiet for a while, and then she said, "Hold your baby girl and hug her for me. I'd love to do it myself to comfort her with a banana popsicle. But I can't." Her tears returned, and her voice revealed her pain.

"I will, honey, don't worry, and thanks for the suggestion. I am going right now and making some mini popsicles! I saw a recipe on Pinterest. Oh, thank you so much, Maddie. Please try not to worry. Rick will fix this. He always does!"

"I know, but I'm still worrying. You've helped me feel better. Let me know how little Mattie is, will you?"

"Sure," Holly said as she ended the call.

Madison walked the floor in front of the large oak deck. She thought of the years when she was young and didn't have adult-size worries. Or had she? As she paced back and forth, she recalled the time she'd been brought to this office after running away from Shirley and the restaurant. Mr. Olsen caught her hiding behind the feed sacks in his hardware. He'd brought her in to see Ole Sheriff Franks, saying that she was a wanted criminal.

The sheriff threatened to lock her in his cell if she ever ran away again. Maddie remembered how terrified she felt thinking the sheriff was serious. She'd hugged Mr. Olsen's legs, hiding behind him. He lifted her into his arms and carried her across the street to her waiting mother.

Shirley took her from Mr. Olsen and kissed her. "What were you planning on doing, honey?" she had asked.

"I don't know. But I'll never run away again." And she hugged the chubby woman that raised her.

In those days, she knew Shirley as her mom, but later, on her sixth birthday, doubt edged into her young brain thanks to her Aunt Denny. All she remembered of the runaway was that she felt close to Mr. Olsen. He was the only grandparent figure she had. But he was not her blood kin...

"Humph, neither was anyone else, except Jess," Maddie said. She felt her tightened gut return.

Bud jumped to his feet, and she heard Rick's heavy footfalls on the wood sidewalk.

"Nothing?" he asked, as he wrapped his strong arms around his trembling wife.

She shook her head and buried it in his neck. They stood silent for a long while, and then she pulled away, saying, "I'm going to see the house." Her voice cracked.

"Okay," Rick said, "but do not touch a thing! Nothing! You hear?"

"Of course," Maddie said. She smacked a quick kiss on his lips and rushed out the door, followed by four quick legs and the tapping of his toenails on the wood floor.

3

Several Volunteer Firemen huddled around the steps of what was left of the back porch at the property. Tim Smith looked up as Maddie neared.

"Hello, Maddie," he said. "Have you heard anything from your folks?"

"No," she shook her head, looking around in disbelief.

Tim stepped away from the other firemen. "Chief says there are no human remains, and I'm sure he's right. He knows his job." A former schoolmate of Maddie's, Tim removed his cap and ran smutted fingers through yellow hair. "The Arsines were careless, left evidence everywhere. They wanted to send a message to someone. I'm guessing that would be your husband."

Maddie looked into concerned blue eyes. She remembered Tim was always a nice boy in high school, and they were close during her senior year. Secretly, she'd wanted him to be her boyfriend but felt she'd never have a chance against the more popular girls. Everyone liked him. Maddie counted herself lucky to be Tim's friend.

"Well?" His voice snapped her into the present.

"What?" she said, staring blankly at him.

"Rick? What does he think about the crime?" Tim's perfectly aligned smile boasted whiter than ever with suet clouding his face.

"Oh, he's pretty sure it has something to do with his former employment with TBI," Maddie said. She felt her face burn. "I just want to know that Jess and Shirley are okay. You know?"

"Of course, we all do."

She turned toward the gravel drive. "Maybe I can find some tire prints from the truck."

"I doubt it. We had a half dozen vehicles running all over this property." Tim walked across the drive. "I did notice one thing. I nearly forgot about it." He bent at his waist to pick up something. "It's an earring."

Maddie crossed the drive and reached for the golden object. "That's Shirley's," she said. "I gave her this set of hoops on Mothers' Day last year." She was surprised. "Shirley would never let these out of her sight!" She turned her attention to the grassy edge of the drive. "Looks like a different print from those over there. This is a smaller tire print coming out of the grass. Look! The larger prints ran over it in that direction." Maddie pointed away from the scene.

Tim walked in the direction she pointed. "I see more of that same track," he said. "It's smaller than the units we use. But there were also police cruisers on scene." He shook his head just slightly. "It's worth following up on, I'd bet. And I know one very determined officer of the law that is motivated to do just that."

"Yeah, *me*," Maddie said and turned, sprinting back toward the sheriff's office. "Thanks, Tim!" she called over her shoulder. "Come on, Bud!"

Rick jumped to his feet when Maddie burst through the front door.

"We found her earring!" Maddie breathed hard.

"She probably dropped it when they took them," Rick said.

"No. If it fell off, it would not have been latched. See, it has a tight catch. She had to refasten it on purpose and then dropped it." Maddie stretched her arm out, showing Rick the clasp. "She never took them off. Said they were comfortable enough to sleep in, and she'd never remove them."

"Alright, but we know they were taken," Rick said. "She's leaving you a bread crumb. But where is the next one?" Rick pulled Maddie into his arms.

"Tire prints! We need to check them." She pulled her phone from her pocket and showed him the pictures she'd taken. "It's worth a look."

"There were so many vehicles there, honey."

"So, we can rule those out," Maddie said. "This might be the very one they were taken away in."

"I'll go and make a cast." Rick grabbed a plaster kit. "I changed the message so they can call my cell number."

"Rick, you've never given out your cell phone number."

"This is important. I had no choice."

Maddie followed him outside just as Ranger Scott pulled up. He and Brooklyn got out.

"Scott, I'm sorry I missed your text," Maddie said. "It's crazy here." Maddie's voice reflected her nerves.

"No problem, Maddie. I heard what happened. Anything I can do?" Scott offered.

"We're not even sure what we can do at this time," Rick said, getting onto his vehicle.

"Then I'll await your call. Don't forget, I am also a qualified police officer and was a sharpshooter in the military." He winked at Maddie, "If you need me—"

"Thanks, I remember," Maddie said and turned to Brooklyn. "Now, let's get you something to eat."

She turned to go and motioned for the teen to follow. They entered Shirley's and were met by Margie.

"I'm sorry, Maddie," Margie said. "Once again, your life is in turmoil."

"Thank you. Nothing new for me, huh?"

"How can I help?" Margie propped both hands on her hips.

"Feed this young lady, and put it on my bill?" Maddie said and turned to go. "Stay here till I get back, Brooklyn."

Brooklyn only nodded.

Maddie returned to the sheriff's office to wait for Rick. She heard a click on the desk phone. She gave Rick time to pick up and then lifted the receiver to listen.

Maddie didn't recognize the voice, but from Rick's tone, she knew he did. And it wasn't a pleasant memory. She listened silently, praying, hoping for a sign of life. Rick didn't ask questions. He responded as needed and then hung up the call. She touched the button, returning the receiver to its cradle. Batting away tears, she turned to see Rick coming through the door.

"You heard?" He set the plaster cast on the desk. "Not much need for this now."

"You know him. Who is it? And why?" Maddie's anger began overriding her tears. She swallowed hard, staring at the man she loved so desperately. "Why, Rick?"

"It was a long time ago. You don't need to know the details. The less you know, the better off you are." He didn't look at her. He was shaken, nervous to the core. Whatever Rick knew about that man was deep and dark.

She backed away as though she feared what her husband might be involved in. Bud lay on the outside part of the doorstep. She turned to step over him. He raised his head, looked at Rick, and chose to follow Maddie back to the house.

Maddie remembered Brooklyn was still at the restaurant. She put Bud inside and walked across the street. Brooklyn sat alone, picking at a plate of food.

"Did you enjoy someone else's cooking for a change?" Maddie asked, pulling out the chair across from Brooklyn. "Margie serves delicious home-made desert. Want one?"

"I can't finish this," Brooklyn said. She looked at Maddie.

"You can take it in a to-go box. Might taste good for lunch tomorrow." Maddie picked up a dessert menu. "My favorite is her chocolate-caramel cheesecake. I think I'll order one." She handed the menu to Brooklyn.

Margie joined them at the small table, pulling a chair from the larger one next to them. "You haven't had a thing to eat, Maddie. What are you doing?"

"We're ordering dessert and a to-go box for Brooklyn's half-eaten meal," Maddie said. She stared at Margie with a "don't bother me" attitude. "Besides, I ate breakfast. Isn't that enough?"

She felt bad that she'd snapped at Margie. Her last words might smooth that over.

"And what would you like, honey?" Margie asked, smiling at the teen.

"Lemon pie?" Brooklyn spoke softly.

"Coming right up." Margie gave Madison a sideways glance. "You want coffee with that cheesecake?"

"No thanks, Margie." Maddie looked out the window, noticing Rick walking toward the restaurant. "Rick might want something substantial to eat."

Rick swung one long leg over the chair Margie left, next to the small table. "What's good today?" he asked, looking toward Brooklyn.

"Everything?" Brooklyn said, grinning.

"Then that's what I'll have." He looked carefully at Madison. "You are eating, right?"

"Yes." She kept her face toward the window.

"Brooklyn, I'm proud of you for owning up to your error. After we eat, Maddie and I will drive you home. Okay?" Rick tilted his head toward Brooklyn. "In the future, when you feel the urge to strike out at the world, come talk to me. We can find a more constructive way to do it."

Brooklyn looked at him long and hard but then said, "Yeah, right." She put her hand on Madison's and asked, "Where's the ladies room?"

Madison pointed toward the sign hanging above the swinging kitchen doors. "Through the doors and to your right."

Brooklyn excused herself and walked toward the restroom.

Margie brought the deserts to the table, setting them down with a glass of water for Madison. "You want the special, Rick?"

"Is that all you're eating, Maddie? You'll make yourself sick." Rick looked at Margie for help. "Yes, Margie, bring two specials."

"Just put it in a to-go box," Maddie said. "I need to drive Brooklyn home." Madison looked into sympathetic eyes of her longtime friend. "Understand, Margie?"

"Sure, Madison." Margie turned away, disappearing into the kitchen.

Brooklyn returned, sat down, and slowly ate her lemon pie. Madison watched her. It was as though the girl was savoring every bite, every morsel.

"I checked on your mom, Brooklyn. She's still in jail in Jonesborough. You aren't eighteen yet. Who's watching out for you?"

"I don't need no watching out," she said. "I'm a grownup now. I can stay by myself. And you can't do nothing about it." She stabbed the fork into the pie and attacked the last bite.

"Okay, but how do you get by? No money...Who is paying the bills?" Madison leaned in closely so as not to be heard by anyone else.

"Everything is paid for," Brooklyn said. "I mean, except the monthly bills, and I pay them. I don't eat a lot. I can manage a couple more months. She'll be out in October. Please, trust me. I can do it."

"So, everything is paid off?" Madison looked at Rick, "That's what your mom did with the money?"

"Yes, and she went to jail. She's paid her dues." Brooklyn's eyes watered, and she looked down at her lap. "Please, Ms. Maddie."

Rick spoke up, "It isn't really up to us, Brooklyn. It's up to the law."

"You are the Law." Brooklyn stood up, knocking her chair over with a loud bang.

Rick stood up, set the chair upright, and said, "Sit down, young lady."

Brooklyn sat, hands in her lap, eyes trained down at the empty pie saucer. "I'm sorry."

"That's better," Rick said, sitting as Margie delivered his meal and set two to-go orders on the table.

Rick ate like he was half-starved. Maddie had only a couple bites of her cheesecake. Brooklyn sat patiently, looking out the window and waiting. There was no conversation until she asked Maddie, "Are you going to throw away the rest of your desert?"

"You want to taste it?" She picked up a clean spoon and offered a bite to Brooklyn.

Brooklyn leaned forward, opening her mouth. "That really is good." She laughed, "I've never tasted cheesecake. I had no idea..."

They all three laughed together. "Finish it up, and we'll get out of here," Rick said. As they walked to the house to get Bud, Rick added, "Stick with us, kid, and you'll learn all kinds of new things. Some you might even like." He playfully nudged her shoulder.

Brooklyn laughed, "My daddy used to do that." She punched Rick on the shoulder. "You remind me of him."

The ride down the mountain was quiet. Brooklyn picked up her left-over food and walked toward the back of the house. Rick and Maddie sat there for a few minutes, assuring she got in the back door safely. Brooklyn waved from the open curtain in the living room.

Driving back to Cold Creek gave Maddie a feeling of dread. She finally asked Rick what he planned to do. He didn't answer immediately, but finally said, "I guess you did not hear the beginning of the conversation with Buck."

"No, I didn't pick up immediately. What else did he say?" Maddie felt her nerves returning. Her heart pounded hard in her chest.

"I have to go with him, and he'll release you folks."

"When?"

"Tonight."

"No, you aren't going anywhere near that mad man!" Maddie pounded her fist on her knee. "Absolutely not! When it comes time for the exchange, you'll just have to outsmart him."

"I can't do that, or he'll kill them," Rick said. "He's a serious bad dude!"

"So am I, and you aren't going anywhere with him!" Maddie said, trying to swallow a well of tears. "Call Ranger Scott. He can help. He's a sharp-shooter!"

"Thought about that, but I've seen what Buck can do and has done in the past. I can't outsmart him. He's pure evil!"

"Rick, I'm just saying, what can you do after he takes you?" Maddie asked, turning in the seat. Her hands clinched in desperation.

Rick stomped the brake, sliding the vehicle to a stop in the center of the highway. Bud flew into the floorboard of the backseat. Madison shrieked, "What are you doing?"

Rick put the car in park and grabbed hold of Maddie by the shoulders, yelling, "I don't need this! I need your support. I need Madison McKenzie right now! The strong woman who followed a serial killer to Alaska, who singlehandedly overcame injuries in a plane crash high upon a snowy mountain, faced down a grizzly, and watched her only known blood kin have her head knocked off her shoulders, and she didn't even flinch! I need Madison, who faced an escaped prisoner and a crooked sheriff in the rugged mountain terrain of Rocky Fork, slithering into a cave to pursue him. The brave woman who joined me on the trek of the Appalachian Trail, talked to the dead, and was responsible for tracking down the Trail Killer. I need that Madison McKenzie! Maddie Malone has turned soft. I want the old Madison back. She can help me figure this out!"

Cars began driving around the sheriff's vehicle, still sitting in the middle of the road. One man stopped to ask if they needed help.

"Thanks, man," Rick told him. "I believe I got this one under control." He released his hold on Maddie.

Madison settled back into the seat, and she sat straight, staring out the front windshield. She took a deep breath and said, "Okay. I'll get in touch with her. Now, get us out of the middle of the road before we cause an accident. Would you, please?"

4

Back in Cold Creek, the sun dropped below the trees. It would soon be dark. Rick drove alone to the River Bend, where Jess and his friend used to fish—straight up the rocky outcroppings of Bald Mountain, where the creek emptied out from the cave and surfaced before tumbling down to join the River. Out of sight from the road, a single rifle scope trained on the vehicles below. Maddie lay belly down on a grassy spot with night vision binoculars waiting for what transpired.

Scott whispered to her, "Notice the river, right next to the bridge. There appears to be two people floating in the water."

She raised the binoculars, looking at the water. "Looks like Jess and Shirley, but I believe its two mannequins dressed like them. They are too stiff and bobbing. Maybe blow-ups. But definitely not real live people." She got a hitch in her breath. "He wants Rick to think they're real."

Rick then stepped from the patrol car, walking toward a tall, thin man with a .357 in his hand. Maddie watched carefully for his every movement. The windows of the truck were tinted dark, not allowing a view inside. A second car pulled in behind Rick. Two rough looking men got out and followed his steps toward the man with the gun. There did not appear to be anyone else in the car. Maddie could not make out any conversation. Time slowed with Maddie's breathing. She could tell by raised voices they were arguing.

The man with the gun fired one shot off into the water. That's when Rick noticed the floating bodies. He lunged at the gun, but one of the men whacked him on the head from behind before he reached the man Maddie assumed was Buck. Rick dropped to his knees, but he wasn't out. He attempted to stand, but the man behind him stuck the gun in Rick's back.

Louder yelling began. The second man behind Rick fired two shots, and the bodies sunk. Rick collapsed forward. Both men grabbed him, one under each arm pulling him toward the black truck. They dumped him into the back seat, tied his hands and feet, and slammed the door. The tall man, presumably Buck, walked to the driver's side and drove away. The other two men followed momentarily in their car.

"I couldn't get a clean shot," Scott said, sitting up quickly. "We have to follow them." He ran down the steep hillside with Madison on his heels. They jumped into the patrol car and gave chase. But they were not able to catch up. When they reached I-26, there was no sign in either direction, east or west, to see which way they'd gone.

"I got the tag number of the truck," Maddie said. "I'll call it in to the North Carolina and Virginia State Troopers to be on alert. I have a good photo of the other car as well." Madison made a third call to the Washington County, Unicoi County, and Sullivan County patrols too. She sent photos to TBI in Knoxville as well as VA, NC, and KY. There was no telling which way they headed.

Reluctantly, Madison turned around and drove Scott back to his car in Cold Creek. "Nothing we can do now but wait."

When they stopped in front of the sheriff's office, Jess and Shirley stood on the sidewalk. Multiple townspeople gathered around, talking excitedly to them. Madison ran to hug her folks.

After several minutes, someone asked where Bud was. Then, Mr. Olsen opened the patrol car door to let him out. "Poor fellow, I believe they forgot about you."

Bud ran straight to Jess and Shirley.

"Well, you have a place to stay," Madison said. "And thanks to the box of old clothes you told me to donate to the Church Bazar, which I never did, you even have clothes to wear at my house."

The crowd dispersed and Maddie, Jess and Shirley, Henry, and Scott all went to Madison's house when it got too dark to see outside.

TBI officers showed up, along with a couple of Washington County police officers. Madison put on a pot of coffee. She knew it was going to be a long night.

Reports came in over scanners till after midnight. All leads fell through. How could two or even one vehicle just vanish? At least they had the tag number of the truck. But it wasn't spotted on I-26 or I-81 either.

"Rick said he couldn't outsmart this guy. He might be right," Madison slurred her words so badly that Jess told her to go to bed. He'd wake her if anything transpired.

Scott left about 11:00, and Henry walked out with him. Mr. Olsen soon followed. Maddie told her folks to take her bedroom, and she'd sleep downstairs, although she knew sleep was far from her abilities right now.

The TBI agent, Samuel Land, said he was used to the night shift. He'd stay at the helm and mind any calls or message that came in. Everyone else dispersed, leaving Maddie and Bud sitting in the bedroom of the cottage.

"Just like old times, huh, Bud? We haven't done this in about three years."

Bud curled up on the braided rug in front of Maddie's bed. It wasn't long till Maddie was all alone. Rick's words kept reverberating in her mind: "I need the old Madison McKenzie to help me figure this out."

She lay her head on his pillow, which she'd removed from their bed upstairs. His words pounded in her memory, all the brave things she'd done before they married. Had she really gotten so soft and complacent? Maybe outwardly, but inside, she was still Madison McKenzie, strong and determined to get her man. The words to a song she loved came to her lips.

"No matter where you go, I will find you," she kept singing over and over. "I will find you. I WILL FIND YOU!"

Bud woke Madison, whining to go outside. She sat up, shaking her head as though to wake from a bad dream. She looked at the bed she was in. Not a dream; this was a reality. She was in her old room. Her hand still wore the wedding band Rick had placed there on the happiest day of her life. Reality hurt. Her husband was gone.

She wore the same clothes she'd fallen asleep in, including her shoes. Hurriedly, she ran a brush through her hair and stepped into the living room of her cottage. Voices from upstairs drew her attention. She opened the front door to allow Bud his morning run. She climbed the stairs to the new section of the house she and Rick built.

Several TBI agents sat in a circular pattern around the coffee table. Some in chairs, some on their knees. All stared at a map of the tristate area. Their eyes fell on her when she entered the room.

"Anything?" she asked.

"Nothing, Madison," an older man in a dark blue suit said. He stood. "I'm Mel Frost, director of the Knox County Division of TBI." He extended his hand.

She stared at the hand as though she didn't understand. "Where's Jack? Why isn't he the director anymore?"

"Jack retired last year. I'm his replacement. I've heard lots about you, Madison. And I worked with Rick in his FBI years in D.C. Fine fellow. We're doing everything we can to locate him." Frost sat back down without a handshake and continued, "This 'Buck' fellow, as Rick called him…Would you recognize him from a photo?"

"Yes," Madison answered quickly.

A younger agent, looking to maybe be in her mid-twenties, stepped forward. On the tablet screen were mug shots of a rough-skinned man, dark hair and darker eyes. Madison looked at the young lady and nodded her head.

"That's Buck, only much older now. Who is he?" Maddie directed her question to Frost.

"He is trouble," Frost replied. "Ruthless, calculating, and meaner than the Devil himself." Frost stood and looked out the front window. "I've been after him for some time. Don't know why he'd go after Malone at this particular time, unless he feels we have him cornered."

"After him for what exactly?" Madison McKenzie stood tall and strong. The question came from her training. "You need to tell me everything, if you expect to find him. Rick and I could have done this alone had he not threatened my parents and burned their house. So, I have to know what you know!"

"This is a need-to-know basis—" Frost started to say.

"Don't give me that bullshit. You know nothing about me. You don't even know Rick, not the Rick I know. And how I got to know him was in the field, under fire. We went through Hell together. So don't stonewall me. I'll find him without you, so you better stay out of my way. And get out of my house. You can set up your pow wow in the sheriff's office."

She threw a set of keys onto the coffee table. Briskly, she trotted downstairs. She and Bud walked to the restaurant across the street. Margie met her at the front door.

"Any news, Maddie?"

"No, except that I have a room full of idiots in my house, and I just told them to get out. They pay for any food they get from you too, understand?"

"Sure. Speaking of food..." Margie smiled, looking very concerned at Madison. "Why don't you sit with your folks, and I'll bring you something to eat. You can't function on an empty stomach."

Maddie nodded and went to the corner table, where Jess and Shirley always sat. Jess stood, hugging his daughter tightly. "I'm worried," Jess said. "What can we do?"

"I have to figure that out," Maddie said. "You know, like Indiana Jones says, 'I'm making this up as I go,'" she laughed.

"Your sense of humor always makes you strong when you're about to collapse. Sit down. We just ordered. I wanted to wait for you, but I'm sure you didn't get any sleep."

"Actually, I did sleep. Bud had to wake me to let him out." Maddie reached for her mom's coffee. "If you're not drinking this, I will."

"Help yourself," Shirley said. "I just don't feel in a coffee mood this morning." She tipped her glass of orange juice.

Margie brought three plates of biscuits and gravy, six over easy eggs, and a plate load of bacon and sausage. "What else can I get you?" she asked.

"This ought to keep us busy for a while," Jess said and helped himself to the bacon. "Maddie needs a bigger mug of coffee, though."

The small family ate in peace until a TV crew from Channel 11 WJHL Johnson City came through the door.

"Sara Diamond, herself!" Jess said. "Oh my god. That's a first." Jess sat up straight in his chair and wiped his napkin across his mouth.

"I've never seen her live on a story," Shirley said, putting her hand on Jess's. "Try to control yourself, sweetie. I know you have a crush on her." She winked at Maddie.

"Good morning, Margie." Sara approached the counter where the owner stood. "We won't even turn on the camera without your permission."

"Thank you, Ms. Sara. But you'll need to ask the family, not me."

Sara looked around the room, and spotting Madison, she strolled over to the table. "Hi, I'm Sara Diamond. I'd like to ask you a few questions. But totally on your call. We aren't going to invade your privacy. I'll let you finish your breakfast. If you'd like to suggest a more private space?"

"Thank you, Sara. Give us a minute. Okay?" Madison said.

Sara walked back to her camera man. He nodded and walked outside.

Margie hurried over to the table where most of the plates were emptied. She began clearing away a few and said, "Out back in the shade by the creek is cool this early, and no one would see you back there. I'll have Ben watch to keep away any onlookers."

"Good idea. Thank you, Margie." Madison stood, bending down to hug Shirley. She said, "Don't do this if you don't want to. I know it's rough on you. I need to give her an interview."

"And you should," Shirley said. She looked to Jess. "Um, uh, what do you think?"

Jess put his hand on Shirley's cheek and said, "I'll talk to her; no need

29

for you to. You'll start crying, and that will upset you needlessly. Why don't you stay in the kitchen and watch out the window?"

Shirley's tears were already dripping onto her blouse. She wiped her eyes with her napkin and stood up. "I'd like that. The kitchen has always been my safe place." She picked up the remaining dishes and plates, carrying them to the kitchen.

"I'll keep a good watch on her," Margie whispered to Jess.

5

Maddie and Jess took their place at a picnic table in the shade of the oak tree with Cold Creek behind them. Sara stood over to their left side, but slightly in front. The camera man had the restaurant to his back. He attached microphones to their clothing and did a sound check. He walked about ten steps away and gave them a thumbs up.

That was Sara's signal to begin talking. At first, the camera zoomed in on Sara. She began with, "I'm Sara Diamond on location in Cold Creek. Normally a quiet, peaceful community, this morning it's buzzing with activity. With me is Jess McKenzie and his daughter, Madison McKenzie-Malone, lifelong residents." The camera panned to Jess and Madison. "Jess, tell me what happened yesterday."

"My wife, Shirley, and I were about to take our morning walk when two strangers approached us at our back door. They only said, 'You're coming with us.' And they forced us into a pickup truck."

"Did they hurt you or threaten you at all?" Sara asked.

"Not until I resisted," Jess said. "One of the men pulled a pistol, and that was the end of my objection."

"After you were in the truck, what happened?" Sara continued the questioning.

"The fellow with the gun drove us away. The other one stayed behind.

It wasn't until we were released that we learned he burned our house to the ground." Jess cleared his throat and wiped away a tear on his cheek. "We had no idea why; we just followed orders. Didn't want no trouble."

"Madison, I know you used to be the sheriff here in Cold Creek," Sara said. "And since your marriage, your husband has assumed that title. Are you his deputy now?"

"Yes, along with Bud, my dog," Maddie said.

"Tell me how you learned about the abduction of your folks and the burned house." Sara's voice cracked, as if in sympathy.

"I was out on business when it all happened. This is an ongoing investigation, so I can't really share any details, Sara. I'm sure you understand."

"Where is Sheriff Malone?" Sara insisted.

"If I knew that, I'd go and get him," Maddie said. She was through talking. "The TBI is in the sheriff's office across the street. Maybe you should talk to them."

"I've already tried," Sara said. She motioned for the camera man to cut the feed. "They told me to talk to you and Jess."

"I have nothing more to say." Maddie walked to the back door of the restaurant. Once inside, she called Ranger Scott's number.

"This is Ranger Scott with the Tennessee Wildlife...Madison, I'm sorry I didn't pick up quicker. Have you heard from Rick?"

"No, but I have an idea. Are you busy?" she asked.

"No, come on up to Rocky Fork," Scott said. "I'm just here for a couple more hours, but we can talk in private. There's hardly anybody been here today."

"Thanks. On my way."

Maddie rounded up Bud and told Shirley she was going to Rocky Fork and would be back before dark.

Rick's words kept playing in her mind: "I can't outsmart him. He's pure Evil." She wondered why her husband feared this man so much.

She pulled to the side of the road as soon as she was out of Cold Creek. Scrolling through her phone contacts, she found TBI contacts. What was the agent's name, the one Rick told her about who was now with NC's Bureau? She went through one name at a time, when finally...

"O'Hair," Maddie said aloud. "That's it. Donnelly O'Hair." Bud tilted his head and then looked out the window as though Maddie had seen someone. "No, Bud, on my phone," she laughed at his interest.

"Agent O'Hair," the voice sounded on her speaker phone.

"Agent Donnelly? This is Madison Malone in Cold Creek. Can we talk a minute?"

"Sure, I'm off duty," he said. "What up with my favorite sheriff's wife? And Madison, please call me Donnelly. Too many syllables in Agent Donnelly. I'm just Donnelly—no agent or sir or mister."

"Well, then, Donnelly, I'm Maddie, and I need your help. Rick told me if I ever needed information, you'd be the one to ask."

"Has something happened to Rick?" he asked.

"Yes, he's been abducted by a very bad guy!" Madison said.

"Tell me what's going on."

For the next ten minutes, she spilled her guts, and a few tears, as she drove up Rocky Fork Creek Road.

"I'll see what I can find right away," Agent Donnelly said. "Can I text it to you?"

"Yes, but I won't have a signal in a few minutes, so don't worry if I can't get right back to you. I might lose you any time."

"Is your email at the office the same?" Donnelly asked.

"Yes, and that's even a better idea," Maddie said. "Thanks, I'd really appreciate it if you don't talk to anyone else about this. Not even your old buddies at TBI."

"No problem...I have no use for that guy, Frost," Donnelly said.

Before any more talk could transpire, Madison lost her cell signal. The high mountains with narrow valleys were hard to get a signal of any kind.

Scott was sitting by the fire pit when Maddie drove in and parked. She walked to his location and sat on one of the stump-like seats. "I am trying to find out from another agency who this Buck guy is," Maddie said. "TBI won't tell me anything. How can I find Rick if I don't know who I'm up against?"

"Maybe you should just let them handle this," Scott said. "They have a lot more manpower, and what good is it for you to die finding Rick?"

"Sounds like you don't have a lot of faith in me," she said.

"I think Rick was warning you when he said he couldn't outsmart the guy. What makes you think you can if Rick can't?"

"I have an advantage—ESP," she said with a serious look.

"Oh, I didn't know that, my bad," Scott laughed. "I'd bet you and Rick have a secret language too."

Maddie stood up and walked toward her vehicle. "Come on, Bud."

"Now, wait, Madison," Scott apologized. "I don't mean any harm. I've just never known that is a real thing."

"Well, it is with me," she said and kept walking.

Scott stayed by the fire pit, and Maddie drove away.

Maddie returned to Cold Creek sheriff's office, finding it unlocked and the keys on the desk. TBI left a note saying they'd handle the investigation from Knox County. There was nothing to work with in Unicoi County or the surrounding areas.

She checked the fax machine. A copy of each BOLO that had been issued had collected in the tray. Nothing new, nothing helpful, nothing from Donnelly. She ran to the other side of the office to check the email on her PC.

"Yes!" she cried out. Bud jumped to his feet, looking toward the door. "No, I'm sorry, Bud. There's an email from Donnelly. He says he'll hand deliver the results of his research. We need to drive to the Visitor's Center on top of the mountain. He didn't want the information falling into anyone else's hands. Oh, boy. Rick, what are you connected with?"

CABIN IN THE COVE

Bud lay back down, satisfied with the explanation.

Maddie looked at her phone. *Still early*, she thought. *I'll tell Jess I'm following up on a lead. That will give me privacy.*

"No one needs to know what I'm dealing with but you and me, Bud," she voiced aloud.

She used a password protected file to store the email from Donnelly, tidied up the office, and walked to her house. Jess sat on the front steps, head in hand.

"What are you thinking, Jess?" Maddie asked, sitting on the porch swing.

"We need to find a place to rent," Jess said. "I can't just take over your home."

"Why not? I'll be all over the place following leads. I certainly don't need it. Consider it yours till you decide what you need to do. Rebuild or whatever, but nothing hasty. This could take weeks, or heaven forbid—longer."

With that note, Maddie got up and walked into the cottage. Bud stayed on the porch with Jess.

After what seemed like an eternity, Maddie loaded a few items into the patrol car and looked toward Bud. "I'm going to put you in charge of the Homefront, boy. No need in you going across the mountain. Who knows when I'll be home?"

She went to locate Shirley or Jess. *Not in the house, so probably over at the restaurant for supper*, she thought.

A crowd had gathered at Shirley's, so Maddie entered through the back door. Just as she'd anticipated, Shirley and Jess sat at the table by the back door. Ben sat backwards on a ladder-back chair, leaning his elbows on the top wrung.

"Hello, Ben. Looking busy in there." Maddie nodded toward the dining area out front. "Jess, I'll be back a little late. Bud is staying to watch over you two."

"Where are you going?" Shirley asked.

"Just to follow up on a lead, probably a dead end, like all the others. But I have to handle the local ones. TBI exited the office and left me the bread-crumbs." Maddie laughed, mostly to herself.

"I can go with you," Jess suggested.

"No, I'm sure it's just a waste of time. You stay with Mom," she said and leaned in to hug Shirley. "Besides, Bud needs to feel useful."

Ben laughed. "Bud is always useful," he said. "I'll send him a doggy bag when they leave."

"Take it easy on that, Ben. He's getting as broad as he is tall."

They all laughed.

"You be careful," Shirley said.

Maddie winked and left by the back door.

The sun had dropped behind the mountain by the time Maddie drove around the lower level of the NC Visitor's Center Parking lot. She noticed a semi-truck pulling away, heading toward the exit ramp of the VC parking lot.

No markings on the trailer—just a small name scripted on the door of the truck. "Hmmm, what a great disguise," Maddie said aloud. "A person could drive several cars into that hauler and no one would be the wiser." As her wheels were turning and she watched the truck's wheels speed up with the southbound traffic, she didn't notice the SUV pull up on her right side.

A tall, well-built, middle-aged man walked around to her window. "Not very alert there, Maddie," he said. "Thought you'd be watching every move around you." Donnelly dropped his head to her level.

"Did you see that semi pulling out?" she asked. "No lettering of identifi-cation on the trailer, only small lettering on the cab, which I couldn't read from here. So many ways to hide a car, or a truck—just drive up into the back, close the door, and the cargo is hidden." She hadn't looked up at Donnelly's face until she watched the rig completely out of sight.

"Oh, so you were in surveillance mode. I see." Donnelly leaned against the fender of her patrol car. "Didn't expect to see you driving this."

She looked at him with no expression. "Why not? I'm on duty."

"But I'm not," Donnelly said. He walked back to his SUV. He took a tote out of the back seat and set it in the back of the patrol car. "It's dark enough now, so nobody will notice. But you be sure you read this stuff in private. You and I both could be prosecuted if we're caught with these secret documents. This is no joke. TBI aren't about to share the information with you. I shouldn't, but I know you. You will solve this single-handedly. Just like your keen eye on that semi. You're always thinking. Rick was right when he said you're a two-legged bloodhound."

"Rick called me a two-legged bloodhound?"

Donnelly laughed, "Yeah, with love in his eyes."

"What do you think my chances are?" Maddie was really looking for an honest answer.

"I've got some off time in two weeks," he said. "If you want me, I'm available. But till then, I'm stacked to the hilt, with the divorce and all my personal life shi—"

He stopped short.

"Rick hadn't told me," Maddie said. "I'm sorry, Donnelly. I'll figure this out; you've got enough to worry about." She thought for a moment. "Are the kids alright?"

"Davie is, but it's messing with Deborah real bad. She dropped out of college. Should have finished up her fall semester. Now she'll lose this semester's progress. She said she couldn't concentrate. Davie joined the Marines back in the spring, never went to college at all."

"I'm sorry, I hesitate to ask—" She looked away, wondering whose decision the divorce was.

"It wasn't my choice," Donnelly said. "And I may not be an angel, but I was sure I'd married one. Turns out, I am not a good judge of character, I guess." He swiped his hand under his nose and turned to get into his SUV. "Call me. Whatever you need, you hear?" Then, he got into the driver's seat. "Be very careful. I mean it."

Madison nodded her head, but no words were spoken.

She'd always understood that Rick believed he'd feel lucky to have a marriage as good as Donnelly's. She could not help feeling emotional over this strong man in his broken state. It's true that not every spouse is cut out to live the life of a law enforcement officer's wife, or husband, for that matter. She and Rick hoped they had what it took to keep their relationship afloat. They understand the risks and strived to hold hands through whatever came across the board.

After twenty-two plus years, even the best were challenged. Who could point the blame? They did not grow together. Donnelly was a good husband and father, and aside from what is only seen on the outside, Rick knew he was the best agent the Bureau had to offer. They'd worked the worst possible cases and always got their man. Was this the result of too much imbalance between home and work?

The tote sat on her back seat, taunting her curiosity. She could not take the chance of having it in the cottage. Someone could see it and know what she was up to. She couldn't sit there in the Visitor's Center parking lot, especially with full darkness surrounding her. She drove to I-26 onramp and proceeded south toward Asheville. Her stomach began to growl, reminding her she'd not eaten lunch, and it was beyond suppertime. The road unfolded ahead of her, almost as though the vehicle drove itself.

Tunnel Road brought back memories of another time she's done undercover work here. She chose a nice restaurant, Carrabba's. While sitting in her vehicle, she pulled up the to-go menu, ordered, paid online, and in ten minutes she walked inside to get her meal.

Returning to her car, she drove to a small hotel at the bottom of the hill. Driving around the parking lot, she looked at all the car tags as she surveyed the possibilities. Each one appeared to be family vehicles, out of town tags, vacationers just passing through. Not a nosy or rowdy bunch of guests, and they were not filled to capacity. "I'll take it," she said.

Madison turned the TV on and found the local news channel. Keeping the volume low, she ate supper as she flipped through the first folder from the tote. She wasn't sure what this story had to do with what's going on at the moment. So, she set it aside, picking out another. After the fourth file folder, she noticed they were in sequence by date. She spread them on the second bed in the room. Beginning with the oldest date, 1987, she lined them up to the present.

As though reading a book, she opened the first file and scanned it. Luckily, Maddie was a fast reader. The files began falling like chapters, painting a scene as it moved though the months and years. Rick was a young rookie, hardly worth mentioning. Until that is, Klaus Burckhardt came to the D.C. Bureau. He moved up the ranks quickly with a ruthless attitude, influencing a young Rick Malone.

Reading intensifying, she began seeing that wherever Klaus got transferred to, Rick soon followed. Notations appeared in all the personnel statements. It became apparent that this Klaus Burckhardt was "Buck," a shortened and not altogether approved of nickname. Maddie read continuously through the night. Wherever she deemed necessary, she made a photocopy to her phone for future reference.

"Note to self; pick up flash drive for safe storage of these photos," she said. Maddie walked to the bathroom for a cloth to wipe her face. She peeked out the window to see the sun rising. She fell across the bed and lay there, just to clear her thoughts momentarily.

Sleep crept in, and she was awakened by a knock at the door. Maddie looked at the clock on the nightstand. 11:43 glared into her eyes. She heard the knock again.

Pulling the curtain aside, she peeked out just as a voice said, "Housekeeping?"

Maddie opened the door just a crack. "I must have overslept. Can you give me a couple more minutes? I'll get out of your way."

"No problemo," the Spanish accent answered with a charming smile. She went on to the next door. Maddie heard her knock and then, "Housekeeping?"

She replaced all the files to the tote and then removed her clothes, stepping into the shower. Hot water proved a welcome shield. She washed her hair and applied cream rinse them stood still for a long rinse. Her muscles ached, but the heat of the water soothed her muscles. She must have slept for, what? Five hours? She reached for the knobs and the final rinse was cold, just to bring her fully awake.

The tote found a settling place behind the back seat covered with a blanket. She pulled her vehicle around to the front and stopped at the office. Inside she noticed the night clerk had gone off duty and a new one had taken over. She probably would not even notice the late checkout. So, she drove on and headed back up Tunnel Road. Spotting a drive-thru coffee brewery, she stopped at the window.

If this concoction didn't give her Drive Power, nothing would. She sipped the hot liquid, routing her SUV into buzzing traffic leading out of Asheville and over the mountain back into Tennessee.

The parking lot at Shirley's Restaurant was full with the lunch crowd, and fish on the menu for Friday. She pulled into her garage and shut the door. The less townspeople knew of her whereabouts these days, the better. She had some serious research to do, and there was no time to waste. Inside her cottage she found Bud resting on the braided rug of the small living room. He ran to her as if she'd been gone a lifetime, not just overnight.

"That you, Maddie?" a sweet voice called from upstairs.

"Yep, I'm back." Maddie went to her room and picked out clothes to change in for this day, whatever remained.

"I was concerned when I saw your bed wasn't slept in. Everything okay?" Shirley stuck her head around the door.

"Yeah, I had some good leads, and it had to be dealt with. Sorry, I let time get away from me, and I didn't want to text you in the middle of the night."

"Guess I'd better get used to that, huh?" Shirley smiled sympathetically. "Not going to be easy for me, but I know you have to do this. Dad and I promise to stay out of your way."

"Trust me, that's all I ask," Madison said. She slipped one arm around her mom's neck. "I love you. And I want you to stand by me, but not in front of me."

Shirley frowned but then nodded. "Okay."

Maddie's phone rang. She didn't recognize the number but wasn't about to miss the possibility of it being Rick. "Hello?" she answered.

She listened for a couple seconds, and her face brightened up. "Nell?"

Twenty minutes later, she walked upstairs, looking for Shirley. "That was Nell on the phone," Maddie said. "She and Drew are staying in Pigeon Forge for a couple days and want me to come over. They hadn't heard about Rick. That's why we talked so long. I'm going to pack a change of clothes and go meet them. They have an extra room in the house they're renting. Oh, this is perfect! Just what I needed. I can run my ideas past Drew and maybe come up with a workable solution as to where to begin."

Shirley hugged her and said, "Yes, definitely, you should go spend some time with them. We'll keep Bud."

"Bud is better off with Holly and Bear. I'll run out to see her."

Maddie packed a canvas bag with Bud's food and a few of his toys. She called Holly as she drove out of Cold Creek to the Jacob's farm.

"I'm so glad Nell called you," Holly said. "This is just what you need. How dare you even ask if we can keep Bud? Come here and give me a hug. I've been so worried about you. Now, maybe I can rest a little easier." Holly had baby Mattie in one arm and squeezed Maddie with the other.

"How's my namesake, Mattie?" Maddie asked. "Those old teeth stop hurting you yet?"

Mattie plunged into Madison's arms so quickly that Holly nearly fell over. "Matt-mat," was all Mattie could say. But that was enough to show how much love she felt. The toddler squealed, hugging tighter. And then she spotted Bud hopping out of the vehicle. She reached out for the dog, and Maddie had to put her down. Bud was very gentle with the tiny baby girl, but gentle was not a word Mattie knew when it came to hugging a dog. Bear ran from around back, joining the roughhousing.

Maddie tried to interfere to keep the little girl from being hurt by the romping dogs.

"You might as well leave them alone," Holly said. "Mattie thinks they are three kids, or she's a dog herself, I'm not sure which." Holly brushed them off and linked her arm into Maddie's "Come up on the porch and tell me what you know so far."

Holly had already brought out glasses filled with lemonade. Maddie snatched one up and sat in the rocker beside her best friend. She and Holly watched the dogs run around the house at full speed as though it was the first time they'd played together in months. This was the way they always did their catch up. Mattie clapped her hands and yelled every time they ran past her. She sat on the step finally, waiting for their energy to settle down.

After a brief conversation, Maddie said, "I need to get home and pack some things."

Holly followed to the vehicle to get Bud's overnight bag. "Try to keep in touch and know that I'm praying every day and night for you and Rick."

Maddie's welled-up tears broke loose. "Oh, Holly, I know you always do, and you know how much I need all the prayers you can give me. And I don't know what's wrong with me. I can't focus on Rick's thoughts. He hasn't even once tried to signal me. Am I losing my touch?"

"You're emotionally attached," Holly said. "Normally you don't know the messengers. Your love might cloud your reception for a while. Give it time. I know you'll figure it out. Besides, you said Rick believed that it was Shirley and Jess laying in the river. He thinks they are dead. Maybe his overwhelming guilt is blocking his thoughts. Did you ever really put yourself in his shoes?"

"You're right, you know? I hadn't thought of it that way. Maybe getting out of Cold Creek will help me think clearly. Or is that clairvoyantly?"

6

As soon as Maddie arrived in Sevierville, she turned on her GPS, following directions to the address Nell had relayed to her earlier. When she came to Middle Creek, she was told to turn left. "Aw, I know where this is going," she said aloud. Just to keep on track, she continued following the voice of the in-car guidance system.

As she suspected, there were more left-hand turns until the road wound up a steep hillside and the valley below got smaller. Homes were scarce and rarely could she even make out shapes of cabins in evergreens. The incline remained steep until she seemed to break out at the top of the ridge. Ahead, she spotted a lonely three-story frame and log house. The GPS told her, "You have arrived at your destination." Noticing a right turn, she pulled onto a narrow concrete drive, winding up toward the large structure.

Sure enough, on a wraparound porch, she saw Nell and Drew sitting in rocking chairs. In her arms, Nell held a small child dressed in bright pink, and sitting on Drew's lap was a small boy squirming to get down. Maddie took in the site and broke into tears.

"Look how big you are, DJ! Have you been eating your dad's food, too?"

"No, oh—" the little guy giggled as she snatched him up.

"How did you grow so big?" Maddie asked and nestled him with hugs and kisses.

By now, Nell handed off the bundle of pink and reached to hug Maddie. "I'm so sorry you're in pain," she said. "What can we do?"

The two women cried for a few minutes, embraced in a warm hug.

Maddie and Nell had become very good friends while dealing with the confusion of her jolt to reality and the tragic death of her aunt in Alaska. Nell and Drew had managed a lasting love connection during the investigation, despite Maddie and Drew butting heads. They'd been through a lifetime of heartbreak and near-death experiences, and all endured as friends.

"It'll be okay, I know," Maddie said. "I just have to figure out where they took him. I already know why." She wiped her face with the back of her hand. "You hadn't even told me about that baby girl. Why you holding out on me?"

"Long story," Nell said. "Come on in, and let's hear your story first." She pulled Maddie toward the porch.

Drew had always been shy, and hugging Maddie was not easy for him. But she didn't let him decide; she grabbed him first.

"Come here, you! I didn't drive here just to cry in Nell's arms. These arms have lifted me up in the past. And I'm counting on that this time more than ever!"

Drew laughed, looking away as she reeled him in. "Okay, I guess you're due a hug this time." He shifted the baby to his shoulder, embracing Maddie with the other arm.

She took the tiny baby girl from him. "What's your name, beautiful?"

Nell stepped up hurriedly and said, "We call her Rosie, her name is Roseland. And we just got her two weeks ago. So, she's still not really used to us. Boy, she had no resistance to you!"

"Oh, that's wonderful, she's beautiful!" Maddie said. "My goodness, Nell, she looks just like you!"

"I know, that's what everyone says. But we got her in Ukraine. I'll tell you all about it in due time. We feel so blessed to have her. She understands some English already, but look at her tiny size. She's ten months old."

"This is amazing. You really should feel blessed. And seems to me, maybe she's the blessed one."

"Indeed." Nell stared at her miracle baby daughter. "We didn't even know we wanted a second child. See, that's the most important thing I've learned from you, my friend."

"From me? What would that be?" Maddie cocked her head. "Nell, you taught me the most important things—everything! I didn't even know who Madison McKenzie was before you came into my world. You're the smartest woman I know."

"I don't remember it that way, but thanks for the compliment." Roseland fell asleep while Nell and Madison talked. "I'm going to put her down. She's a little mixed up since we aren't in a routine."

Maddie approached Drew. He walked out the door of the cabin and said, "This place is the best! I'm happy you joined us. I'm sorry hearing about Rick. Do you have any leads?"

The two of them looked across the valleys below. Ribbons of color lay before them like tails of a kite. All seemingly attached to the dark green forested mountain jutting up even higher than their present elevation.

"That's Mount Le Conte," Drew said calmly, and added, "Did you know it's the highest peak contained within Tennessee? 6,593 feet and the third highest in the Great Smokey Mountains National Park."

"Key wording there, 'contained within Tennessee,'" Maddie said. She smiled in an appreciative manner. "I think I've read every book, every tourist guide, and brochure about our home state. I had forgotten the exact height. Thanks for reminding me."

Drew studied her eyes. "You've cried too much in your young years, Maddie." His strong hand touched her cheek with a handkerchief. "Maybe you need this more than I do." He returned his gaze to the Mountain Peak and said, "Did they leave the area?"

"Don't know. We never saw the car or truck after they drove away with Rick hogtied in the backseat. We had the tag numbers, type of vehicles, colors, everything to complete the BOLO. Nothing from any direction. They must have driven into a wormhole." Maddie blew her nose on the handkerchief. "I promise to wash this before I return it."

"What did you call this man…Buck?" Drew's years in law enforcement had the wheels turning. "Why does that sound so familiar to me?" He glanced at Maddie. "Last name or first?"

"Nickname, from a shortened last name, Klaus Burkhardt. Buck was all most people ever called him." Madison remembered the tote with Top Secret files in her SUV. "I need to move some things into the cabin, but I don't want you to know anything about them. The less you know, the safer you and your family are. Maybe I shouldn't even be here myself."

Drew looked eye to eye with her, and then he burst out laughing. "No one is looking for you, or they would already have you. No one knows we're here, unless you told. And as for Top Secret, honey, seriously, I hope you aren't out on one of your usual limbs."

Madison didn't laugh. She turned and walked to her vehicle. "I removed the Unicoi County sheriff's decal from this car, but I was also very careful that no one followed me. Wonder who I learned that from?"

Drew followed, and seeing the size of the tote, he frowned. "Where'd you get this?"

"Someone I trust with Rick's life." She lifted the square box and started toward the porch.

Drew walked ahead and opened a different door. "Down here," he said. The door opened to a set of stairs. "This is better—quiet and no outside windows."

He followed Maddie into the basement. "Here, put that on this table. I wondered what this would come in handy for. Who knew?"

Madison tapped her hand on top of the tote. "Only if you are sure you want to be involved. We can keep it quite from Nell."

"Nell already knows," Nell said as she reached the landing of the stairs. "What makes you think you two are the only snoops in the family? Both kids are asleep, and I have the monitor in my pocket. Let's get started. Time is wasting."

The next couple hours were taken up by Madison pouring her heart out with the painful details which had taken place those days before her beloved husband was abducted. Drew listened, and Nell asked questions that even Madison had not entertained yet.

Hours passed. Nell listened carefully to the baby monitor. "Oh, I think Rose is awake. I'll be back soon. You two keep at it. You're making interesting stacks and little conversation. I call that progress."

After a while, Nell returned. From the top of the stairs, she called out, "One of you come get this while I go back for the kids."

Drew slid away from the stool he'd occupying long enough to put a crick in his back. He stretched a couple times and then took three steps to the top of the landing. Returning with a tray of warm ham 'n cheese sliders and a bowl of freshly cut up cantaloupe, he set it down on the one clear spot of the table surface. He raced back up the stairs, balancing a pitcher of tea in one hand and his little Drew Jr. in the other.

"Why are we hiding out down here, Daddy?"

"Not hiding; we're playing detective," Drew said. "There's your tricycle. You can ride all over the basement." He put his toddler down.

Little DJ ran to his "bike," as he called it. Maddie watched the young child on the tiniest tricycle she'd ever seen.

"I didn't even know they made one that small," she said. "How cute!" She pulled her phone out of her pocket and snapped a photo. "Jess and Shirley are going to love this shot."

"But not right away." Drew smiled as he cautioned her, "No one needs to know where we are just yet."

"Of course," she said and lay the phone on the table. At the top of the stairs, she noticed Nell returning. Meeting her on the landing, she took a basket filled with cups and paper plates, some plastic utensils, napkins, and several other items buried in the bottom. Nell followed with Rose wrapped in a blanket.

"One thing's for sure; if we do buy this place—" Drew stopped midsentence.

"I thought that was going to remain quiet for a while," Nell smiled at her husband.

"I agree," Maddie said. "I'd have a door to the inside the house, not just this dark stairway."

Drew and Nell laughed with their friend. Drew had leaked that he was offered a position at the local police department. It didn't take Maddie long to put two and two together. Especially when she noticed the "For Sale by Owner" flyer upstairs in the living room.

"When will you give them an answer, Drew?" Maddie asked as she munched on a warm sandwich.

"All depends on what we learn in this can of worms. From what I've seen so far, this rookie is most likely Rick in his early years. Evidentially, he found himself in a position not easily removed from. In fact, I'd say Buck compromised Rick as an alibi and has controlled the situation over these last two decades." Drew scratched his neck. "Why now? What caused the change in his plan?"

Maddie had silenced her phone but noticed the screen lit up, showing she had a message. She touched the unlock button and scanned a long line of incoming communications. "Wow, I've been missed by everyone just in this short time," she said. She chose to answer Jess's message with an icon of a big heart and added, "Having a great time catching up...Will call you tomorrow."

"This is from Don," Maddie said. "I better read it."

She walked to the stairs and sat by herself.

Drew joined her after a few minutes. He said, "I figured it was Donnelly. Rick and I became very close when I was recovering from my fall. I know more about his past probably than he ever shared with you. That's why I'm glad you turned to me for help. I think I know where he is."

Maddie jumped to her feet and said, "Then you have to tell me how I can get to him and bring him home."

"We can plan that together. You aren't doing this alone. So, get that notion out of your head. In due time, I promise." Drew returned to the table for another sandwich. "Buck didn't burn Jess's house, and he won't hurt Rick. He needs him. He cared for him like his own from the very beginning. He won't hurt him now."

"But he has hurt him," Maddie said. "And whose idea was it to use my folks to draw him out?" Madison propped her fists on her hips.

"Those goons he hired to help him," Drew said. "He dumped them as soon as they cleared the county line. Probably turn up in body bags off a mountain."

Maddie whirled around and walked back to the stairs. She pulled up the message from Donnelly and read, "Two unidentified men found just off the Blue Ridge Parkway near Grandfather Mountain today. Both shot once in the head from close range. No fingerprints, no ID on them, but when we get the DNA tests back, we'll have some idea if they were ever connected to Buck. Now, we know he's capable of murder."

Maddie blinked away tears and stared at Drew. "You so sure he won't hurt Rick?" she asked.

Nell led Junior by the hand to the stairs. Drew picked him up and carried him ahead of her. She followed with the baby.

Madison returned to the table, hoping to see something she'd missed.

Time dragged by before Nell came back down the steps. "Sweetie, you need some rest," she said. "I have your room ready. Please come on up and try to let your body recover from your nightmare. You should listen to Drew. I know you've always had a love/hate relationship, but he's a good detective, and he loves you. He only has your best interest at heart."

"I know, Nell. But he has never given me credit for what I've learned. Rick worked with me on cases, he knows what I am capable of..."

"He knows," Nell said. "Rick bragged on you all the time. Drew is shy. He's very different from Rick, and he hides his feelings. But I know him. He doesn't show all his cards. You have no poker face. He says you'd be the first one naked in a game of strip poker. And he's right!"

"I'd never!" Maddie couldn't help laughing. "Maybe he's right about that. Not that I'd ever even play poker anyway. I know I'm a sore loser! Okay, my eyes are killing me. I do need a break, that's for sure."

She joined arms with Nell, and they ascended the stairs.

7

Maddie opened her eyes to bright light strips cutting through the blinds in her room. She'd hoped to wake early, before Nell and Drew, so she could go for a run.

She dressed and walked into the open area of the great room. Nell sat at the bar in the kitchen feeding Rosie. DJ sat next to his mom, attempting to eat a bowl of Cheerios, which had become life preservers for the blueberries bobbing in a sea of milk.

"Say, those blueberries with life preservers look like a great breakfast for me. Or have you captured all of them?" Maddie sat next to the little boy, kissing him on top of his golden curls.

"I saved some for you," he laughed, throwing her a kiss with milk-dripping fingers.

"Good, I was afraid I might have to eat some mushy stuff like Rosie." Maddie winked at Nell when she said it.

"Help yourself to coffee," Nell said, nodding toward the Keurig on the counter. "I hope you're feeling a bit better. Did we wake you?"

Maddie chose a dark brew cup, slipped it into the machine, and pulled a tall mug from the cabinet. "I wish I'd wakened earlier. Where's Drew?"

"He went into town about thirty minutes ago. Had a breakfast meeting with the Town Council. He is going to accept the position but tell them he needs a full week to get moved."

Nell took a moment to sip her coffee. Rosie sat like a baby bird with mouth open wide, anticipating the next bite.

"I'm sure they'll be happy having him," Maddie said. "Can you move into here, or will you need to move twice?"

"We hope only one trip will do it," Nell said. "I think the owner is motivated to sell, so she'll probably go for his offer and okay us to move right away. Her husband has been transferred to Hawaii. She is ready to go!"

"Hawaii...Not sure I'd want that location. But I'm a mountain goat!" Maddie laughed.

"I've lived in lots of different places, and I can honestly say Tennessee is my favorite," Nell said. She wiped Rosie's face and offered her a cup of water. Rosie promptly slapped it out of her hand and began whining. "She's got some really bad habits for a child so young." Nell got up, made a bottle, and lifted the petite girl from the highchair, sitting down with the baby in her arms. Rosie held the bottle herself, settling into a calm mode.

"What about Louisville? Too big and busy for you?" Maddie asked. She sat across from Nell.

"No, it was okay. We were far enough out of the city. I didn't mind it, but I have grown very fond of these mountains."

"I'm happy having you back in our lives. I know Rick will be also." Maddie's voice dropped off in a low sigh.

"Chin up, girl," Nell said. "He'll be back with us soon. Drew is sure you can find him. He even said this morning that he hoped to stop by the TBI office to see if they'll share any news with him."

"They won't! This bunch they have now don't know their A-Hum from a whole in the ground. I hope he won't mention anything we read in those papers. I don't want to cause trouble for Donnelly. He's with the NC Bureau now. And they have no reason to even learn that I know him."

"Drew would never volunteer any information. You know how quiet he is."

Rosie drifted off to sleep, and Nell went to put her in the port-a crib. She guided DJ to the bathroom to brush his teeth. And upon returning to the kitchen, she asked, "Have you and Rick discussed having children?"

"Not really." Madison's phone rang, so she dodged that heartache. "It's Jess. I better talk to him."

Maddie took her coffee outside onto the wraparound porch and said, "Good morning."

Nell washed the few dishes and watched out the window. She noticed Maddie's face turn from a sunny smile to a clouded frown. She'd learned to read Maddie while they worked to help Drew on the case of the hometown skeletons in Cold Creek a few years earlier. Maddie appeared more upset with every word from Jess. Nell stepped onto the porch to see what bothered her friend.

Maddie disconnected the call. She blew air out slowly, like the slow leak of a tire. And then she turned to Nell. "I have to go," she said. "Something is going on, and I need to stop it."

She brushed past Nell to gather her things from the basement. Once the tote was loaded into her SUV, Nell came out with the bag from the room Maddie slept in.

"Thanks for not asking questions, Nell," Maddie said. "I'll be in touch." She tossed her bag into the passenger seat and gave Nell a hug. "I'll be back, I promise."

"You better," Nell said. "You know that you always have a place with us."

Maddie traced the curvy road back down the mountain to Middle Creek Road. An oncoming car flashed his lights; she soon realized it was Drew. She pulled to the side at an abandoned building and waited for him to pull up next to her.

"Where are you off to?" he asked.

"Back to Cold Creek," Maddie said. "I got a call from Jess."

"Glad I caught you. Don't go. Listen to me. Did you tell him where you are?"

"No, just said catching up with old friends. He knew I was coming to meet you and Nell. Why?"

"I learned from that new prick in charge where Rick used to work, that the men they found were agents. He is blaming Rick. He has Jess's phone tapped and everyone else you might call. Turn around and get back up the mountain. We're keeping you under house arrest."

Drew scratched off, motioning for her to follow.

"What the heck?" Maddie said aloud to only herself. But she trusted Drew and whipped her car around, following him. *What is going on with TBI?* she thought.

She felt they were not trustworthy, but hiding from them? Something was really out of whack. And she'd take Drew up on staying out of sight for a while. Besides, staying away from Cold Creek might give her an advantage. Rarely did she have those extra senses while in her hometown.

Once at the cabin, Drew told Maddie to put the tote in the basement under the stairs. When she came back out, her vehicle had been backed into some overhanging trees above the cabin. Drew was busy covering the tire tracks and pulling loose foliage closer to conceal her SUV. He ran down the steps, returning with a camo tarp.

"Help me with this," he instructed as he shook the tarp out to its full length. "At the bottom of the stairs, I saw some bungie cords. Bring them."

Maddie did as he told her and didn't ask questions until they got back inside the house.

"This is for your safety. I have no idea how far that idiot will go." Drew tipped up a beer he pulled from the fridge.

"Which one?" Maddie asked.

"TBI, anyone associated with that branch. You won't believe what he blabbed to me when I introduced myself as the new chief of police of Sevier-ville." Drew turned up the beer and chugged it. "Guess he wanted to impress me. He's taking this abduction of Rick's as a self-designed disappearance. I didn't make any statements of connection to you or Cold Creek, so for a while at least, he's in the dark. All he knows is that my wife and family are moving with me from Kentucky to take the position as chief of police. So, my dear, your best bet is to become part of our family. Have you ever wanted to be a nanny? You are now."

"This is so bizarre!" Maddie said. "What is going on with our law enforcement?"

"We don't know who can be trusted and who can't, so don't talk to any of them. Let me see your phone." Drew reached for the cell phone next to Maddie. "I'll get you a burner. Pull the plug on this one." He removed the sim-card and the battery. "I'll let Jess know not to worry, and he can notify Holly for you." Drew looked out the side window for a moment. "There's a self-store-it at the bottom of the mountain. I'll rent a unit, and we can hide your vehicle in there after dark. Someone will eventually spot your SUV in the bushes. We don't want any connection between us and you."

"You're really scaring me, Drew," Nell said. She looked at Madison. "You probably need a disguise of some kind."

Maddie nodded to Nell. "I'm way ahead of you. There's a small beauty shop down the road. I noticed it on my way up here."

"The sooner the better," Drew said, following her thinking. "Did you notice the name of it?"

"I sure did. Holly's House of Hair. I remember laughing when I noticed it."

Drew fumbled with his phone. "Here it is, Holly's. Call to see how soon she can get you in. We should leave ASAP to get moved." He handed his cell to Maddie.

"Hello, you must be Holly?" Maddie said. She smiled, trying not to laugh. "I've had it with my hair. How soon can you work in a new patron?"

She listened for a few moments and said, "I could use a good makeover. Been thinking about it for too long. Made up my mind to go all out!" She listened, then said, "I'd be happy to come this afternoon."

The call disconnected.

"Was that fast enough?" Maddie asked.

"Let's get going," Drew said, turning to his wife. "Honey, get the bare necessities together for our trip back to Kentucky. We'll leave as soon as Madison is done."

"She's not staying here by herself, is she?" Nell asked.

"No, she's our nanny, remember? She's going to Kentucky with us."

Maddie and Drew rode in his Cadillac Escalade back down the mountain toward Sevierville. Drew ran inside a Walmart and purchased the burner phone. Upon returning, he instructed, "Always keep it shut off when you aren't using it. It's just like your own phone, only untraceable. I've already talked to Jess, and he's notified Holly and Henry. No one else will need to know anything about you. Is that clear?"

"Yeah, but what about Bud? And who's looking out for the sheriff's office?"

"That's all taken care of. You are on a vacation, wherever everyone else is concerned."

Drew parked down the block from the storage place, making sure he was not on any surveillance cameras. Now, he had to think like the criminals, and he was very careful not to make any mistakes. In a few minutes, he returned with a key and a piece of paper. "Now, what time did she tell you to come?" he asked.

"Around 1:30, and it's almost that now," Maddie said.

"Do you need something to eat before I drop you off?" Drew took a deep breath and looked straight at Maddie. "You can certainly be a pain in the ass. But I know you're worth it. This is the best thing I can think of to stay ahead of what's about to happen. You trust me, don't you?"

Maddie stared out the front windshield. "I'm not hungry. What will you do while I'm in there?"

"I have several things that still need done before we head to Kentucky. You only worry about yourself. Don't use your real name. Make something up. I don't care what you tell this Holly, and don't tell your friend Holly anything. You got that?"

"Sure," Maddie said. "But, Drew, are you telling me everything I need to know? Jess said there's some details about their burned-out house. Insurance is not helpful. I need to help him get Shirley settled."

"No, you do not," Drew said. "Henry has everything under his control. They will be better off not knowing anything about you. And that's all I intend to say for now."

He drove back to Middle Creek Road to Holly's House of Hair.

Maddie carried nothing in with her, except cash in her pocket and the burner phone.

"Don't say anything when you're done," Drew said. "Just let my cell ring three times and hang up. I'll be here within a couple minutes."

Maddie pushed the brightly colored turquoise door open, walking into a great, big, untrue story.

"Welcome," a woman said. "Please come in and make yourself comfortable. There are some style books you can look at while I finish up this haircut. I didn't catch your name earlier when you called. I'm Holly. And you are?" She stopped talking just long enough for Maddie to respond.

"I'm Nan...Nancy. Thanks for getting me in while I'm in the mood." Maddie sat on a straight back chair and picked up a color and style book.

Holly never stopped snipping on the lovely red hair she had in the turquoise salon chair. She and the redhead resumed their conversation as though Maddie wasn't there.

Maddie thought how quickly she'd come out with Nancy as her name. So, maybe that was a good one to pull this disguise off. New name, new job, new look! And now, she'd better find that new look, because she was sure Holly was fast-paced!

She turned to the middle of the styles for medium-length look. No, that would not change her own look very much. She'd better go shorter. As she thumbed through the short styles, she came across a golden blonde pixy cut that appeared an easy style to keep. And luckily, the model in the photos had a similar-shaped face. Holly had told her previously that her dark level of color was too dark to be a white blonde without turning her healthy hair into mush.

Maddie looked to the color section and found a variety of darker blonds. Holly had already explained to her that those had high maintenance because they required a double process. If she was to keep this disguise for a few weeks, or even months, she'd better stick with easy. Something she and Nell can do on their own up at the cabin.

The redhead was blown dry and dismissed. Now it was Maddie's turn. Her stomach flip-flopped as she stood up. Ms. Holly quickly swept the red hair into a dustpan on a long handle and set it aside. She sprayed the turquoise chair down and wiped with a clean dry towel. She sprayed the sink with the same disinfectant. Momentarily, she wiped it away with another clean dry towel.

"This isn't just because of Covid," Holly said. "I've always sanitized my unit as if it was a dental chair. You can have a seat here now."

Maddie moved toward the clean chair and sat, wondering all the while if she'd recognize herself when this was over. She was second-guessing her decision now.

8

Ms. Holly combed through Maddie's thick hair.
"Wow, you have avoided a beauty shop, haven't you?" Holly said. Not
allowing for an answer, she continued, "Such a rich healthy color, and mid-
way down your back. This is a shame cutting it short. But I have a grand idea
for a style for you. You okay with blow drying it every few days?" She looked
at the solemn face in the mirror.

Maddie fought tears, but one slid out from the corner of her eye. "I have
only had it cut once or twice. Never shorter than my shoulders. I've always
had it long enough to put into a ponytail if I wanted to."

Ms. Holly waddled over to the table and picked up a different book. She
flipped right to a certain page and showed Maddie. "This is a lovely and
lively cut, but it only works well on hair as thick as yours. Do you like it?"

"Yes," Maddie said. "It's short but long in the front. I kind of do like
that." She batted away any other tears and smiled at Ms. Holly. "Yes, that's
good. And what about the color?"

"Why are you so bent on changing the color?" she asked.

"I've never known anything but semi-sweet or dark chocolate. I'm ready
for a change. I was thinking of blonde, but I realize that's out of the question."

"Did you like the red that just walked out of here?" Ms. Holly asked.

"I guess. I just never imagined myself as a redhead." Maddie furrowed her brow. "Doesn't that require a bleaching too?"

"Yes, but the first stage of lightening hair is red. Even most blondes have to go through a shade of red before it whitens up to blonde. We call it lifting stages; sounds less harsh than bleaching. With your creamy skin and dark eyes, you'd fit in the parameters of a natural redhead. What do you think?"

"Does that mean fewer weeks between touching up the roots?" Maddie asked.

"No, not really," Holly said. "But dark at the roots won't show as quickly in a deep autumn red. Since I started using Redkin Color Product, I've had the best reds ever. And Redkin doesn't wash out like so many other brands. They really have a great depth of deposit. Clara, who just left here...Her natural color is almost as dark as yours."

"How long ago did you do her color?"

"It's been a couple years! She was just here for the haircut. I did her roots three weeks ago. Didn't see a lot of dark chocolate showing up, did you?"

"No, I assumed you did the color today, too," Maddie said. "It looked so fresh." She smiled at her reflection. "Nancy, you're gonna be a redhead!"

"Then it's settled?" Holly asked, and Maddie nodded. "Okay, I'll cut the bulk of the length off first." Holly wrapped a rubber band tightly around the hair at the nape of her neck. "This way, we can save this much for Locks of Love. You ever heard of that?"

"Yes. The first time I had my hair cut, we managed to send 24 inches to Locks of Love. I wasn't sure I had enough now for them."

"Sure, and as thick as this is, they can make a couple of short wigs out of it. It's a great contribution for someone with no hair at all." Ms. Holly began snipping away at the long lock of hair. She measured it, then said, "Almost 18 inches. That's a plenty all right."

The color was done next, and after 90 minutes, Ms. Holly began carving out the long sides and shortened the back. She washed the hair one last time and conditioned it before starting the blow drying.

"This is best done if you put your head down and bend from the waste to get the most volume," Holly said. "I can only build so much by pulling yours up. Use a round brush like this one to give it a slight under curve. Try not to use a heating iron unless you absolutely have to. You'll need good strong muscles to achieve the best swing."

"Even when mine was just touching my shoulders, I dried it with my head upside down," Maddie said. "So, I'm familiar with that torture."

Ms. Holly turned the back of Maddie's head toward the mirror, handed her a hand mirror, and said, "What do you think of this?"

Maddie turned from side to side, then she looked up at Ms. Holly. "You've done a lovely job," Maddie said. "I like the color a lot, and I love the way my hair swings when I move. It's alive again. And it feels great." She stood up and removed the cape from her shoulders. "How much do I owe you for this miracle?"

"Since you donated your hair, you automatically earn a 25% discount on the works," Ms. Holly said. "It makes me feel so good sending beautiful healthy hair to LOL. Thank you for your business. And take my card so that when you need a touch up, you'll remember to call me."

Madison handed the hairdresser a hundred-dollar bill and said, "Will this cover it?"

"I'll owe you $25 back."

"No, ma'am, you keep it all. And thank you for making me feel so much better about myself. You'd have made a good therapist."

"You're not the first I've heard that from," Ms. Holly said. She laughed as Maddie stepped into the fading sunlight.

"How does it look in the sun?" Maddie asked.

"Autumn red. And beautiful."

Maddie had already punched in the numbers of Drew's phone. She ended the call at the third ring. Less than five minutes later, she saw Drew's Escalade coming toward the turn-in. She waved in case Drew might not recognize her.

As the vehicle came closer, she realized it was Nell driving. She was so happy seeing her friend instead of the man of the house.

"Oh, gosh!" Nell squealed as soon as Maddie opened the door. "Good thing I remembered what you were wearing, or I'd have never recognized you. Girl! You look amazing."

"So, it's okay?" Maddie asked.

"It's better than okay! It's remarkable! I want mine done like that."

"No, you can't be my twin. We get in enough trouble just the way we are."

Both women laughed like silly schoolgirls. It was a good feeling being together again.

They drove back up the mountain to the cabin. Drew pulled Maddie's SUV out of the bushes.

"Where did you get this, Maddie?" Drew asked, stepping up close to her and turning her face to look at his. "That you? Really?"

"My name is Nancy. I'm the nanny. Pleased to meet you, Chief." Maddie thought she even sounded different. And she liked it.

"You follow me in your vehicle, Nancy the Nanny," Drew said. "We'll take it to the storage unit. I had a close look today, and there are no cameras on the back side. That's where your unit is located. Nell, we'll be back within thirty minutes."

Drew led the way to the unit on the backside the felicity. He opened the door and helped Maddie back it into the empty room. "Did you remove everything personal?" he asked.

"Yes, I did that when you corralled me earlier," Maddie said. She watched him close and lock the door.

As they drove away, Drew looked at her long and hard. "I doubt that Rick could even recognize you with that change," he said. "Damn, you're beautiful. You might draw more attention to yourself with that look. How do you like it?"

"It's not me," Maddie said. "But that might be a good thing from the way you've scared the crap out of me." She looked at Drew with cold, dark eyes. "My name is Nancy."

"Let's not go too far with that disguise."

The look Drew gave Maddie was not any she'd ever seen from him. She hoped he was the same Drew Perry she'd known in her single years. She'd put him through a lot of trouble when she found the skeletons of Cold Creek. She was not sure he'd actually forgiven her for the way she went over his head as the town sheriff, finding the details he and his deputy had not.

She had not set out to make him angry or cause him trouble. However, she'd managed to do both, and severely at that. Led by her intuition and untapped boldness, she won over the handsome TBI agent, Rick Malone, to confront Cold Creek's lawman. Did he harbor a grudge for her even now? She had dropped out of school at UT in Knoxville to take over the sheriff position when Drew nearly died from a broken back, and he became what many feared—a broken man. Nell had nursed him with enough love that they married, and Drew brought his strength up above the former man he'd been. He should thank Maddie for pushing him to be his best. Or did he see it another way?

Nell had the children tucked in for the night. She warmed supper and insisted Maddie eat. She knew all too well how Maddie easily fell into a bulimic condition when she was upset or deeply troubled. Rick was kidnapped, and the desperado had no compassion. Maddie needed her strength more than ever to help her husband free himself from the notorious former FBI agent who'd trained and groomed him.

Was Rick involved in the mayhem himself? How had he been so easily led away from his beloved Madison? Nell feared Rick might never return. Not only did the law suspect him, but the unlawful had it in for him, too. Keeping Maddie healthy was now her main goal. No one will recognize the new woman, Nancy, unless Maddie tips them off by her old habits. Nell would not stand for that. She'd helped Maddie climb out of the grips of her domineering aunt, and now she had another battle ahead, maybe even bigger than the first.

Maddie woke the next morning to the smell of coffee brewing. It was the best start she could imagine considering her lack of restful sleep. She'd heard Drew pacing in the kitchen numerous times throughout the night. Carefully, she gathered everything of hers and stepped softly so as not to wake anyone. Nell mentioned she'd set the coffee maker for 6:00 a.m., so they could get their car packed before the kids awakened.

To Maddie's surprise, Drew sat with a steaming mug in front of him and a paper road map. He looked up smiling when she entered the kitchen.

"Get any sleep?" he asked.

"A little," Maddie answered at the end of a yawn. She carried her duffel bag, setting it by the front door. "Coffee smells good."

"I bet you haven't seen anyone actually use a paper road map recently, have you?"

She shook her head as she poured a cup of wake-up.

"I like having the bird's eye view," Drew said. "Not just following a line on the GPS."

Maddie nodded but said nothing. She sat down in the living room in front of the TV, which was muted on the Weather Channel. After a couple of warnings about the storms moving from west to east, she noticed the path looked clear from TN to north KY. The coffee went down quickly, so she returned for a refill.

"Drew, I don't want you getting caught harboring a 'pain in your ass.' Are you sure you don't want me to call someone to come and get me?"

"No, you're safer with us," he said. "And until I see your picture in the post office, I'm not worried. Besides, Nell can really use your help. She has her hands full right now. Are you okay with being part of the family for a while?"

"I guess," Maddie said. "As long as I'm not too much trouble." She returned to the seat in front of the TV.

Nell came downstairs with two brightly colored suitcases. Drew stood up quickly to take them from her.

"I would have gotten those for you, honey," he said. He pulled up the handles and rolled them across the hardwood floor to the front door. "Ours are already in the car. I'll come back for yours, Maddie." He opened the front door.

Nell walked over and smoothed the back of Maddie's hair. "This is such a cute look for you. Do you like it?"

"Yeah, I do, but I wonder if blonde might have been better." Maddie shook the long pieces down in front of her face. "I mean, is it enough of a change that I won't be recognized?"

"Yes, I believe it is," Nell said. "I'd like to show you some make-up tips, too. Drew even suggested we shop for a new wardrobe for you. That could be fun."

"Maybe a couple of items, but I can't really afford a whole new wardrobe," Maddie said as she finished her second cup of coffee.

"You can where I shop. I never pay full price for clothes and have even bought at consignment shops. We have some great ones in Knoxville."

Nell busied herself with oatmeal and fresh fruit for the children, explaining to Maddie that at least that was something they can eat on the road. She didn't plan on waking them until time to get in the car.

Both Drew and Nell hurriedly strapped the children in the back seats, leaving the center open for Maddie to climb into the third-row seating. She carried her pillow and a light blanket in case she felt the urge to sleep. Drew told her she could drive, and he'd snore in the back. But she didn't feel the need for that at the beginning of their trip.

"I'll spell you in a couple of hours if you'd like," Maddie said, leaning her head against the pillow at the side window.

"I can drive very well in my sleep," Drew said and glanced at the rearview mirror.

Maddie thought from the map that the trip might be about five hours. She woke form her sleep as they passed a sign indicating, *Louisville, 30 miles.*

Little DJ and Rosie watched a lively cartoon on the overhead screen. "Oh, good, I love this one," Maddie said, leaning toward the two giggling youngsters. "That is, unless you want me to drive?"

"No, I'm good, but I will stop at the next exit for everyone to stretch their legs or anything else necessary," Drew said. "I didn't think you'd ever wake up. Nell's eyeballs are floating!" He laughed loudly.

After a few minutes of wandering around inside the gas station, everyone loaded back up and they were on the road again.

That afternoon, with the U-Haul truck loaded, they set back on the route south.

"Do you want me driving the truck or the Escalade?" Maddie asked.

"You and Nell take the car and the kids," Drew said. "I'll handle the truck." He kissed Nell and both babies before climbing into the cab. "I'm going to stop in about two hours at a restaurant and motel. If you need to stop for anything before then, flash your lights at me." He smiled at Maddie.

"This was an easy move. Who did all the packing?" Maddie asked Nell once they were tucked in line behind Drew in the truck.

"We had movers take most of our things," Nell said. "What we have here is only personal items. We packed it up before we drove to Sevierville. The truck with our furniture and the rest of the boxes will be there tomorrow. But I don't think we can use all our furniture. The cabin was sold to us furnished. Drew says we can pick what we want to keep and donate or sell the rest."

"That's a good idea," Maddie said. "And I like the idea Drew mentioned about putting a drive down to the basement and having a garage door put in. That's a great space down there, just sort of impractical."

"I think that's why we got a good buy on the property. It won't be easy having that drive put in. But it does make better sense than using it the way we have it now. I love our view, though."

Drew chose a Comfort Inn next door to an Applebee's restaurant. The children were ready to get out of their car seat, and so were the ladies. Drew opened the back of the truck, getting out a double stroller. DJ was having no part of the pushing him in a stroller. He held Maddie's hand and walked with her.

"I'll take the stroller," Drew said. "Rosie and I are going on ahead to get a nice table with a view." He winked at Nell and went down the sidewalk.

DJ had to stop to investigate everything along the pathway, including a little black snake. Nell let out a squeal and jumped off the sidewalk. DJ laughed at his mom, and Maddie picked up the snake.

"This is how you tell if he's a good snake," Maddie said. "See how his head and body join straight at what should be his neck?"

DJ nodded and reached to touch it.

"This is how the 'friend to you' snake looks," Maddie went on. "Now, if he was a bad snake, you could see his head shape was different, right there." She pointed behind his eye. "A poison one has jaws that look like an arrowhead. Do you know what I mean?"

DJ laughed and said, "Yes, it would be fat there." Again, he touched the snake right where Maddie pointed.

"That's right! I'll show you on my pone when we get inside. Now, where do you think he might have been heading when we stopped him?"

"Into the grass?" DJ pointed at some tall grass off the side of the pathway.

"I bet you're right." Maddie set the wiggly snake down, and he slipped out of sight in no time. DJ watched him as long as he could see the grass moving.

"Enough science for today," Nell said, narrowing her eyes at Maddie. "Let's get some hands washed up so we can eat. You wash yours too, girl."

After taking an hour to eat the evening meal, Drew led them to the third floor. He carried one of the kids' suitcases, and Maddie carried hers. Immediately, DJ found the sliding door and saw there was a playground below on the back side of the hotel.

"Can we go out and swing?" DJ pleaded.

Maddie thought he had a good idea. "How about if I take both of the children out while you guys settle in and rest a bit?"

"I won't argue with that. But no snake handling this time?" Nell said.

The sun was dipping below the trees, and DJ wore himself out running up and down the slide, climbing the rope ladder, and finally wiggling into a swing. Maddie put Rosie in a toddler swing next to him and pushed them both.

After a while, Maddie felt a mosquito bite her arm, so she picked up Rosie, instructing DJ to lead her to the front lobby so they could return to the room.

Nell had the bathtub ready with floating ducks and boats. Rosie squealed, grabbing for the purple duck before she even had her diaper off. Drew took DJ into the shower with him. Maddie dropped on the sofa to wait. The next thing she knew, Nell shook her to wake her up.

"Your turn in the shower, or the bed, whichever you want," she laughed. "I hope you don't mind a guy sleeping with you. He's very small."

"Not at all," Maddie said. "He can't be any worse than sleeping with Bud." She turned away to hide the tears flowing from her eyes.

"Drew says you can call Holly from my phone," Nell said. "I know you miss him, and you need to talk to Holly."

After a quick shower, Maddie walked onto the balcony to call Holly. She chose to send a text first: *Call me at this #.* Then, Maddie waited a couple of minutes.

Holly's cell number showed on the phone screen.

"Hello," Maddie answered.

"There's a four-legged mutt jumping for the phone," Holly said. "He heard me tell Henry I was calling you."

Maddie laughed and cried at the same time. "I miss him," she said. She cleared her throat and added, "I miss everybody!"

"We miss you, too. But it's best this way. Are you alright?" Holly sounded tearful. She waited for Maddie to answer.

Finally, Maddie said, "Under the circumstance, I'm great! How about Shirley and Jess?"

"They're okay, too. We're fine; no need worrying about any of us. Do your thing. You're the only one who can!"

The call dropped.

Maddie's hands shook. Why would Holly hang up like that? Was some-one there? Was someone listening?

Maddie's restless sleep had nothing to do with her bed buddy, DJ. He was easier to lay next to than Bud. She watched his chest rise and fall with each breath. His lips moved as though he were dreaming of sucking a bottle. But he was totally on table food, and no need for bottles. She thought about that—what would a two-year-old dream of? His sleep was so peaceful, she felt envious. Watching his tiny little movements caused her heart to ache.

Will Rick and I ever have a child? Do I even want to bring one into this cruel world? She wiped a tear and breathed deeply. The tiny form rolled over, mov-ing closer to her. She lay an extra pillow between them so she wouldn't turn over and bump him out into the floor.

Drew had pulled the blackout curtain all the way closed. The next time Maddie awoke, she couldn't tell what time it was. She'd neglected to put her watch back on after she showered. She looked into tiny blue eyes, wide open and staring at her. Then, DJ smiled as though he remembered why she was there. He went back to sleep, so she got up to look outside. The sun was high already. Had Drew not set his alarm? He said he wanted to leave early to get things unloaded at the house in Sevierville. Maybe she should wake Nell?

After making a trip to the bathroom, Maddie returned to her bedside. Nell signaled to her. "Shhh," she said, then whispered, "Let's let them sleep while we get the car reloaded."

Maddie nodded. She carried her clothes to the bathroom to quickly dress before Drew woke up. A couple minutes later, she made a trip to the vehicle with her small suitcase. She went to the lobby and retrieved a carafe of coffee and a couple packages of orange and apple juice. She found the door to their room open and the babies still sleeping.

Drew walked out with the remaining personal items for the car. "Nell is almost ready. I'll be back for a cup of coffee. Save me some?"

Maddie just smiled and nodded.

With a new cartoon on the overhead screen, the women and children were tucked in behind the truck heading south again, just a couple hours behind schedule. Conversation was sparse between the friends. Maddie had too much on her mind to listen when Nell did speak. After a while, DJ asked if he could have a cookie. His quick bowl of cereal had not been enough for this growing boy.

Nell moved toward the canvas bag on the floor behind her seat. She pulled out snacks and even handed a teething biscuit to Rosie. "She'll have that mess all over her and the back seat," Nell said. "But I know she loves them. Watch your sister so she doesn't get choked, will you, DJ?"

"I will. She makes a mess," he warned his mom. "Big messy."

"We'll let her enjoy her mess today. Is that okay with you?"

DJ was already consumed by the TV screen.

"He speaks clearly for a two-year-old," Maddie said.

"He really does," Nell said. "We marvel at things he repeats."

They both laughed.

The long, monotonous interstate drive came to a sudden halt as they reached the outskirts of Knoxville. Traffic came to a slow crawl.

"There must be a game today," Maddie said. "Or somewhere up ahead, there's a wreck. Call Drew and ask him if he'll let me lead. I can reroute us on a couple backroads and escape this congestion."

Drew was glad to oblige Maddie. He followed her through curvy backroads, and they made their destination without losing any additional time. When he pulled into the drive at their new house, Mattie pulled into the tracks in the grass from where her SUV had driven.

"We might as well make that the driveway to the garage," Drew said. "I'm going to get someone on that project ASAP." He picked up DJ and swung him around. "Have you had enough riding and TV for today?"

"Too much ridin'," DJ said in his sweet little mature-sounding voice. "More swing."

Drew looked toward Nell with an adoring smile. "Thank you for the gift of this precious life."

Nell smiled with a glow.

"You sound different now, Drew," Maddie said. "I believe you've absorbed a little of Nell's sweetness. You're a lucky guy, having this family." She tried not to show her pain as it sunk in that she and Rick might never have what her friends enjoyed.

Drew put his free arm around her and squeezed her tightly. "Maddie, you're going to be happy and back with Rick soon. You are too optimistic for those thoughts."

After helping unload the car and the rental truck, Maddie came out with her hiking boots on. She saw Drew surveying the potential drive around to the lower level and garage. "You mind if I go for a hike?" she asked.

"If you promise not to get lost," Drew said as he waved to her with a big smile.

"I'll be back before dark. I have my burner and won't use it unless I have to."

Maddie waved bye and headed up the hill to the left of the house. She'd already decided it was a game trail and hoped she'd come across some deer, and maybe even a bear.

9

The afternoon air was warm with a cool breeze. Maddie walked along the highly traveled trail, paying close attention to all she passed so she could retrace her steps. How she wished her Bud was with her. This was all new for her, and with some marvelous views of Mount Le Conte, she continued walking, feeling less stress than she had for several days. All of a sudden, she felt a hand touched her arm. She stopped, looking all around. She thought she must have brushed against a tree branch or something. Not seeing what might have touched her, she leaned against a rock. There was no one around her, yet she felt a tug on her arm.

Closing her eyes, she breathed deep several times. Her head felt light, so she sat on the path thinking she might pass out. A chill tingled through her body. A voice whispered in her left ear, like sound coming from within the rock.

She listened but couldn't make sense of it. She crossed her legs, sitting Indian style, and again, closed her eyes. She'd felt this way before. It was when she entered the tent in Georgia where the rangers placed the body of a dead hiker they found along the Appalachian Trail. She sat still and let her breathing slow. Her head felt lighter now, and her face burned. Glancing at her arm, she felt a cool presence; quietly, she awaited a message. Previously, the dead communicated with her. Was this voice from a living, breathing person? Was it Rick?

She thought of one of their hikes up to Whitehouse Cliff Trail. She had been trying to pace herself to catch up with Bud, as he was far ahead of her. Rick had grabbed her left arm and stopped her, saying, "What's your hurry? Bud is on a mission, but we are not. You know he won't go out of our sight. Slow down and see all that's around you."

What was she missing? Was it even Rick speaking to her? Slowly, she stood up, holding on to the rock face for support. Then, she heard a scuffing sound farther up the trail. A large, dark form moved toward her. It was a single bear, meandering down the path right toward her. As carefully as she could, she climbed up the rock, high as she could reach. The bear continued on toward her. Distracted by something other than her, he walked right on past her and took a lower trail down the steep mountain.

Maddie sat on the rock ledge, watching him go out of sight and wondering what just happened. She had bear spray in her small backpack, but she hadn't even thought to take it out. The bear was not the least bit concerned about her. He hadn't even seen her. Was she lucky or what? Giving the wild critter plenty of space, she waited a few minutes before she climbed down and began retracing her steps back down the trail she'd been walking.

Maddie could not shake the feeling that she'd been warned. Why had she thought of the exact incident when Rick grabbed her arm to get her attention, and why did she remember his words so clearly?

"Yes, I was warned," she said aloud. "Okay now, Rick, talk to me. Tell me where you are being held! I'm listening!"

Back at the house, Maddie found Drew waiting on the deck when she walked across the driveway.

"I was beginning to worry as I watched that beautiful sunset," Drew said. "Thanks for getting back before dark."

Maddie swung her backpack off her shoulders and set it next to the front door. "It's a great trail," she said. "But keep your bear spray handy. I want to bring Rick and Bud up here to hike up to Mount Le Conte. You guys will want to see it too. The views are awesome."

"Even the views of the bears?" Drew grinned.

"Yes, even the bears." She said no more—just walked into the house.

Nell came out of the kitchen. She asked, "Can you believe we got everything put away?"

"Even the furniture?" Maddie asked, looking around the room. "I see some nice pieces that were not here before. Where's the rest of it?"

"We fit it all in, except for a couple of chairs," Nell said. "Drew wrangled them down the steps to the basement. I wouldn't say they are in the same condition, but they will be okay there."

Nell's laughter told Maddie her friend was way beyond tired.

"You need to go to bed early, girl," Maddie said. "I can get the children to bed." She walked to the kitchen stove and checked out a covered pot. "Did you save me something for supper?"

"You know I did. Do you feel like potato soup?" Nell dropped into a chair. "How was the walk?"

"It's a wonderful trail. I bumped into a rather large bear, but he didn't even notice me."

"What? You saw a bear, but he didn't see you? I can't believe that!"

"Got any crackers?" Maddie asked, ignoring Nell's comment. "Oh, I see them...That's perfect. I like the oyster crackers with potato soup." She helped herself to a bottle of water and sat in the chair across from Nell.

"I can't believe the way this encounter came about," Maddie said, trying her soup. She proceeded to tell Nell what had transpired.

Later that evening, with everyone in bed but her, Maddie bundled up and went out onto the back deck. She sat in a lounge chair and stared at the sky. After a couple of minutes, she noticed a shooting star. And shortly after, there was another. *Hmmm, must be a meteor shower tonight. Well, I know where I'm sleeping,* she told herself.

Meanwhile in Cold Creek, Doc caught up with Henry as he arrived at the sheriff's office early the next morning.

"Hey, Henry," Doc said. "You have any idea where Maddie is? I've been trying for days to get in touch with her."

"I'm really sorry, but we can't tell anyone where she is," Henry said. "Some bad dudes are looking for her. And now, they even suspect Rick of staging his own kidnapping. It's completely out of the question, but someone cooked it up. So, I'm checking on messages and fax machine a couple times a day. What do you need to tell her?" Henry unlocked the door to Rick's office.

"I visit a patient of mine up near Sam's Gap about once a month," Doc said. "Seeing her yesterday, she told me some interesting information. And her grandson shared some photos with me that he took from his drone. I don't know who to take the photos to." Doc pulled up the video on his phone first. "Notice the date? It's the same day Rick was taken. And look at these vehicles. Look, he even got in close enough to read the license plate on the black truck."

Henry sat in Rick's chair, watching the video the young boy caught by accident. "This was taken up near Sam's Gap?"

"Yeah, right about where Maddie drove off, crashing her Blazer that time."

"I'm not even sure who to trust with this. TBI over at the Knoxville office are a bunch of jerks! Maddie must know someone, but she hasn't shared any names with me. Well, except for Scott, one of the rangers at Rocky Fort State Park."

"I'll download these to a flash drive if you happen to have one?" Doc said, fumbling with his phone.

"I remember seeing one on that desk," Henry said, stepping over to Maddie's desk.

Doc succeeded in adding the still shots to the flash drive.

"I'll give Scott a call," Henry said.

"I have a patient coming in shortly," Doc said. "Let me know what you can find out." He left the office.

Henry called Scott. He was on a fishing trip.

"Scott, Henry Jacobs," he said. "Listen, I have some information, but not sure who to refer it to. Did Maddie mention anyone to you?"

"No, Henry, she kind of left here in a huff," Scott replied. "I didn't know she and Rick had any voodoo powers between them. I guess I hurt her feelings."

"I'm not sure how much Rick believes in it, but Maddie sure has something that makes her sense things before they happen," Henry said. "I'd certainly never laugh it off."

"Have you not talked with her?" Scott asked.

"She's out of contact for the time being. I'll try getting a message to her. But I have no way to reach out to her. If you hear from her, please let me know?"

And with that, Henry hung up the phone. Their conversation threw up a red flag for Henry. He'd been around Rick enough to smell something fishy. He called Jess.

"Hello, are you at home?" Henry asked. He walked toward the fax machine, snatched up the copies to put on file, and then walked next door to Maddie's house, where he and Shirley were staying.

Jess met him outside, saying, "Shirley is napping. I thought we ought to talk out here."

Henry showed the drone video to Jess and commented on the still shots.

"Henry, you feel like going hunting?" Jess asked with such enthusiasm that Henry had to laugh.

"Heck yeah!" Henry said. "We've been left in charge of things, haven't we? Let's go."

The two men drove toward the North Carolina-Tennessee state line at Sam's Gap via the old Hwy 23. Henry made a call as they proceeded up the old road. He requested that Jess stop in at Mrs. Whitson's house to talk with her grandson.

Mrs. Whitson sat in a rocking chair on the front porch of her house.

Henry approached, saying, "You're looking good, Mrs. Whitson."

"Hello, Henry," she said. "Come on up here and visit a spell."

"How'd you know it was me?" Henry said. He climbed the stairs, stepping directly in front of the elderly lady.

Mrs. Whitson extended her hand. Henry caught it for a shake. "When you lose one of your senses, the others gain more perception," she said. "Since I lost my sight, voices are uniquely keen to my ears. We just spoke by phone. Of course I recognize you." She laughed. "Who you got with you?"

"Maybe you'll recognize my voice too, Ms. Wilma?" Jess said, stopping at the bottom of the steps.

"Why, Jess McKenzie, is that you? Lordy, I haven't seen you in a decade. Come on up here, close to me."

Jess put his hand on hers. "It's been a long time, for sure."

"How's your Shirley? I heard you all sold the restaurant."

"Yes, ma'am, and we have done some traveling. We're enjoying retirement."

"I might be out in the country, but not out of touch. I heard your house got burned. Now, tell me how your wife is, please."

"Pardon me, Mrs. Wilma. Shirley is not great. We're staying at Maddie's right now. But she's gonna be just fine. We will be okay. Just a bump in the road."

"If anybody can do it, you two can," Mrs. Whitson said. "You're strong minded. And that's a good thing."

"When I spoke with you, Mrs. Whitson, you said you'd heard strange sounds going on," Henry cut in. "What type of sounds?"

"Gabe told me what I heard was the sounds from his videos," she said. "He was over on the mountain above Spivey. I reckon he was trying to spot some deer with his drone. Anyway, I asked why he'd been in the area, around a sawmill or a construction site. He said there wasn't supposed to be anything like that there. He couldn't figure it out."

"When will Gabe be home?" Jess asked.

"He's down in South Carolina at his dad's right now. I've sent him my phone number, and he's supposed to call me."

Henry stood up, stretched his legs, and placed his hand on the elderly woman's. "It was good seeing you, doing so well. If you ever need help, like when Gabe is not here, just call me. I can put my number in your phone if you'd like?"

"Thank you, Henry, but it's already in there...as 007," Mrs. Whitson said. She laughed and added, "Gabe done it as a joke, but it's easy to remember."

"And if Henry is tied up, tell him to call me and Shirley," Jess said. "Matter of fact, I'd love to bring her up here for a while just to make her feel needed. You got anything she could give you help with? Canning food or planting flowers? She's got so much energy now that she's thin again."

"Shirley always had energy, but I'm pleased hearing she's done so good on her weight loss," Mrs. Whitson said. "I'll think of something she can do for me, or at least make her think I need help with." She pulled her phone out of her apron pocket. "Go on and put yours in my phone, and file it under 0007. That is easy to recall after this meeting today. I have a strange filling system." She laughed even harder this time.

Jess grasped her chin gently and bent to kiss her cheek. "We've always loved you, Ms. Wilma. Shirley will be here to see you soon, I promise."

Back on the road, heading up Spivey Mountain, Henry told Jess of his suspicions: "When my brother and I were teens, we used to go bear hunting. We never got one, thank goodness. But we heard about a meadow which was supposed to be home to plenty of wildlife. We walked our legs off and camped out two nights before we realized we were on the wrong side of Spivey. Just because the waterfall is on the south side of the mountain, that doesn't discount the north side. That's part of Spivey Mountain, too. And a really large area."

"Did you ever go back to the north side for hunting?" Jess pondered the thought.

"Yes, but not until Holly and I were married. She and I spent a weekend camping out and walking trails. The only thing we found was The Lost Cove."

"I've never hiked to The Lost Cove," Jess said. "Always wanted to, but never made the time. I wouldn't have ever thought you'd get to that location from Spivey."

"Told you it's a vast area," Henry said. "If you look as the crow flies, you'd make sense of the location."

Jess pulled the vehicle off the side of Hwy 19 onto a forestry road with a locked gate.

"This is where we started our escapade," Henry said. "By the time we got back to my old truck, it had a note on the windshield with a strong word from Division of Forestry."

The men climbed out of the truck and checked around the gate, looking for any recent activity. They discovered plenty in front of the gate, but nothing seemed to go beyond. Henry continued walking up the mostly grassy, gravel road. A couple hundred yards, and the creek cut across the road. Henry stepped on stable rocks to make his way to the other side the creek.

"Jess, I got something on this side," Henry said. "Tracks—ATV tracks, and they look to be recent. We might be onto something for sure." He tiptoed back across the rocky creek and joined Jess.

"I found some tracks in that sandy area," Jess said. "I photographed them. I'll compare to the tire prints Maddie found in our yard. I bet you they will match."

"Okay, time to head back to the sheriff office and make a plan," Henry said. "I have a four-wheeler. You still have yours?"

"No, Shirley worried that I might get hurt, so I got rid of it."

"I'm sure my brother will loan us his. He might even want to go with us," Henry said. "We need a plan. I think I'll talk to Ranger Scott. You and I can't do anything if they are holding Rick up there. Scott is part of the Division of Forestry; he can."

On the return trip to Cold Water Creek, Jess tried calling Maddie. "No luck," he said to Henry. "Her phone is still turned off."

"Holly said Maddie called her last night," Henry said. "They didn't get to talk, though. Holly heard something on the line that she claims sounded like someone listening in. So, she quickly hung up. She said the cell Maddie called from was based in Kentucky. Who can you think of that is in Kentucky?"

Henry looked toward Jess.

"Nell and Drew are in Louisville, Kentucky," Jess admitted. "In fact, they are in Sevierville, and Maddie went to visit them. We can call Drew."

"Do you have his number?"

"I believe so." Jess scrolled through a lifetime collection of numbers. "I need to clear most of these outta here." He shook his head in frustration.

"Try looking under 'sheriff.' I bet you never updated it after Drew was hurt," Henry said.

"I'll be darned, you're right. Drew is listed under the S's. Like I said, I gotta eliminate most of these."

Jess pressed send, and in just a minute, he answered the incoming call.

"Drew, its Jess McKenzie."

After a lengthy conversation, Jess said, "He's coming here tomorrow. But he doesn't want to get Maddie's hopes up. So, he's not going to tell her."

10

Early the following morning, Henry started out while Holly and the kids slept. He left a note on the kitchen counter that read, *Sweet thing, I gotta get on the job early. I'll call you later. Love you.*

He parked next to the sheriff's office and walked across the street to Shirley's Restaurant. He noticed a car in the parking lot with a Kentucky tag. Inside, he found Drew sipping coffee and talking with Ben, the owner of the restaurant.

"Henry," Drew called out. "Top of the morning, ole buddy." He stood, meeting Henry halfway across the room.

"Good seeing you, Drew," Henry said. "How ya been?" Henry took a quick look around, hoping no locals were up this early. They had the restaurant to themselves. "Glad you came. We need some guidance on this."

In a low voice, Henry unloaded the dread on his shoulders. He and Drew ate a hardy breakfast and drank at least a full pot of coffee as they shared ideas of how this strategic mission was to go. Drew elected not to contact Scott, so as to keep the team as small as possible.

"If we need reinforcement, we can call on a few more," Drew explained. "But we'd better keep things quiet about scanning that area first."

Jess joined them as the sun lighted his way. "Good morning, boys!" he said.

Jess settled on a seat at the counter where Ben poured a mug of coffee for the former owner of the restaurant.

Drew approached with open arms, embracing an old friend. "I'm glad you called me. This visit is long overdue."

"I agree with you on keeping Maddie out of the mix today," Jess said. "Where Rick is concerned, she thinks with her heart. Best not cause her any more depression if we are wrong with our assumptions." He sat back onto the stool, finishing his coffee. "Sorry I missed the planning. What are we doing?"

As locals began gathering in the restaurant, Ben suggested the three men relocate to the kitchen table, where they could make a plan of attack, away from ears not needing involvement.

Drew made a sort of plan on a napkin. Henry and Jess were to ride in as close as they dared on one ATV, and Drew would circle the opposite side on the other. They were just waiting for Henry's brother to bring the two ATVs into town. He had them both at his house a short way from town. Arriving right on time, the men thanked Ben for the secret meeting place, and they hit the road in the truck Ross brought them, pulling the trailer with four wheelers.

Drew unloaded several rifles and handguns from his car, thoughtfully disguised as golf clubs. They all got a huge laugh out of the covert disguise.

The woods dripped of morning dew with shards of sunlight cutting a directional path up the overgrown forest road. If it weren't for this being a very serious, possibly lifesaving matter of someone they all three genuinely loved, this could be classified as a fun trip. Each man had his own private thoughts of what Agent Rick Malone meant to them. How he'd stolen the heart of not only the town's favorite daughter, Madison McKenzie, but theirs as well.

Rick's devotion to the citizens of Cold Creek and their task of uncovering, literally, the bones of injustice was unmatched. He'd poured his heart into backing Maddie all the way to Alaska to bring closure to the horrors of the young woman's lifelong deception. Rick was a good man, and by no fault of his own, someone challenged the people of the community by taking their beloved sheriff. Now, this team represented those citizens.

Drew explained that he had studied a map of the area known as The Lost Cove, which is where the team was heading. Originally, the community was a booming population with two main industries: lumber and whisky. The Cove was surrounded by steep mountains, difficult to access but filled with trees for harvesting, which were floated down the Nolichucky River to Erwin and the waiting sawmills. As for whisky, the location of the small settlement was enough to keep out any snooping from the law in North Carolina and Tennessee; neither one felt obligated to enforce the issue, considering The Lost Cove was right smack on their state lines.

The only transportation besides walking in, or horseback, was the railroad and the river. The deep gorge cut through some of the steepest terrane of the Blue Ridge Mountains. Naturally, in the 1950s, when the railroad quit stopping for community access, people began moving away. Thus, the settlement shrank until, in 1957, the final resident left the Cove.

Nowadays, the homes and buildings were mostly deteriorated, leaving only steps to nowhere or foundations of a dwelling long forgotten. Vandals made off with any worthy items left by its people, or else the forests overtook them. Mostly, curious hikers trekked in by walking the tracks next to the river or hiking miles up the steep mountainside. Even the skeleton on an ancient truck in the midst of a now uninhabited wilderness suggested there was once an actual road. Decades of nature reclaiming her territory hid it beyond recognition.

Drew brought his ATV to a halt. He suggested the others stay at this point. He pointed out a split in the walking trail. "As I studied the aerial map last night, I noticed this split," he said. "I'll go on the right side and work my way around approximately two miles and come in from the other side. Wait here fifteen minutes before you go on foot the rest of the way, maybe a half mile. The only distinguishing landmark I saw was what remains of one house with an old truck frame amongst the tree growth. Move slowly, stay hidden best you can, and by all means, stay quiet. You're slipping up on the worst monster you ever hope to come across. And he might still have some eyes on lookout besides his own."

"What about the bodies they found off the Parkway?" Henry asked.

"No connection. Those were illegals escaped from the border. They just aren't letting any details out locally. But they were not our kidnappers. Don't know how that story even got started. So, are we good here? No shooting. This is just reconnaissance today."

Henry and Jess nodded their heads. Jess got off and pulled some branches up for Henry to drive the ATV underneath in an attempt to hide the vehicle. Jess noted the time on his watch: 9:20. He and Henry grabbed the two rifles they'd gotten from Drew. Both had great scopes on the barrels for close viewing. If they could keep hidden and still view the area, this might just work.

Luckily, the soft ferns jutting through the forest floor and the ground covered with bulbs coming to life for May's blooms provided them with quiet footsteps. They crouched at any sound they heard. With each step, they surveyed their surroundings. Edging toward the remains of any community was far from the scenes of what they were encountering. Jess must have looked doubtful. Henry gave him a thumbs-up sign rather than speaking. Jess nodded slowly and shrugged his shoulders.

Another stretch of thick underbrush passed slowly before they reached what might have once been a clearing. There were lots of skinny trees and no old growth in the forest as far as the eye could see. Henry squatted down and raised the scope of the rifle. He swung the barrel from one side to the other and then quickly back. He lowered the rifle and pointed in the direction he'd viewed.

Jess raised his barrel and looked through his scope. He nodded, still moving slightly side to side. They chose the largest clumps for coverage and approached closer to the remains of the last standing house and, sure enough, they spotted the antique truck frame over to the side.

Henry moved toward his left to gain a vantage point closer to the structure. That's when the memory Mrs. Whitson recalled from hearing the video came to Henry's mind.

The video picked up sounds like a saw. "Those are small logs on the side of that house, unlike the boards on the remainder of the house," Henry said. "It's been reconstructed." He raised the scope again and studied the logs closely. "There's bark on the logs. That's not right."

He motioned to Jess to join him. Slowly, carefully, he made his way to Henry's side. Raising his scope, he immediately knew what Henry saw. He nodded his head. Henry took out his phone, checking for a signal. Nothing! They couldn't text Drew. They sat tight, waiting for some sign or movement.

After what seemed an eternity, Henry raised the scope again to look at something moving. It was a man in a suit. Close behind him was another movement. That one went back away from sight. So, there were two, possibly. Henry watched. Jess tapped his arm softly and pointed to another man walking toward the one in the suit. This one was wearing camouflage like a hunter. The man in the suit began yelling, and the other turned to go back where he had come from. They were too far away to distinguish any dialogue.

The man in the suit lit a cigar, puffing out a billow of smoke. He followed the camouflage guy, now out of sight of Henry and Jess. They sunk to the ground to wait for whatever developed, or to hear from Drew.

"Can you recognize the suit guy?" Henry asked.

"I can't see him that well from here," Jess answered. "The voice sounds right, but he was not wearing a suit when he abducted Shirley and me."

"There could be more than the original three men in on this."

At that moment, something rustled in the bush behind them. They both focused scopes toward that direction.

"Put 'em down, boys, it's me," Drew whispered. "There's more than three of them up there. I'm thinking one of us needs to stay here. The other two go out and call up reinforcements. If Rick is there, we can't get to him without more backup." Drew took a deep breath. "I accepted the position of chief of police in Sevierville starting next week. They can't help us, but TBI can. I hate the idea, the way they've acted so far, but I don't know who else to turn to. Unicoi County officers..." He stopped. "Well, I'm not sure how experienced they are at this kind of thing. These fellows are professionals."

"Let's meet back up at the ATV," Henry suggested. "You find yours, and let's pull back. I'll stay in the woods. You and Jess go get reinforcements."

The group split again, meeting back at the vehicles half an hour later. Jess left with Drew in the truck, and Henry returned to the trail on one of the ATVs. He guarded the position where he could watch the guys move around the recently renovated cabin. He pulled a candy bar from his shirt pocket and settled against a tree to eat a bite of lunch.

All of a sudden, he heard a motor starting up. Then, the man in the suit came around the cabin on a side-by-side.

"So, that's your mode of transportation?" Henry scooted back into the underbrush and focused the scope on the movement. It appeared the suit was going for a ride. He watched as the side-by-side moved down the hill toward the river. Henry followed at a safe distance.

Steep as the hill sloped, he wondered if the vehicle could move all the way to the river. It sure didn't take long to find out. The man parked and slid down the hillside the last one hundred yards, leaving the vehicle parked against a large rock and covered by a large pine branch.

Sneaky, aren't you? No one would ever spot that from the tracks or the river, Henry thought as he slid carefully down to watch.

A river raft waited at the bottom where the old dock once provided a stopping place for boats. Nowadays, only kayaks and rafters ventured along the cliffs below the old settlement. The river rapids can become dangerous in the area depending on the water level. Henry was well aware the rapids were no place for amateurs. He had a close friend who'd gotten injured badly trying to run the rapids without a guide.

He watched and photographed with his phone as the suit man stepped aboard the raft. Then, they vanished among the rocky outcroppings as the river flowed away from Henry's view. He tried his phone, but as he suspected, there was no signal in the depth of the canyon cutting between the steep mountains.

Meanwhile, back at the cottage Nell and Drew purchased for their new home, Maddie helped her friend organize the basement contents. The bare room now looked like a man-cave. Nell explained Drew's imaginary plan for adding the garage door and a wall to separate the two rooms.

"I suggested he have a window or two cut into that wall," she said and pointed beyond the area where a car was to park.

"It would be nice having natural light," Maddie said. "Guess he'll have to discuss that with the builder. This is perfect for finishing off your new home. Drew will come down here to hide from the kids." She laughed.

"He's saving that side of the room to build a swing set and climbing wall for them," Nell said. "I can't believe he's serious, but it was his idea."

Nell smiled with a look that made Maddie fill with envy. She turned to keep her tears from showing. "Where will the elevator be?" Maddie asked.

"Oh, in the garage side. He's already sketched it, so he can relay an accurate picture to the builder. He's really fired up with this whole idea. I've never seen him this excited about spending money."

They both laughed.

The baby monitor notified them that the children were awake, so they hurried back upstairs.

Both children were in good moods as they ate their lunch. Maddie felt an energy overflow.

"You and the kids will have fun playing today," Maddie said. "Will you allow me to take your car and go someplace? I hate to leave alone, but I can't stay cooped up on a day as pretty as it is out there."

"Drew took my car," Nell said. "He needed to do some personal running around and couldn't use his police car. I'm sorry."

"It's okay. I just can't sit still. I need to be out there, in the open. I am going to call a cab and take my own vehicle. I don't like being held prisoner."

"I wish you wouldn't, but I won't stop you. I understand and wish I could help you." Nell gave Maddie a big hug and handed her phone to her best friend. "I'm sorry, I have no idea when Drew will be home. Take my phone with you. You can use it freely. I'll keep your burner just in case of an emergency."

"Are you sure?" Maddie asked. "It's one thing with me at odds with Drew, but it's totally another if he gets mad at you."

"Well, you leaving won't sit well with him, so taking my phone is the least of our worries," Nell laughed.

"No, I don't want you involved. I'm doing this on my own."

Maddie walked briskly up the stairs and packed her bag. She had no idea where she was going or what she might need. She was not sure Drew was being completely honest with her. She had a gut feeling he was hiding something. She had to get away before he returned.

11

Drew called Scott as soon as he had a cell signal. Scott said it was his day off and agreed to meet him at the sheriff's office.

He thought about Agent Donnelly in Asheville, and as luck would have it, he had made note of the private cell number in his phone. He called the number.

In a few seconds, Agent Donnelly answered: "Agent Donnelly,"

"Hello, Donnelly. Drew Perry here. I, um, need a favor, brother. We believe we've located Rick Malone. But we're outnumbered. I don't believe the locals here in the area can safely handle this. I know who has him, as do you. Maddie is at my home, safe, and doesn't know what I've discovered. Can you help us?"

"Obviously, Maddie confided in you," the agent said, "even though I asked her not to tell anyone. But I'll help. Where do I need to be?"

"Do you know the location of The Lost Cove on the Tennessee-North Carolina state line?" Drew asked.

"I do. Are you referring to the walk-in trail?"

"Yes. We'll meet there on Highway 19 as soon as possible. There are four or five men, but there could be more. Henry Jacobs is still there, keeping an eye on them. I'm trying to round up as many men as I dare trust. The TBI hasn't been notified yet," Drew reluctantly mentioned.

"Don't," Donnelly said. "I have some good men I can contact. We'll see you in a couple hours. Thanks for calling, Drew. Be careful, buddy."

Next, Drew called the sheriff of Hancock County, an old friend, tough as nails and a really shady character. But he was trustworthy and knew how to fight. After a short conversation, they made a plan to meet in two hours.

A couple more phone calls, and Drew phoned Jess.

"I've got all the help I need," Drew told him. "You stay behind in case we need you here."

He started to hang up, but Jess interjected with, "No, Drew, I'm going with you. We lost everything in the fire. I have to go!"

"All the more reason you need to stay here with Shirley and not give her any more grief."

Drew made one more call and walked to the restaurant, going in through the back door. Ben met him and offered a sandwich. Drew accepted the chicken salad and ordered a dozen of any kind Ben could whip up quickly. He loaded a case of water offered by the restaurant, then sped out of town with everything he needed loaded into Henry's truck.

As he arrived at the forestry gate on Hwy 19, there were multiple trucks on the side the road, and he counted ten men gathered around one vehicle. He parked and joined them, carrying the box of sandwiches.

"If any of you have not eaten, Shirley's Restaurant sent a good supply of sandwiches, and I have a couple cases of water also," Drew said. "Help yourselves, please." He put one wrapped sandwich in his jacket pocket and then briefly spoke before turning the plan over to Donnelly.

"This is flying by the seat of our pants, but if we can save Sheriff Malone, it's worth our time trying," Donnelly said. He delivered all the information he was aware of and asked the men to hold their fire no matter what, unless they were told to shoot. "I'm familiar with a couple of you and thank you for coming. This is a volunteer-only mission. Use your best judgement, and let's try not to fire a shot."

Additional four-wheelers and side-by-sides had been unloaded before Drew arrived. He was happy seeing the promising turnout. He took a moment to pray quietly to himself as he led the procession out the forestry trail.

At that same time, Maddie walked briskly toward the storage unit where Drew locked away her SUV. She'd picked up the key from the kitchen drawer where she'd seen him toss it. She drove the vehicle out and replaced the lock. She drove toward Gatlinburg by a back road, trying to stay off the main highways.

She noticed that her heart was racing as she turned onto Old Middle Creek Road. Why was she nervous? Was it a fear of Drew getting upset at her for taking off? Or was she guilty for leaving Nell alone? At this particular time, she didn't really care what Drew thought. Her husband was kidnapped, and her family's home burned, and she could not just sit around on her hands and do nothing. She had to be out in the wild trying to read any thoughts she might intercept from Rick. She'd had good results in the past and knew she could do it again.

Traffic was tolerable when she entered the bypass heading up toward the Smokey Mountain National Park. She stopped at the Visitor's Center for a couple bottles of water and a snack before she turned right onto the road toward Townsend. Following the creek in the midst of the woodlands was a lovely drive. Maddie noticed the creek was full, so she thought she'd like to stop at the waterfall and see if anyone was jumping off the cliff above. Everyone knew the authorities didn't like it; they even posted signs, hoping no one would be hurt. She'd seen teens—boys and girls—jump to the water below. But she'd never heard of anyone being hurt.

There were no spaces to park when she passed the bridge, so Maddie drove on past. *Oh well, I better keep on track anyway,* she thought.

When she came to the curve in the river, she felt chills. She'd been run off the road once and pushed into the flooding river in that very spot. It caused an uneasy feeling as she passed the pool were the car she drove had gone over. She escaped by swimming against the current of the drainpipe running under the road, and at the other end, she was rescued by a handsome state trooper. Luck was really on her side that day. She hoped Rick had some luck in his lifeline. She couldn't even imagine how she'd live without him. He was her best friend, and she loved him more than she'd ever thought possible.

Continuing straight, she saw the sign put out by the rangers estimating how long the drive through the eleven-mile circle around the Loop Road in the Cove might be on a day with today's traffic. She was pleased noting that the time was estimated on the lower side. Sometimes the traffic was so heavy it backed up for a mile or more. That was usually caused by the sight of a bear. Maddie laughed out loud when she remembered traffic had backed up because of a turkey on the side of the Loop Road. Signs everywhere said, "Be considerate. Don't stop in the road. Use the pull-offs where provided."

There were always those who couldn't or wouldn't read. They really caused a traffic jam with multiple bears.

Maddie recalled one trip, she got out of the car, leaving Rick to sit by himself. She walked at least a mile to the head of the traffic jam only to find it had been a momma bear with two cubs causing a two-mile backup. Eventually, the traffic moved, and she waited for Rick to drive by and pick her up.

After that, Rick refused to drive through the Cove anymore. She missed it so much. It had been one of her very favorite places to visit. Once, it was soothing to drive the Loop, but too many rude people spoiled it for her from that day forward.

Today, the access road into the Cove was void of all traffic. Maddie was sure she'd never seen zero cars entering the eleven-mile, one-way Loop. She drove past the pasture where the stables and horses were. The horses were all in the pasture grazing.

In the first stretch, there was not a car as far as she could see. "Wow, this is odd," she said aloud. When Maddie came to the first donation box, she pulled in. She never passed the box without making a donation. The park was free to visit, and yet so many cars zipped right on past it. She looked carefully as she pulled back onto the road, but still no cars.

Driving in silence with the windows down, she enjoyed the freshness of the forest mixed with wildflowers. Butterflies and bees flew close to the ground, not missing a single bloom. The first creek crossing was unique, the road dips and the water flowing over smoothly. She loved this spot but never had the opportunity to take a photo of the water upon her tires. She even noticed a couple of tiny minnows swimming almost within touching distance below her window.

This was way too quiet to believe. But when she rounded the next curve, there were the cars. They were all pulled over at a cabin where a special display was set up, showing a nature exhibit.

"Enjoy," Maddie said. "Take your time as I drive the Loop all by myself." She waved at a couple that smiled as she passed.

In the field below the crowded cabin, she saw a momma deer with two spotted fawns. She slowed to a stop and watched them graze on tender green grass. The fawns played, running to and fro like children. She felt saddened, thinking about Nell and her lovely children back at the house. She quickly blotted the thought from her mind.

She thought she heard a voice. It sounded so real that she turned her head to look back and see if someone had called her name. No one was even close. She drove on, but not so cheerful now.

The next curve in the road reminded her—that was where she'd had her famous bear encounter. She thought it was the perfect place to wander on a trail for a while. She parked and locked the vehicle. Walking up toward the gully between the two steep ridges caused a stir inside her gut.

I'm not afraid. What is this feeling? She continued walking slowly, watching for any movement. Intensely green ferns covered the ground all around, except the path she was on.

"Is this the game trail where deer and bears come out?" she said aloud. She smiled when she noticed the sweet purple violets low to the ground, next to some tall ferns.

"That's a nice picture," she spoke to no one but herself. Just to the left of them, she saw the white violets nestled below another stand of ferns. She snapped another picture.

Walking along, she felt the trail begin to rise toward the game trail where she'd met the momma bear. Maddie heard a voice on the wind. She stopped and turned her head all different ways. She spoke, "Rick? Are you thinking of me?"

The woods drowned out her thoughts with birds and bugs singing or chirping their songs. Maddie stopped to photograph a blue bird picking a bug out of the grass. She followed its flight into a maple tree overhead. A brighter blue, the male landed next to the first bird. She zoomed in to capture the mates side by side on the branch.

While Maddie stood looking at the screen on her camera, she missed the movement on the ridge ahead. Walking again, she heard a female voice.

"Over here," the low voice whispered.

Maddie looked off the trail next to a large tree; there was a lady holding a camera with a long lens. The woman motioned her to come toward her. Maddie approached, wondering what this was about.

"There's a momma bear at the top of the ridge," the woman said. "I'm waiting to take her picture. You can't see her yet. I noticed her as she climbed down from a tree higher up the trail. I see her often. I didn't want her to scare you. Or you to scare her off."

"Oh, good, I want to see her," Maddie said. "I was looking at the photos I got of the violets. I'm sorry. Hope I didn't spoil your shot."

"You didn't; she hasn't spotted us yet. I'm Liz. I come out here a couple days of the week just to find her. I named her Delilah. She has three cubs this year."

"I'm Maddie. I think I met Delilah a couple years ago. I was up on top of the ridge, and she walked from that ridge to this one. I was excited but unsure if she would hurt me. She came within about fifty or seventy-five feet," Maddie said softly. It felt good telling a fellow bear watcher about her encounter.

"There, she's starting down the trail now," Liz said, focusing the camera and snapping several pictures in succession. She kept shooting until Delilah was out of sight on the game trail.

"Wow, you must have some terrific photos there!" Maddie said. She felt like such an amateur.

"I do this for a living," Liz said. "The camera does all the work."

"You did the work, learning your camera and studying your subject. I'm happy meeting a professional."

"What do you do?" Liz asked.

Maddie dropped her head, suddenly reminded of her situation. Tears trickled from her eyes as she searched for what to say. "Um, I came to the Cove to gather my thoughts," she said. "My husband, the sheriff of Cold Creek...Well, he's been kidnapped. I don't know how to help him. I came here to think." She looked at the ground. "You must find that odd. But for me, it sometimes works."

Suddenly, she felt shaky. Settling onto a stump, she kept herself from falling.

Liz grasped Maddie's shoulder to steady her. "Oh, I'm so sorry."

After a few minutes, Maddie regained control of her emotions. "I'm sorry, I don't usually get this emotional. I don't understand what's going on with me."

Liz pulled a tissue from her camera bag. She handed it to Maddie. "You aren't pregnant, are you? I mean, you turned pure white. I just wondered."

"No, no, it's..." She paused. "I sometimes have ESP. It was a shot in the dark, but I thought if Rick is able, maybe he could communicate with me. He knows I have abilities. I'm sorry I fell apart in front of you. You're very kind."

"Oh, no, don't apologize," Liz said. "I think it's a good thing. I've heard of people, you know, clairvoyant?" Liz offered her hand to Maddie. "Do you feel like standing? I'll walk you to your vehicle."

"Thank you, I'm okay. This is really unusual for me. I haven't eaten to-day—well, only a snack. I tend to do that when I'm upset." She took a long pause. "I'm embarrassed." She stood. "I'd love seeing your photos. Do you have a shop? Maybe I can stop in sometime?"

"Yeah, my husband and I have a shop near Gatlinburg," Liz said. "I'd rather be out here taking the photos than selling them. I like the quiet here too. We all have our reasons. I respect yours."

"I can relate to that." Maddie took a deep breath. "I'm glad you were here."

The two women walked together out the trail to where Maddie parked. She unlocked her SUV and turned to Liz. "Where are you parked?" she asked.

"Around the curve, on the other side the hill. I walked across."

"That's the way I walked up the time I first saw Delilah. Let me give you a ride back."

"Oh, that's okay. I walk constantly."

"I'm not ready to leave here," Maddie said. "It's nice without so much traffic. I want to stay a while. I'd like to get to talk with you. And I need one of your cards so I can find your shop."

"Okay, I'll ride with you," Liz said. "Thanks." She walked to the passenger side and got in.

After parking next to Liz's car, the two sat and talked. Liz showed Maddie the photos of the bear and others she'd taken earlier. "I have some protein bars in my car," she said. "Let me get us both one." She got the protein bars and a couple of cold water bottles.

While eating, they noticed another bear coming out of the bushes farther up the road. Liz focused her long lens and snapped off a few shots.

"I'd welcome the company if you'd like to walk with me to see what else we might run into," Liz said. "This is a great location for foxes and coyotes. We might even see some bear cubs. That road leads to one of the houses, former residents living in the Cove." She pointed to a well-worn path. "It's a nice walk, level and not more than a mile. With so few people here today, we could see all kinds of wildlife."

"I'd like that," Maddie said. "I've never been to that cabin. Thanks for the protein bar. I feel fine now. I haven't been eating right. I'm my own worst enemy." She laughed.

The walk was peaceful, and they came across a fox with its young. Liz took a few shots of the cute playful fox kits and promised she'd share copies with Maddie. After reaching the cabin and photographing a few shots, a family of deer walked out from the woods and drank from a creek coming from an enclosed spring next to the house. Liz showed Maddie the wild irises coming up next to the smokehouse on the property.

Liz told of how this family was the first in the Cove to build a guest room on the front porch. She explained that people passing through the area were welcome to stay in the room with a warm bed and feel comfortable, while the family was inside the house, apart from the room on the front porch. Their guests also felt at ease with strangers. It worked as a good stopover for travelers. The residences were often miles apart, yet everyone knew their neighbors.

While walking back to the parking lot, Maddie felt that strange sensation she'd had the day before while hiking toward Mount Le Conte. She felt pulled, like Rick was in a painful situation. She stopped at a spring next to the trail, fell to her knees, and looked into the water. It wasn't her reflection she saw but the form of Rick laying on the ground.

Liz watched her with concern, then spoke softly, "Do you see something?" She looked into the water and saw her image standing next to Maddie.

"It was Rick." Knowing Liz's answer before she spoke, Maddie continued, "Of course you didn't see him. I saw blood on the side of his head."

Maddie's own hand felt her left temple. She lowered her hand, now with blood on her fingers, yet there was none on her head.

Liz knelt beside her. Maddie had no blood, but Liz's fingers were red when she pulled them away.

"Did he speak to you?" Liz asked.

"No."

The women began walking again. The blood dried clean on their fingers, leaving no sign. "I'm sorry, Liz. No one has ever witnessed these experiences I have."

"No, don't," Liz hushed her. "I come from a family of clairvoyant women." She looked away for a moment. "I tried denying my gift. But I always knew it would come back."

"Really?" Madison smiled. "I don't know anyone else. I won't tell anybody, but I'm glad you understand."

"He's alive," Liz said. "I felt his heart beating. But the men who have him are really bad. I felt their hearts too. And they terrified me." Liz put her hand on Maddie's arm. "It's been a long time since I felt or saw anything."

"What can I do?" Maddie felt like she was failing her husband.

"He's far from here; it's a steep mountain. I hear a river and a train. So many trees, so thick and cool. No sunshine. The trees are tall and thick. No, he's inside, under a roof. One side is open, old, earthy, damp, but clean."

"How many men can you see?" Maddie asked.

"Three, no, four. They all have guns."

"They would—they're crooks. If I could only find them." Maddie walked into the sunlight off the beaten trail. "Sounds like it's sort of like the Cove. I felt the steep mountainside and the rapids. The river is shallow and rough." She stopped, looking at Liz. "I know where they are. You helped me see more! Do you have a map in your car?"

"I have an atlas. It's old, but it might help."

The two walked quickly to Liz's car. Liz pulled the atlas from her back seat. "Here, this is where we are. Where are you thinking?"

"Find the North Carolina and Tennessee state line," Maddie said. "There, Erwin. There's Highway 23. It is an old map. Interstate 26 has been built since this." She studied the map. "Here, this is Spivey Mountain. Somewhere on this side is The Lost Cove." She slid her finger along the tiny lettering.

"There, it says Lost Cove," Liz said and touched the map. "I've read about it. I always wanted to hike up there and see what's left to photograph."

"I've got to go," Maddie said. "Thank you for helping me. I might save

97

Rick's life, if I can get in touch with my friends. I'll see you again, Liz. Here, put your phone number in my phone."

With that, Maddie raced out the parking area, churning up a cloud of dust. She knew there'd be no cell signal until she was almost in Pigeon Forge. It didn't matter that she could be stopped for speeding; she'd welcome that. But Rick's life could depend on how long it took her to get back to Unicoi County.

12

Meanwhile, in The Lost Cove on the North Carolina-Tennessee state line, the mixture of divisions of law enforcement edged closer to the cabin. They surrounded it and lay low out of sight until the first movement. The man in camouflage was first to walk out. He lit up a cigarette and found a tree to relieve himself before he walked back to the shell of a house.

A voice from inside called out to him. The stealth officers outside couldn't understand the words, but a man walked to the door. His bare feet were in leg irons, and he was handcuffed.

The camo man unlocked his cuffs and pulled out a pistol. He nudged the prisoner toward the trees. Drew was certain, it was Rick. This was the first sight of him, and now they were sure this was the right time. Henry had told of seeing the man in the suit leaving by the river. Where were the other men he had seen earlier?

He motioned for everyone to hold their positions. He and Donnelly moved farther around the perimeter toward the back side of the cabin. They worked their way closer and counted three other men playing cards inside where other side-by-sides were parked. One of the men threw the cards down and stood up. He yelled to the other men, and the argument ensued.

This might be the chance to overtake them. Drew signaled to Scott and the other men. The plan was to cover them as they approach the men. Two of them began fighting and rolling on the ground. The other one walked down the hill a way and squatted next to a bush with his pants down.

Drew hit him with the butt of his rifle, and he was on the ground, out cold. Drew cuffed him and nodded for Donnelly to move to the fight. About that time, the one taking the beating was knocked out, so the other guy started getting up. Donnelly grabbed him and wrestled him to the ground into cuffs with a pistol in his face, warning him not to call out to his buddy. Scott and Henry came around the side of the cabin, where Rick had just returned. He noticed Henry and fell to the ground as a distraction.

"Get up!" The pistol was quickly in his face. But Donnelly struck him with the rifle, knocking the gun out of Camo's hand. The next hit went to the man's chin, and he hit the ground next to Rick.

Donnelly tossed the handcuffs to Rick and said, "Well, do something to help yourself. We can't do everything for you, Malone."

Rick pulled the man's hands behind his back and snapped the cuffs. Donnelly knelt down to unlock the leg-irons on Rick's feet. Henry helped him stand, and the two embraced in relief.

"What took you so long?" Rick said when Drew walked around the side of the cabin.

"We've been playing poker with those goons around back!"

The two friends embraced in a manly and appreciative hug.

"What the hell have you been doing, Malone?" Scott asked, joining in on the embrace.

The rest of the men came from behind the cabin, prodding the three poker players ahead like cattle. After a discussion of who was to remain behind and who'd deliver the prisoners, the sheriff of Cocke County volunteered he and his two men would stay behind to surprise Buck, the one Rick called the ringleader.

During the trip to Erwin, Rick enlightened the rescuers as to what was happening and why Buck left. Uncertain when he'd return, Rick said he overheard him and Camo Man discussing a meeting in Kingsport. Rick wanted to be with the others when they apprehend his captor. Drew shot that idea down, saying he had to go to the hospital to be checked out. The blood on the side of his head needed stitches and some cleaning. He added that Rick's brain needed all the help it could get. And besides, he had an extra woman at his house that was causing lots of trouble.

Drew called Nell to notify Maddie that Rick was free. Nell slowly explained Maddie had flown the coop. She didn't know when she'd return. Rick had no reaction as he listened to Drew.

"She's not there," Drew said. "I told her to stay put. She was safe, but she left!"

Drew disconnected the call.

Rick glanced at Henry. "What's he talking about?"

Henry studied Rick's face. "Maddie was with Nell. But she's left. He doesn't know where she went." Rick's expression confused Henry. "Madison, your deputy."

"Oh," was all Rick said.

This reaction bothered Henry, but no one else seemed to notice.

It was almost dark by the time Maddie returned to the Perrys' house. Nell was on the deck waiting. "Rick is okay," she said. "Drew and some more officers found him, and he's okay. They took him to the ER in Johnson City to check him over. Come on; you need to call and talk to him."

Maddie said, "I'm going home. I'm sorry, Nell, I should have not even been here. I should have been with them. Why didn't Drew take me with him? Why didn't you tell me?"

She backed out of the driveway, turned the vehicle around, and spun off.

All the way back to Johnson City, Maddie was sure she'd get pulled over, driving 80 to 90 the entire time. But she never even saw a police car. Actually, she wished she would so that she'd get an escort. 90 minutes, record time, she screeched into the parking lot at the med center ER. At the door, Henry waited for her.

He didn't recognize her when she ran up to him until she spoke. "What have you done to Maddie?" he asked. "Rick won't even recognize you."

She started to explain but threw her hands up and said, "What's the difference?"

"You drove dangerously. Come on in. They're doing an MRI on Rick. He has a concussion, and his head is a little cracked. But he's okay."

"Were you there for the rescue too?" Maddie asked. "Why didn't one of you let me in on the plan?"

"Come on, Maddie," Henry said. "We did the best we could, and he's going to be fine. Just be happy for that."

"I'm sorry, Henry. But he's my husband. I'm a deputy sheriff, not just his wife! How did you even know where he was? I figured it out. I was going to get him when Nell said you and Drew were already there. Why, Henry? Why?"

Maddie's emotions were on overload. She brushed past Henry and stormed the ER. The first person she saw was Drew. "Where is he?" she demanded.

Drew just pointed through the double doors and said, "First room on your left." He walked past Henry on his way back in. "I better go back to Nell and the kids."

Then, Drew left without speaking again to Maddie.

Rick was still down the hall, having the MRI. Maddie called to speak with Shirley and Jess. They were relived she made it back safely. Maddie caught them up on the news of Rick's MRI and said if they kept him, she'd stay too.

A young male nurse wheeled Rick into the room. He didn't look at the redhead waiting for him. Instead, he high-fives all the law officers in the room who pulled off his release. Maddie waited patiently and finally stepped into the hall, where his doctor stood reviewing Rick's cart. "He doesn't recognize his own wife," Maddie said. Tears tracked down her face. She turned away as Henry walked up.

"Did you speak with him?" Henry asked.

"He didn't recognize me, Henry. My own husband doesn't know me."

"I wouldn't have recognized you if I hadn't already spoken to you, Maddie."

Dr. Reynolds, propping a fist on his hip, asked, "Why the disguise?"

"Drew said the TBI and other agencies were looking for me when they first suspected Rick was in on his own kidnapping, so I changed my hair," she said in a low voice. "What's going on with his skull fracture?"

"What makes you think it's a fracture?" The doctor looked surprised. "You might have been trained in reading dental X-rays, but this is different."

"No, it isn't, not really. Besides, don't forget I took forensic classes at UT. This skull has one temple fracture and possibly a brain bleed at the occipital bone. That's why you sent him for the MRI. What's next, a brain scan?"

"Come with me, Maddie." He stepped into a room behind the nurses' station. Maddie followed. "Let's play this by ear. I'll tell his buddies to leave, and then I am going to question Rick. You may be in there as an observer. Get a lab coat to look the part."

Dr. Reynolds shooed all the spectators out, saying Rick would be moved upstairs. He was being admitted for observation for the night. After a couple minutes, everyone was gone. Maddie walked into the room carrying a clipboard and wearing a white lab jacket with no name tag. She stood on the opposite side of the bed from the doctor. She listened to her husband struggling to answer the simplest of questions.

After about five minutes, two male nurses entered the room. One said, "Got you a room with a view, sheriff. We're going for a ride."

Rick looked toward the doctor. "Sheriff?" He looked quizzically at the two men, then at the doctor. Finally, his eyes settled on the redhead at the foot of his bed. "If you come with the title, I'm game."

Maddie smiled and stepped out of the room without a word. Rick was wheeled down the hallway and through a series of double doors. Maddie blinked away tears and watched till he was out of site.

"Madison, what's going on?" a voice asked. It was Donnelly, standing behind her.

"He doesn't recognize me," Maddie replied. "He doesn't even remember that he's the sheriff." She bit her lip, trying not to cry in front of the FBI agent who Rick used to be close friends with.

"He didn't know me, either," the agent said. "I'm sorry." The large man placed his arm along her shoulders. "I'm sure it's just a temporary condition."

"What if it isn't?" Maddie said.

Madison returned the lab coat to the nurses' station and walked out of the ER with Donnelly. She asked, "What do you know? About Buck, I mean."

"One of the goons told us he had a meeting in Kingsport with some political official. Evidently, the two have some kind of arrangement worked out with the prosecuting attorney."

"Then I'm going to Kingsport. I have a pretty good idea where they are meeting."

"How could you know that?" Donnelly asked.

"Because, while I was by myself, I got a message. I hoped it was from Rick. But after I learned you heroes had made your move, someone spoke to me. The only living thing there was a bear. But I had a vision. Even though it did not make any sense at the time, I figured out the connection."

"Do you know how ridiculous that sounds?" He smiled at her and stepped back to look her in the face. "You keep talking like that, and they will put you in a padded room, honey."

Maddie looked stern and then burst out laughing. "You're right. The bear didn't say Kingsport. It could have been on the river in Knoxville. What made me think Kingsport? Oh, you said he was meeting there." She turned to walk away. "Where is the Netherland Inn?"

"In Kingsport," Donnelly said. "But explain to me how a bear connects to the Netherland Inn?"

"I'm not sure, but I'm going to find out. You with me or against me?"

"I'm going back to Asheville. Call me to bail you out of jail."

Donnelly walked away.

"Keep your phone handy," Maddie called after him.

She unlocked her SUV as Jess and Shirley pulled into the ER parking area. Jess stopped next to her, rolling down his window. He asked, "What are you doing out here?"

"They moved Rick to a room upstairs for an overnight stay," Maddie said. "He didn't even know who I was. I'll be back in a little while. Go through the front entrance so you can learn his room number. I'll be in touch. Call me if anything changes. I'll talk to you in a little while."

Madison drove to the onramp of I-26 north toward Kingsport. Her heart ached, and tears sometimes blocked her vision. She pulled into the Visitor's Center and washed her face to try and clear away evidence of the tear tracks. She called a friend in Erwin at the city police department and asked for Amber.

"Hello, Maddie," Amber answered. "I got the report you asked for. How is Rick?"

"They're keeping him overnight for observation," she replied. "You didn't mention I'd called about the stolen cars, did you?"

"Heavens, no. You know I wouldn't rat you out." Amber laughed.

"That's why I called you. What did you learn?"

"The only vehicle reported stolen on that day was a 2019 Ford F150, denim blue, with a topper on it. Unicoi County tag."

"Anything in Unicoi or Johnson City?" Maddie asked.

"No, it was a quiet night."

"Thanks, Amber. If you hear anything at all about Kingsport, call me?"

"Okay, you be careful. I sense you're up to something." Amber chuckled.

"You know it, girl!"

Maddie disconnected the call. Returning to I-26, she drove to Hwy 11 West, and exited. She drove to the Netherland Inn Museum, circling the block slowly. Not seeing any sign of a blue F150 truck, she drove down to the river's edge where several vehicles were parked at a boat ramp. But none matched the stolen vehicle. She noticed a couple of men sitting on a bench next to the river, both wearing suits. She pulled into a parking space to watch them for a moment.

While she sat there observing, a truck passed, creeping slowly by her. She watched as it passed; there was a Unicoi County tag on the F150, but it had no topper on and appeared to be black, not blue. She watched it pull into a driveway and turn around. As it came back toward her, she saw it was a woman driving.

"Unless he's wearing a wig and makeup, that's not Buck," Maddie said aloud. The truck parked behind her, and the woman stepped out with her dog on a leash.

The men on the bench stood and shook hands. One walked toward the woman with the dog, and the other sat back down.

"What are you waiting for?" Maddie asked aloud. The man pulled a phone from his coat pocket and seemed to be listening. After a minute or two, he stood again and walked down to the river's edge.

A family of ducks swam by. The man took a photo with his phone and continued with his conversation. Maddie heard a vehicle drive by her again. It was a blue F150 with a topper. She felt her stomach flip-flop. Checking her pistol, she placed it back into her carry bag and stepped from her SUV. She was glad the woman parked behind her, concealing the tag. She walked in the direction the woman had gone. And as luck would have it, they turned and were walking back. So, Madison walked directly to her. The dog was friendly, so she stopped to pet him and talked briefly with the woman, who also turned out to be very talkative. She used this as an angle to watch the men. After a few minutes, the men got up, walking toward the river.

Maddie thanked the dog and woman for the visit and went to the bench to pretend to adjust her shoe. She slipped a receiver, a bug, under the boards of the bench. Replacing her shoe, she walked away from the bench and circled back to her SUV, all the while keeping the men in her sight.

She noticed the ducks coming closer, so she took her phone out to photograph them. They came to her as though they expected feed. "Sorry, guys, I don't have anything to give you."

She deliberately played around with the small ones to keep her eyes glued on the men.

They appeared to be in an argument. The first man returned to the bench. Buck stayed back on the riverbank. He picked up a handful of rocks, skipping them one at a time across the river. Finally, the other man called to him, "Come here, I need you to understand what you're facing with this."

Buck threw the rest of the stones before he returned to the bench. He didn't say a word; he just stood looking down at the other man. "Let me see the video," Buck said.

"I'll admit, it doesn't look like you, but the DA says otherwise. He's got your prints."

"He could have gotten my prints from anywhere. I worked there!"

"But your prints were on the briefcase."

"I could have handled it before he put the gun in there. That's not what I'd call a smoking gun." Buck laughed. "You got nothing! I'm telling you, nothing!"

"There's a lot more than I could get my hands on. And as for that rookie, Rick, all he has to do is show up in court, and the prosecutor is undermined. You have to tell me what to expect. What will Rick say?"

Maddie listened from the bug she'd placed under the bench. Apparently, this was the defending attorney. But what were they talking about. What did Rick witness?

The ducks returned to the river, floating away. She had to find something else to give her an excuse to be there. Would the SUV be too far from the bench to listen in on their conversation? What choice did she have? She strolled farther away from the men, while keeping her phone watching over her shoulder. She circled back to her truck at the same time the woman and dog arrived at the black truck.

Maddie approached them. "Hey, I noticed your tag is Unicoi County. That's where I live."

"It's my dad's truck," the woman said. "I live in Boone. Just came over to visit a friend. This is his dog. We're waiting for him to get off work."

"I see. Well, enjoy your visit," Maddie said.

Opening her SUV door, she pretended to look in the back seat for something. Then, she settled into the driver's side with a magazine in her hand. The voices were lower, but she could still hear their talking. She set the phone on her dash and pressed record. "I should have already recorded what I've heard."

"I gotta get back to Knoxville," the man said. "You better have that fellow there on Tuesday. I can't help you without him. Don't let him out of your sight." The man walked down the riverbank and soon disappeared into some trees.

Buck walked toward the stolen truck. He paused, looking at her SUV still parked on the side the road. Maddie swallowed hard and placed her hand inside her carry bag. Had he seen the Unicoi County tag? He was coming up to the window. She reached for her phone and started talking into it.

When he reached her window, she said, "Honey, will you hold on just a moment?" She smiled at Buck. "Can I help you?" she asked, hand shaking so that she was sure he'd notice.

"Are you having car trouble?" he asked with a seductive smile spread across his face.

"Oh, no, thanks. I'm waiting on my boyfriend. He's just getting off the interstate." Maddie hoped her voice was not shaking.

"Good, just checking. It'll be dark soon. You shouldn't be out here alone." Buck stepped back from the SUV.

"It's a very nice gentleman making sure I'm not having car trouble," Maddie said into the phone. "Yeah, love you too. Hurry up. I'm hungry." Then, she added, "Thank you, sir. I appreciate your kindness."

Buck answered, "Have a nice evening, ma'am."

He walked away quickly, stepping into the blue truck. He spun around in the middle of the road and went back toward the way she'd driven in.

Maddie started her vehicle and turned to follow, keeping a long distance from the taillights of the stolen truck. He drove straight to the interstate, and she followed at a safe distance. The closer she got to Johnson City, the darker the sky got. She'd for sure lose him in the traffic. She thought the only way to get him was to notify someone up ahead. So, she called Drew.

"I'm going back to my family, as if you'd care," Drew's voice scolded.

"I found Buck," Maddie said. "I'm following him. As we head into Johnson City traffic, I could lose him. I can't get too close in my SUV. He'll recognize it."

"What's he driving?" Drew asked, a little nicer now.

"An F150, denim blue, with a topper on, and it has Unicoi plates. It's a stolen vehicle."

"How on earth—never mind," Drew said. "Tell me the last mile marker you passed."

"Exit 17, coming up," she said.

"Got it. Okay, stay on until I get an unmarked car on him."

In a couple minutes, Drew called her back.

"Have you passed Okolona Road?" Maddie asked. "Coming up in just a minute, I think he's right in front of me. He's sticking right on the speed limit."

"Do you see a car entering the on-ramp in front of you?" Drew asked.

"Yes, a white SUV, maybe a Ford Explorer?" Maddie asked.

"That's him. He will pass you and pull back in front. He's sporting a government tag."

"Okay, I'll back him up," Maddie said.

"No, you're getting off the interstate and going back to Johnson City," Drew said sharply.

But Maddie had hung up on him. She watched for the white SUV to pass her. She nodded her head, and he waved his hand, then took off quickly around her. She stayed back. Watching the white vehicle was so much easier. Traffic sped up. She glanced at the speed odometer. She was doing 80, and the white SUV was losing her. So, she sped up to get close enough to observe where he turned. Sure enough, he took the Temple Hill exit behind another SUV. She held back. There were only a couple of roads they could take. And she thought they'd turn left, going up Spivey Mountain.

Spivey was a curvy, narrow two-lane, up one of the steepest mountains around. She could stay a curve back and not lose them. However, she was not sure where the Forest Service Road turned off. Hopefully, Drew was still in contact via his radio. Cells don't work up on these mountains. Looking ahead a couple curves, she saw two vehicles. She continued as fast as she dared. At the top where the road runs level for a ways, she noticed the front car stopped. But the white SUV continued. After it passed, the dark car pulled out again. She stayed on him, barely seeing his lights. In a wooded area, suddenly, the dark SUV pulled onto a side road. It drove around the gate and continued up the gravel road. Maddie drove past and stopped around the next curve. That's where she caught up with the white SUV. She pulled in.

"You weren't supposed to follow anymore," the plain-clothed officer said.

"I don't know if you are aware how evil this man is," Maddie explained. "What are your orders?"

"What were your orders?" he asked.

"I found the scum. I make my own orders. Drew doesn't tell me what to do."

"So, how do we go in behind him? Walk?" The officer smiled.

"Yes, we walk in, otherwise he'll know we're coming." She got out of her SUV with a gun in hand and a rifle with scope slung over her back. "You got any cuffs?'

"Yes, ma'am."

"Bring your flashlight, ammo, and let's get after him," Maddie said. "When he finds his men are gone, he won't stick around long." She turned and started back up the dark road.

"I'm Tommy. I assume you're Madison Malone?"

"Call me Maddie," she said. "Nice to meet you, Tommy. Once we get on the gravel road, we don't talk."

"Okay, I'm right behind you."

After a 15-minute walk, they came to the split in the trail. Maddie scoured the ground and whispered, "This way. He plowed right through there. What does he care? He stole the truck." She led the way.

Another five minutes, and the truck lights appeared, coming back toward them.

"Now, how do we stop him?" Tommy asked.

"He's already seen me today. You'll have to make the stop. I'll cover you from here, where he can't see me."

"Okay." He pulled out his Glock, chambered a shell, and blasted his light right at the driver.

"What the hell are you doing?" Buck asked as he came to a stop in front of Tommy.

"This is a private road. Are you with the Forest Service?" The Glock was trained at Buck's face. "I need you to turn the truck off, sir."

"No need to scare a man to death, officer. I must be on the wrong road. I'm looking for Coffee Ridge," Buck lied.

"Step out of the truck, please."

"Now, just a minute," he said. "I haven't seen any ID from you. How do I know you're not going to rob me or something?"

Maddie made sure Buck heard her cock her Sig. She said, "Out of the truck, Buck. This is the end of the road." Her headlamp caused him to turn his head away from its brightness.

"Who are you? I'm not getting out." Buck resisted.

"Okay, I'll shoot you right where you are," Maddie said. She carefully aimed right over his head, firing off a round. "Don't give me an excuse. The next one will be between your evil eyes."

"Okay, okay, I'm coming out."

"Engine off. Key on the dash!" Tommy ordered, raising his Glock higher.

Buck put his right hand up and reached toward the key. Slowly, as if he was contemplating another move, he turned the key silencing the engine. The key slapped the dash.

"Keep those hands high. Tommy will open the door." Maddie kept the light blinding Buck. "One slip; that's all I need to squeeze the trigger."

"Okay, I'm trying here," Buck stalled. Tommy squeezed the door handle. Buck was halfway out the door, when in one smooth move, Maddie grabbed his arm, spinning him around, and slapped Buck's face against the side of the truck. Tommy pulled the right arm down and locked the other side of the cuff.

"Wow, you're one surprising bitch," Buck said, spitting blood from his busted lip.

"You haven't seen the bitch in me. I'd still rather pump a round or two into your head. You don't have any idea who you're messing with. Do you, Buck?"

"I'd like to meet you one-on-one. What's your name, honey?" he continued, trying to insult Maddie.

"I wouldn't mess with this lady, Bud," Tommy said. "She's pretty pissed, and you don't want to rile a beautiful redhead. Not this one, you don't." He laughed. He opened the back door to the truck, shoved Buck in, and clicked cuffs around his ankles.

Maddie climbed in the front passenger side, keeping the head lamp on the prisoner, and Tommy drove back to the hard road.

Once back at Hwy 19, they elected to move Buck to Maddie's SUV, leaving the stolen truck behind the locked gate. Tommy got into the sheriff vehicle and drove off the mountain with Maddie's trigger finger still pointing at Buck.

"Obviously, you think you have a good reason for this inhumane treatment, but you're going to be sorry, lady," Buck mumbled with his face in the floor of her SUV.

"Why don't you go ahead and introduce yourself?" Tommy looked at Maddie. "I think that's the only way to put fear in this monster."

"Okay, okay. But I was savoring the moment of his brain working so hard to figure it out for himself. I'm Deputy Sheriff Madison McKenzie Malone."

Silence from the back seat.

"What was that you said?" Maddie asked. "I didn't quite catch it. You're mumbling." She leaned over the seat slightly. "That's right...Sheriff Rick Malone is my husband. And you are in deep shit, I promise you. Have you ever prayed, Buck?"

Tommy pulled into the Erwin County Sheriff's Office, where he was met by Henry and several Erwin police officers. Maddie slipped out of the front seat, opened the back door, and pulled Buck to a sitting position.

"Get this scum out of my vehicle, please." She turned to Tommy and offered her hand. "If you ever want to change jobs, come see me in Cold Creek?"

"Thank you, ma'am, I'll keep that in mind," Tommy said. "Now, go see your husband."

Maddie walked to her SUV. Henry waited for her.

"Get in, Maddie, I'll drive you to the hospital," Henry said. He put her hand in his and walked to the passenger side of the car.

"I got him, Henry," Maddie said. "Drew didn't think I could handle it. I found him on my own. I followed him to the woods. I wanted to kill him. I could have, too. But Tommy was so scared; I took it as a sign that I had to let him take over. I wanted to kill Buck. He might have killed Rick. I don't know how to deal with this. What will I do if Rick doesn't remember me?"

"Everything will be fine, eventually. You'll see. Rick's momentarily injured, but he's going to come out of this like he always does."

Maddie stared straight forward, without a word.

13

Jess slept in the recliner in room 603. Shirley stood in front of the window, looking out into the blank sky. Rick was sleeping.

Maddie bent over her dad, kissing him on the cheek. "I'm here. Has Rick talked?"

Jess sat up straight. "We had a conversation, but he changed the subject whenever we mentioned anything he'd need his memory for. Where were you?"

"I caught Buck. He's in jail now in Erwin. I'm staying; you should take Mom home. You both need rest."

"She's right, Jess," Shirley said, giving Maddie a hug.

"Okay, Momma, let's go." Jess stood up, catching Shirley's hand. "Call us if there's any change. Will you?"

"Of course," Maddie said. "Henry, you go home, too. Holly needs you there. You've been absent too long."

After everyone left, Maddie settled into the recliner and pulled it as close as she could get to Rick's bed. She rolled over onto her side so she could watch him breathe. She felt exhausted, but she didn't want her eyes to close. She fought to keep them open. They were heavy, trying to close, for just a moment. *Just let them rest for a short while.*

When she opened her eyes to the light coming through the open blinds, she turned to look at Rick. He smiled at her.

"What have I done to deserve such a lovely angel visiting with me?" Rick asked, leaning his head to one side, kind of like Bud did when Maddie talked to him.

She reached her hand out, touching Rick's face. "You made me fall in love with you."

His head tilted the other way. "How'd I do that?"

"We've been through a lot, Rick. It'll take some time to tell you all the wonderful things I know about you." Tears slipped down her face, dripping onto her neck.

"I've never met such a beauty. Why would I not remember that?" Rick sat the bed up slightly so that he could turn and face Maddie. "What's your name?"

Maddie blinked her eyes; there were more tears than she could handle this time. She blubbered like a hurt puppy. After a few seconds, she managed to say, "I'm Madison. You call me Maddie."

"What happened? Why can't I remember I have a girlfriend?" Rick turned his attention to the window. "Can we go outside and take a walk in the sun?"

"Let me ask one of the nurses." Maddie wiped away tears. She found a nurse and said, "Excuse me, Charity. What does Rick's chart say about his movement?"

The nurse smiled and flipped a file open. "No restrictions, except he has to be in a wheelchair."

"Where can I get that chair?" Maddie rubbed her head. "And is there any place I can get an aspirin for myself?"

"I'll deny it if you tell I gave you these," Charity said and pulled a little bottle from her pocket. "I'll get that wheelchair now."

"Thank you, Charity. My husband wants to walk in the sunshine."

Maddie gave up on wiping away the constant evidence of tears.

Maddie wheeled Rick onto the patio level off the sixth floor. She remained quiet, just praying that her husband's memory might be restored by the energy of the sun. She walked slowly onto the charcoal tile path leading among the potted trees and occasional bench.

Finally, Rick asked her to stop. He reached for her hand and guided her to the bench in front of him. "I'm sorry, can we work through this?"

"What do you want me to say?" Maddie said. "My husband doesn't know me. How do I erase that little obstacle?" Tear traces turned to streams.

"We're married?" Rick's eyes welled up. He turned his face from her. "How long?"

"We celebrated our third anniversary last month," Maddie answered.

He looked back toward her and stood up, the movement causing the wheelchair to roll. Maddie quickly jumped up and set the break.

"The last thing we need is for you to fall. Sit here beside me?" She returned to the bench.

Rick remained standing. He stared down at her. It made chills run down her spine. Not the stare of her loving husband, but the cold stare of a stranger searching for words to express his feelings.

At that moment, a woman in a white lab coat walked onto the patio garden. After looking around at no one else enjoying the warmth of the sunshine, she approached. "Rick Malone, I presume?"

"Yes, ma'am."

"I'm Dr. Simms. And are you Mrs. Malone?"

"Maddie," Maddie replied, remaining seated.

"You've picked a lovely place to have this discussion." Dr. Simms took her seat in the wheelchair. "Mind if I join you for a while?"

Neither Rick nor Maddie answered. Dr. Simms pulled a tablet from the pocket of her lab coat. "Rick, please sit down next to Maddie. First of all, I'm not a shrink, and Rick, you don't have a permanent brain injury. But you do have bleeding on your brain. Bleeding that we need to stop."

Maddie looked at Rick. He looked at his wife and back to Dr. Simms. "How do you fix me?" he asked.

"Your case will require surgery. You're lucky I happened to be here at this time. You see, I'm the number one surgeon in the eastern U.S. who's done this procedure. Not bragging, just stating the facts. You are welcome to check it out."

"I'm not questioning your ability; it's mine that worries me," Rick said. "What are my chances?" Rick slipped his hand into Maddie's. She squeezed his slightly.

"I believe your chances are excellent. There will be some recovery time, and you'll need constant care for months. You may have to relearn to walk, talk, and possibly there could be other side effects—some I'm not even aware of. But without it, you're a ticking time bomb with months, or years, but there are drawbacks as well. You could die within week, days, maybe the next fifteen minutes. This is nothing to fool around with. I could give you the worst-case scenario, but that would just worry you."

"Telling us he can drop dead any minute sounds like the worst case," Maddie said. "What can we do?"

"Just what you're doing now, supporting your husband. Tell him about the life you two had together. Show him photos, videos, whatever you have with fond, heartfelt memories. He needs to know what he has to look forward to with you."

Rick let go of Maddie's hand and put his arm around her shoulders. She leaned in closer to him. "I'll do whatever it takes to remember this beautiful partner of mine," Rick said. He looked into Maddie's eyes. She blinked back tears. "I feel comfortable with you, even though I don't remember you personally. I have to take this chance. Can you?"

She nodded her head slowly and leaned her head on his shoulder. "You were my first and only love," she said. "I can't imagine life without you. Even if the surgery changes you, I know who you are, were, and who you'll always be. But if you don't ever remember the 'us' in our lives, I can learn to accept what you need."

"Wow, that's the best anyone could ask from you," Dr. Simms said. "Rick, you're a lucky man, and one day soon, you'll realize it." Dr. Simms shook their hands and walked to the door. She stopped and said, "You might want to settle any business before I see you again. Your surgery will be at the facility in Knoxville. I'll contact you with all the details. Any questions?"

When neither Rick nor Maddie responded, the doctor turned and disappeared inside the hospital.

The couple sat deep in thought, not really knowing what to say. Finally, Rick said, "You got any photos on your phone?"

Maddie burst out laughing. "I sure do."

The next hour, the two strangers laughed and cried together in an attempt to revive Rick's memory.

"This is the best one yet," Maddie said. "This is from last Christmas. It had begun to snow. Bud was so excited to go out and play that when you opened the inside door, he ran slam into the storm door and knocked himself backwards across the kitchen floor." She turned the photo to where Rick could see Bud laying on his back on the hardwood floor.

"I remember this," Rick said. "Bud's our dog." He looked to Maddie for conformation.

"He was my dog, until you came along," she smiled, still staring at the photo.

One of his nurses came outside looking for Rick. She said, "There you are. Thought you might have run away. Come back in, Sheriff Malone. The doctor released you."

In an hour, Maddie pulled into the driveway beside her house—the house she had been sharing with her parents since theirs burned. She hadn't mentioned that detail at all to Rick.

"This is our house?" he asked.

"The cottage was mine. It's one of the oldest remaining structures from the original settlement of Cold Creek. You and I chose to add onto the garage and the upstairs bedroom suite." After a couple minutes, she added, "Jess and Shirley are staying here too, since theirs—Well, we can talk about that later."

"Your folks?" Rick asked. "Their names feel familiar."

At that moment, the kitchen door opened, and Jess walked out. "Good, you're home," he said. He opened the door for Rick. "Does your doctor know you left?" He laughed.

"They sent me home," Rick said as he stepped from the SUV.

Maddie offered the key to her dad and asked, "Will you drive out to Holly's and pick up Bud?"

"Why don't you and I do it?" Rick looked to his wife.

"We can, if you want." She sounded surprised. "Where's Mom?"

"She's sleeping," Jess said. "This has been hard on her, you know?"

"How did your house burn, Jess?" Rick asked.

Jess and Maddie looked at each other, and then Maddie said, "I haven't told him about that yet."

"The men who took you held us hostage and set fire to our house."

"So, your home is gone because of me?" Rick looked straight at Jess.

"Yes, but we don't blame you, Rick. Not at all. Don't you either. Buck is an animal."

Rick got back into the SUV. He nodded his head at Jess.

The drive to the Jacobs house was irritatingly quiet. When they arrived, Bear and Bud ran to greet their vehicle. Rick opened his door and Bud leapt into his arms. The dog was excited beyond belief. He put both front feet on Rick's shoulders and literally hugged the man. And then he stayed pressed against Rick's chest, his head nuzzled against his neck.

Maddie stared in disbelief, tears streaming down her face. "Bud didn't even react to me returning from Alaska, bandaged with my arm in a cast. Does he sense yours? Why else would he react so strongly?"

Holly and Henry came out of the house to greet them.

"Okay, same Henry," Rick said. "I know him, and this must be Holly?" Rick started to stand but fell back onto the car seat. "Wow." He sat for a moment. Holly was right next to him.

Holly grabbed Rick's arm. "You must be on the good stuff. Let me give you a hand." She pulled him up slowly and continued, "In case you've forgotten, I'm Holly. So, get used to being hugged." She laughed her signature Holly laugh.

"Henry, you were at the hospital. But you were involved with my rescue also. Are you a deputy?" Rick kept his arm around Holly.

"Um, no, I've never been that dependable. I'm a friend." Henry smiled the best he could knowing his best friend in Cold Creek didn't know him, either.

Holly pulled away and hugged Maddie. They both began crying.

"We thought we'd come for the Bud; he can stay with Jess and Shirley while we go to the big city for my repair work," Rick laughed.

"Why can't he stay with us?" Holly turned to Rick in defiance. "He and Bear are good together."

"I guess he could," Maddie said. She looked at Rick. It would be better for him. "But we had to see him."

"Of course," Henry said. "Come in, and let's hear the plan."

Maddie took Rick's hand and said, "We can only stay a few minutes, okay?"

"Sure," Rick said. He walked along with his stranger-wife.

They discussed the plan Dr. Simms had for Rick. Maddie mostly kept quiet and let her husband do the talking. After a while, they told Bud bye again and left. On the way home, Rick reminded Maddie that Dr. Simms mentioned he'd need a long convalescence.

"Maybe we should find a place to rent while I'm under her care," Rick suggested.

"Rick, you own an apartment in Knoxville. It isn't rented right now. The painters should be finished. Why can't we stay there?" Maddie asked.

"I guess I've forgotten a lot of things."

Rick was quiet again the rest of the way back to the house.

14

Shirley and Jess attempted to move their things downstairs, but Rick put a stop to it. "Listen," he said, "I'm going to be in Knoxville for a while anyway. Maddie and I are going there tomorrow. We'll be comfortable in her old room. We probably won't get any sleep anyway. Stay where you are with my blessing."

"Of course, Rick," Jess said. "Thanks." He carried their bags back up the stairs.

Madison was surprised by Rick's plan. That was his nature—to take over and carry the weight. Each day is a gift in his life, and they both realized it. She spent the evening on the phone talking to Holly and getting a suitcase packed. Rick had taken a few shirts and pants from the upstairs closet for her to put in for him. She'd already gotten socks and underwear, toiletries, and everything she could think they'd need.

Leaving early the next morning, Maddie drove to Knoxville. It was almost as if she'd been in a trance. Rick asked her lots of questions. She answered as simply as she could.

"Why not stop and eat a nice breakfast before we go to my apartment? You need to eat. You probably won't once we get to the hospital."

He suggested they stop at Strawberry Plains to eat at Cracker Barrel. Maddie wondered if he remembered how often they had met there. But how did he remember she had an eating disorder?

"You've always liked the Cracker Barrel, remember?" she commented.

"Even if I never remember our past, I'm sure I'll fall in love with you all over again," Rick said.

After lingering over their brunch, Rick called the phone Dr. Simms had supplied so he could find out what time to check into the hospital. "Well, good, that gives us another night to get settled here in Knoxville." He hung up from the call and said, "Let's go to the apartment. I don't need to be there until 6 o'clock in the morning."

The apartment was indeed finished and had been cleaned well. The on-site manager, Sally, met them when they walked upstairs to his unit.

"I took the liberty to get everything cleaned for you, Sheriff Malone. I'm sorry hearing that you're having surgery." Sally opened the door for them. She handed the key to Maddie. "I'm always here if you need anything, Mrs. Malone."

"Call me Maddie, and thanks for all you've done."

Madison didn't sleep a wink. She couldn't take her eyes off Rick, watching his every move. She touched his neck to check his pulse if he breathed too shallow. She watched his chest rise and fall. This could very well be the last time she'd sleep with the love of her life. She prayed constantly, asking for strength in the days ahead.

When morning came, Rick hit the shower first. He looked surprised when she was fully dressed and waiting to leave.

"I showered late last night. I couldn't sleep anyway."

Maddie drove, but Rick showed her the easiest way with less traffic to get to and from the UT hospital. As she pulled into the parking garage, her stomach began churning. Now, she felt very nervous.

"It's okay, really," Rick said. "I'm ready. You don't need to worry about me. I'm going to be the best patient they've ever seen! And I'm looking forward to getting to know my sweetheart all over again."

Maddie walked alone down a cold, quiet hallway to the surgical waiting room. Lack of sleep caught up with her the first few minutes. She chose a recliner as far in the back corner as she could in an attempt to hide. The world around her came to a standstill, and she fell into a fitful sleep. Visions of tubes and hoses and instruments flicked on and off throughout her thoughts.

She felt as though she was on a walkway overlooking a pit far below. The wind blew her from side to side on the swaying path. Sometimes, she'd lose her grip and fall, then catch herself on the hoses. It didn't make any sense. She couldn't wake from the situation. She found herself helplessly fighting an unseen force. The harder she fought, the darker the pit became. The path began crumbling.

A voice repeated over and over, "In recovery."

She tried to hold onto a rail beside her.

"Can you wake up? Madison, wake up. Maddie?"

The voice was clear, and louder. She blinked her eyes. But she saw only a tiny light at the other end of the room, where the TV had been on earlier. Now, all she could make out was a dim light. And the voice again said, "Maddie, can you wake up?"

She tried sitting, but her feet were high up. She realized she was still in the recliner. "I'm awake," she said. "I'm sorry, I am awake. Is he okay? Is Rick okay?"

"Yes, your husband is in recovery," a nurse said. "The surgery went well. He'll be in a room in a few minutes. Let me show you." The lady put her hand out to right Madison in the chair. She helped her to her feet. "Get up slowly...You were really out."

"I'm so sorry—"

"No, you're fine. I'll help you. I'm sure you've been under tremendous stress this week."

Maddie squinted her eyes against the bright light of the hall. "I haven't slept in nearly a week. Thank you for helping me."

"There's a sofa in the room you can rest on that." The nurse continued supporting Maddie's arm. "I'm Joy, your husband's personal nurse. I can help you with everything you need, too."

"Thank you, Joy. I'll be okay. I guess I reached my limit. I felt comatose." Maddie laughed nervously.

"The entire surgery took less than two hours. Dr. Simms was elated. She accused you of praying extremely hard. We were glad you did. This was the smoothest I've ever seen this surgery go. It is truly a miracle, believe me." Joy's face glowed.

"It's great hearing Rick set a record," Maddie said. "He'll have something to brag about when he's well again."

Joy showed Maddie the break room as they walked down the hall. "Anything you or Rick need, you can get in this room. It's at your disposal—no charge for anything to eat or drink, or even magazines, books, whatever is in there. And if you need more, tell me and I'll get it."

"Thanks, Joy. Any idea how long Rick will be in here?"

"Normally, a week to ten days. However, Rick is setting records, so he might not stay with us that long." Joy smiled. "It won't be long now."

Joy walked into the hall.

Maddie looked out the window. The sun shined brightly, as though to lift her spirit. "Thank you, Lord, for bringing Rick through this in good form. Please keep him in your grip!" She spoke as if the Heavens were expecting to hear from her.

Finally, the door opened, and Rick was wheeled into the room. Two hefty male nurses lifted him into the bed. They attached all types of monitors. One connected a drip to the port in his left arm. Rick wore a sort of soft helmet around his head from the occipital bone to his forehead. His eyes were closed, and he appeared to be sound asleep.

"Our sheriff is going to sleep for the rest of the day and night," one nurse said. "I suggest you do the same. It'll be about twelve hours before we have a sense of how he's reacting to his surgery. We have a visual monitor on him as well as these connections. We'll know what he does before you'll know. Don't worry, he's in good hands."

The two men left the room, and Joy returned immediately. "Would you like a lunch tray? I can get you whatever you'd like."

"Thanks, Joy, I'm good," Maddie said. "I brought a large bottle of water. That's all I need." She looked around. "I bet I left it in the surgical waiting room."

"No, it's in the fridge in that break room I showed you," Joy said. "I'll get it for you. Would you like a cup with ice?"

"That would be nice." Maddie stepped close to Rick. "Can I touch him?"

"You can. Just try not to move his head or wake him. He's kind of in a semi-coma for the next twelve hours. We'll move him in four hours; you won't need to do anything but relax."

Maddie nodded her head and didn't speak, fearing tears were about to erupt.

Joy returned in a couple minutes with Maddie's water bottle and the cup of ice. She pointed out the emergency call button next to Rick's bed. "You won't need it, but just so you feel more at ease. It's here for you. I brought a chicken salad sandwich that I'm sure you don't need, but just in case, and there's a package of chips. There are more things in the break room—in case you do get hungry." She winked at Maddie. "Just in case?"

"Thank you, Joy. I don't intend to be a bother. I do appreciate you, don't misunderstand."

"I've been in this business a while," Joy said. "It takes all kinds. And the last thing you are is a bother."

Maddie angled the sofa so that she could put her feet up and rest against a couple pillows, while keeping her eyes aimed at Rick. She kicked off her shoes and pulled her feet and legs up under a blanket. "I should have worn jeans. I'll change tomorrow," she told Rick.

Maddie felt as though the dream she was having was a summation of her thoughts since Rick had been taken. What did it mean? As always, she realized she was too involved in every detail, but that's natural for her, and it's very personal considering it is her husband she's worried about.

Her eyes felt like lead. She blinked a couple times from dryness. Not helping, so she sat up and reached for the bag with the sandwich and chips in it.

"That was sweet of Joy," Maddie said to herself. "She knew I needed something, whether I wanted it or not. Oh, well, let me see if I can tolerate the chicken salad." That's when she remembered the nurses said Rick was on a monitor. *Maybe I shouldn't talk out loud. They'll think I'm crazy,* Maddie thought.

She finished the sandwich and the chips, much to her pleasure. Then, she thought that maybe if there was a magazine in that room, she might read herself to sleep, so she wandered down the hall.

The day was long. People walked in and out all day. She didn't get much rest. The night was uneventful, and she even slept four hours straight until the team came in to move Rick slightly. After the second movement by the team, Rick was restless. Maddie talked softly to try and sooth his restlessness. She noticed it worked, so she told him a story about a young girl who fell in love with a TBI agent. When she remembered a camera was monitoring him, she felt embarrassed. But she spoke so low, she didn't think they heard her anyway.

The first sign of light the next morning, Madison took a walk down the hall so she could call Shirley and Jess. After a couple minutes assuring them that Rick was not out of the woods yet, she called Henry and Holly. On her way back up the hall, she thought maybe she should call Nell. After all, Nell wasn't the person she was upset with concerning Rick. She stopped at the break room, fixed herself a cup of coffee, and called Nell.

After talking with her friend for a half hour, Maddie continued back to Rick's room. The team was there waking him. She moved into the far corner of the room and waited. She hadn't realized her hands were formed in the shape of praying hands. Joy stepped into the room and stood close to her. Maddie moved her hands down to her side.

"Are you on a 24-hour shift?" Maddie whispered.

"No, I'm off. I just wanted to see him as he comes out of the induced coma."

"Praying for more records?" Maddie asked.

"I'm betting on him!" Joy rubbed her hands together.

Rick opened his eyes, looking around the room. When they stopped at Maddie, he smiled. Her insides flip-flopped with encouragement.

"Rick," she mouthed but made no sound.

One of the nurses stepped forward, blocking his view. Maddie punched Joy lightly and said, "Look, he's trying to see around the nurse."

Joy grinned. "I see. That's a great sign!"

When Dr. Simms came in the room, she waved to Joy and Maddie. She walked close and spoke to Rick, "How's my patient today?"

Rick trained his eyes on the doctor but didn't speak. He looked toward Maddie again, but this time Dr. Simms was the one he needed looking around. He moved his head and then closed his eyes again.

"Did he move on his own?" Dr. Simms leaned closer, examining his neck.

"He must have; I didn't move his head," the male nurse answered. "Rick, open your eyes."

Rick blinked several times.

"Put drops in them," Dr. Simms said.

The nurse braced his hand on Rick's forehead and dripped a couple drops from a vile into both eyes. Rick blinked, moving his head again. He was still trying to see around the doctor.

"Are you looking at that beautiful redhead over there?" Dr. Simms asked.

Ricked looked up at her and said, "My wife."

Joy and Maddie gasped.

"Well, come on over here, Maddie. Your husband wants to see you."

She stepped slowly and carefully closer, where she had a clear view of Rick's face. "Hi, honey," she said. "How do you feel?"

"Good. You look rested."

"Well, I am guessing you've managed one hurdle," Dr. Simms said.

"You're moving and talking. That's a heck of a good start, Rick. I'd pat myself on the back, but I have to give someone else credit for your success. With the Lord on your side, you've got this recovery whipped." Dr. Simms had tears in her eyes too. "I'll be back to check on you in a while."

After a couple hours, Rick asked to get up. He was already tired of the bed. Dr. Simms told him not to rush it. She wished he'd remain on the bed for another hour. She gave him the okay to sit up, but not to let his feet touch the floor—not just yet. Rick just groaned his dissatisfaction.

Maddie waited for the doctor and her nurse to leave, and then she walked to Rick's bedside. "Let me rub your back. That always makes you feel better." But Rick stiffened at her touch.

"I understand," Maddie said, returning to the sofa.

"I'm sorry, Maddie," Rick said. "It isn't your fault. Don't take this personal."

"I don't know how to fix our problem. I'm at a loss here, Rick. Dr. Simms said you'd be indifferent. But please don't push me away." She stood, walking to the door. "Would you rather be alone for a while?"

"Just for a little while," he said. "You need a break too." Rick tried smiling. It came through as a failed effort.

She threw him a kiss and went into the hallway.

Joy approached with her soothing smile. "What's the weather like in there?" she asked.

"He's so moody, I don't know how to help him," Maddie said. "So, I'm leaving him to think by himself."

"He wants to know if all his parts are working. Can he walk? Can he feel normal again? There's a lot of psychological issues after any brain surgery. Give him space and time; he'll come around. And he'll want you with him. He still loves you. And he'll remember that." Joy made her best effort to encourage Maddie.

"Thanks, you're probably right. I'll be back later. You have my number?"

Joy nodded her head.

Maddie felt guilty leaving Rick, but she had pride and needed to deal with his difference in the only way she knew how—alone, watching nothing on TV, but at the same time talking to her best friend, Holly.

Holly answered on the first ring.

"Hello, are you tied up with children?" Maddie asked.

"No. Everyone is occupied and Little Mattie is sleeping. How's Rick?"

"He's being difficult," Maddie said. "Doesn't want to do what he's told and doesn't want me to touch him."

"Uh-oh," Holly said. "Sounds like you're ticked. As you probably should be." Holly knew Maddie better than she knew herself.

"I'm at the apartment. I just walked out. He can call me if he needs me. I might not answer."

The girls laughed for an hour, and finally Maddie said, "I'll let you go to your babes. Talk to you again tomorrow. I love you, Holly."

"You be careful, girl," Holly said. "Love you, too."

The next morning, Madison awoke with a start. Would Rick be in a better mood after spending a night alone? She dressed and drove back to the hospital. The food trays were getting to the rooms. She slipped in quietly to see Rick sitting up and feeding himself.

"Good morning."

"Hey, I thought you might have gone home," Rick said. "I'm glad you didn't." His smile was genuine this time.

"You handling that shovel okay?" Maddie asked. She watched him lift the fork to his mouth.

"Why'd you change your hair?" Rick asked. He moved his fingers to thread them though the silken red strands. "Your dark chocolate color was beautiful."

"You noticed?"

"It was dark chocolate in all the photos you showed me. I just wondered why and when you became a redhead."

"It was Drew's idea," Maddie said. "He worried someone might come after me."

"Why is Drew such an influence on you?" Rick set the fork down

"He isn't. He was worried about us. He's married to Nell, my friend. You don't remember them, do you?"

"Why should I?" Rick picked up a piece of toast.

"We were all friends," Maddie said. "When they moved to Louisville, we kind of drifted apart, naturally. He was offered the position as chief of police in Sevierville, so they just moved back to Tennessee. He started that position this week."

"So, while I was missing, he took care of you?"

"I was going crazy in Cold Creek. Nobody was really looking for you. I went to see Nell after she and Drew came here for what I thought was a vacation."

She explained about her joy spending time in the woods with Bud from the time he was a puppy, and how she loved running. That always cleared her head and provided time to think without someone interrupting her thoughts.

Rick put the toast down. Was he beginning to realize how independent his wife was?

"Oh, Rick, I've been worried sick about you."

"The new hair color?" He reminded her of his question.

"Drew was afraid for my safety," Maddie finally said. "I can get it back to normal, except for the length."

"I like the cut, but you're not mean enough to be a redhead," Rick said and pulled her slender body closer to the bed. "You've lost weight. You're not eating, are you?"

"My body doesn't want food. You know how—" She stopped short of finishing her sentence. "No, I guess you don't."

The door swung open. In walked Dr. Simms, Joy, and a Dr. Sebastian.

"Are you up for company?" Dr. Simms asked. "We can return in an hour or so."

Madison stepped from the edge of the bed, red-faced. "Sorry, I've been trying to explain some details Rick hasn't pieced together yet."

"I see," Joy said and walked quickly to the back side of the bed, opening the window blinds and allowing sunlight into the room.

Dr. Simms said, "Rick, do you remember meeting Dr. Sebastian yesterday?"

"No, I'm sorry, I don't." Rick looked closely as the doctor approached. "But you resemble someone."

"Apparently someone named Buck," the doctor said, offering his hand. "I'm happy you don't want to kill me today."

Maddie slipped close to Joy. "You neglected to tell me that part," she whispered.

"Maddie, I'd like you to meet Dr. Sebastian," Dr. Simms introduced the large doctor.

"I'm pleased to meet you," Maddie said, offering her handshake. "I'm going to the break room for a cup of coffee. I'll give you doctors time to talk to your patient." She started out of the room.

"Don't worry, we won't be here long," Dr. Sebastian said and flipped open a laptop, making some strokes on the keys.

Joy walked into the hall with Maddie. "I'll get that for you. Dr. Simms wants you to hear what they have to tell Rick. Dark coffee today, with extra cream?"

"Yes," Maddie said. "Thank you, Joy."

Dr. Simms instructed Rick to get away from all stress and anyone who might upset him. As Maddie listened to his explanation of places they shouldn't go, she had an idea. She recalled that Liz mentioned she had a cabin in Cades Cove where she liked spending time whenever possible.

After the two doctors said their peace and left Rick's room, she sat down on the sofa again.

"I met a very sweet lady in Cades Cove the other day," Maddie began. "She's a photographer. We talked quite a while, and she showed me a cabin I'd never been to before. During the time we spent together, she told me her family owns property at the edge of the Cove on one of the gravel roads lead-ing away from the park. It has a cabin way back up in the woods that nobody lives in now. She sometimes stays in it to get an early start in the Cove before the main gate opens. Since you still have at least another week to stay here under doctors' care, I can go look at the cabin. It might be someplace we can rent for the summer."

"Or it might be a bear's hideout," Rick said, smiling.

Madison walked to the break room for privacy and called Liz. "Hey, Liz. It's Maddie. Can you talk?"

"Of course," Liz answered. "I'm glad to hear from you. How is Rick?"

Maddie filled in all the gaps quickly and came straight to the point. "When we were looking at your photos, you mentioned your grandpa had a cabin on the mountain near Cades Cove."

"Yes, and I told you I stay there sometimes to enable me to make it to the Cove before sunrise. Are you thinking what I think you're thinking?" Liz sounded excited, figuring she had a solution for Madison and a hiding place for Rick.

"Then we're okay to come there?" Maddie couldn't believe her luck at meeting Liz when she did. "This is perfect. I believe you and I were meant to meet."

They set up a meeting time for the next day so that Maddie could see the cabin in the Cove.

"Did you call Holly to talk to our boy?" Rick asked as Maddie returned to the room.

They both laughed.

"You didn't mention you had a boy," Joy said, appearing puzzled at what she'd overhead.

"He's our dog," Rick explained. "And my deputy."

"Oh, well then, I completely understand," Joy said. She finished up her duties and left the room.

The following morning, Maddie got up early and headed out on Alcoa Highway toward Maryville and the road to the Cove. At this point, she had no real idea of what to expect. A cabin, and a very old one at that.

"Oh, I hope it's a decent place to stay," Maddie said. "This is helpful, and we can maybe have Bud with us."

This idea caused her heart to race. It seemed like she had been away from Bud for so long. The only really long time away from her beloved dog was her trip to Alaska. She missed him and his cute antics. Having him back in her daily life was necessary. Leaving him with Holly had been better until now, because he and Bear were best friends. He might not miss her as much that way, but she sure missed him.

As her route led her through Maryville, she noticed a drive-thru restaurant. Remembering how she'd nearly fainted in front of Liz, she didn't want that to happen again. She was not taking any chances of getting shaky from low blood sugar. She could use a big cup of coffee and a breakfast sandwich.

Back on the road, cleanly and quickly she drove on toward Townsend. She was meeting Liz on a side road and entering the Cove from a different direction. Being careful not to arrive late, she'd already entered the name of the road and all details Liz gave her into the GPS.

She saw a sign that read, *Apple Valley Mountain Village, 1 mile*. At that moment, her GPS sounded, "Turn right onto Old Tuckaleechee Road in .5 miles."

Maddie checked her rearview mirror, gave her signal, and turned onto the narrow road. She followed the road to Tuckaleechee Methodist Church. She turned into the parking area on her right and noticed only one vehicle, which she recognized as Liz's SUV.

She pulled up next to Liz and put her window down. "I hope I haven't kept you long," she said.

"Not at all, I haven't been here even five minutes," Liz said. "I'm excited about seeing you again, and most of all I'm happy showing you my cabin. I think you're going to love it!" Liz glowed in the dim light of this early mountain morning.

"I can't believe my luck of meeting you the way I did," Maddie said. "I've decided the bear is my spirit animal." She laughed.

"I know the bear is my spirit animal," Liz said. "You must walk with me someday on the trails where I find them. I know them all by name. You'll enjoy seeing my many spirits. Let's get going. Come on, follow me."

With that, she turned onto Old Cades Cove Road with Maddie following close behind. The road passed a few small houses as they climbed a steep hill. The higher they drove, the farther the homesites were apart. The roughly paved road ran out as they rounded a sharp curve to the right. In Maddie's thoughts, civilization ran out as well.

She moved closer to the back of Liz's SUV. *I can't afford to lose my leader,* she thought.

They drove up and down a snake-like road that felt as though it went on forever. Maddie watched her mileage and realized it was the condition of the road that made it seem so long. But it had only been about 7 miles. The terrane was forested and up one hill and down another. No way would she ever attempt this in winter.

All of a sudden, they came to Davy Crockett riding stables. "OMG, way out here in the middle of nowhere?" Maddie laughed to herself.

The road forked, and Liz took the right fork, heading up an even steeper hill. "Oh, boy, here we go again," she said.

About halfway to the mountain ridge, Liz turned right onto a gravel road and across a little bridge. Maddie pulled up beside her to ask, "Are we stopping for lunch?" She laughed.

"I told you it seems a lot longer than it is." Liz laughed with Maddie. "This is Hesse Creek, the beginning of my property." She took a deep breath, still smiling.

"I see you are proud of your ancestry," Maddie said.

"You bet I am."

Liz drove up the narrow drive for another quarter of a mile. Maddie parked next to her in the front of an eighteenth-century log mansion.

She stared at the house. "That's no cabin," she said.

Liz ran up to the vehicle. "Come on in. Let's take a look around."

Maddie walked the rocky path leading to wooden steps. The logs were hand hewed with a gray stain on them. The outside walls appeared to be well cared for.

Liz quickly unlocked the front door, running inside. Maddie followed as her eyes were treated to a wonderful historic education. She stood inside the door, looking around. She'd stepped back in time, loving what she saw. "Rick is going to fall in love with this," she said.

Liz had disappeared, but momentarily she returned. "I always open the back door to let a fresh breeze rush in," she said. "It hasn't been opened up in weeks."

"This is not a cabin, Liz. It's a glorified mansion! I love it! And I don't detect a stale odor. Yes, it has an old smell, but that's homey and historical. I lived in a nearly two-hundred-year-old cottage until Rick and I added a master bedroom over a three-car garage. You have a lovely treasure here."

The two walked from room to room as Liz explained things she hoped to update or areas that had been updated at least a little. Maddie grew more excited with each doorway they walked through. The kitchen definitely needed help. It was the size of a living room and had a second fireplace showing it was still capable of whipping up a full-course family meal.

"In the 19th century, the wood cooking stove was added. Before that, all the cooking was done on the fireplace. Look, that little rock oven bakes the best biscuits and cornbread you've ever tasted. And those arms swing around to hold a pot the size of a witch's caldron. Not that anyone in my family were witches," Liz laughed with pride-filled joy. "It still warms this room and the upstairs."

They turned to the stairs situated between the kitchen and dining room. They were smoothly worn and slightly scuffed. Maddie noticed the wood had been beautifully carved and wider than she imagined for a home such as this.

"Someone put a lot of love and craftsmanship into this stairwell," Maddie said and ran her hand up the dark-stained and shiny railing.

"That was my great grandfather," Liz said. "He and my great grandmother built this themselves. She was as good a carpenter as him, or so my grandpa said."

"The frontier women had to do plenty of things women aren't capable of today."

Liz stopped at the top of the stairs. She said, "I have taken the old beds out. They held old smells and weren't comfortable. I thought, someday, I'll have all these rooms filled again, but for now this is my room. And it will be yours while you're here, if you think Rick will go for it."

She led Maddie into the largest bedroom. Furnished with a queen bed, a tall, antique armoire stood stately on an interior wall and stretched nearly to the ceiling. Maddie ran her hand gently over the smooth surface. "May I open it?" she asked.

"Sure." The double doors exposed a row of drawers on one side and spacious hanging on the other. There were only a couple of sachets in the drawers and empty wooden hangers on the hanging side. A sweet mix of cedar and lilac drifted to Maddie's nose.

"They didn't make this?" Maddie asked.

"No, I got that from an estate sale in Atlanta years ago. It just called out to be include in this room. That little round table came from the same sale. See, no closets."

"That's right." Maddie took great care to notice the lace bed coverings and matching curtains. "You've dressed this room beautifully."

"Thank you," Liz said. "Randy hasn't stayed here yet; he's a city boy. So, I come here alone." She walked to the window. "The windows work well and can all be opened whenever you want. I haven't gotten the ceiling fan installed yet. But I hope to soon. It's exquisite; I wish it was up now."

They left the master suite and went into the "twin room," as Liz called it. There were two twin beds with thick mattresses, a big fluffy beige rug, and a small nightstand between them. A ladder-back chair and a long narrow table sat across one wall. The room held one window with a pull-down shade and a sheer curtain. With the furnishings of this room, Maddie could imagine children playing on the hardwood floors with toys of the earlier centuries.

The remaining two bedrooms were empty except for a few storage shelves and a couple of chairs. "See, I still have a lot of work to do to get it complete. But someday..." Liz trailed off, sounding as if she was apologizing.

"Liz, you have an amazing treasure here. Don't diminish it. You are young and have plenty of years ahead to do whatever you and Randy choose to do. I think it's terrific. You just need to tell me how much money to bring you when we come out to stay."

"Don't you think Rick might want to see it first?" Liz asked.

"No," Maddie said. "I'm the boss until he gets well!" She started down the stairs and stopped. "Oh, are you allowing pets?"

"Yes, you can bring Bud. I can't wait to meet him. From what you've said about him, I think he'll spend his time out exploring."

The two laughed as they continued down to the last room off the back of the house.

"This is the latest update, but it's not quite what I hope to have permanently," Liz said and opened a door off the left of the small room. It held a toilet and a small shower. A pedestal sink stood conspicuously behind the door to the back yard. "That's not staying there. And I only have a washer because I got a new one at home, so my uncle hooked this one up for when we do come out here in the summers. But there are no plans to do that this year. They've chosen to go to Disney World and a Florida beach instead."

A laundry tub sat next to the washer. Liz added, "I have not gotten that hooked up yet."

"I think you've done very well," Maddie said. "Consider it rented." She offered a handshake. Liz took it and gave her quick hug.

"I might come out to visit you when I'm in the Cove, if you don't mind," Liz said.

"That'd be great." Maddie looked at her watch. "I hope I can find my way out of here. I wouldn't dare try to make it after dark."

The girls talked for a few more minutes before Maddie left. She drove back the way she came in and succeeded in finding civilization.

15

Maddie made it back to the hospital in time to help Rick eat his supper. "Can I help you with that?" Maddie asked as she watched Rick try to open a milk carton. "You know you don't have all of your strength back yet. Remember, Dr. Simms told you simple things we take for granted can be difficult until you're completely well." She took the small red and white carton into her hands. "This is skim milk. Are you sure you want it? You always drink whole milk."

"So, you're telling me I can't change my mind?" Rick gave her a long, irritated look.

"Of course you can." She handed the milk back to him with a straw in it. She was hurt by his look, but she reminded herself that her husband wasn't himself and chose to ignore it.

"I'd like telling you about the cabin in the Cove," Maddie said. "That's what I went to see today."

"Oh, no doubt I'm going to get the blow-by-blow full report," Rick said. He didn't look at her. He stabbed his fork into a chicken breast.

"Not if you don't want to hear about it." Maddie looked up at the TV screen. The show was not one she'd ever seen Rick interested in. "Maybe you'd like me to find a better program on the TV?"

"I can't drink skim milk or watch a game show?" Rick knocked the carton of milk over onto the tray, trying to reach the remote control.

Maddie quickly uprated the carton and grabbed his napkin to absorb the spilled milk. Then, she went to the bathroom for a washcloth to replace his napkin.

She lowered the volume on the TV. "You can watch whatever you like," she said. "I am only trying to be helpful." Leaning her head back in the recliner, she sat quietly for a while.

Finally, Rick said, "I thought you were going to enlighten me."

"And I got the hint that you didn't want to hear about it," Maddie replied without the hurt she felt.

Maddie began with, "If someone doesn't have really good directions, they'd never find this place. There's a fireplace on each end of the house, with four rooms accessing the warmth of the wood burning fixtures. When Liz stays at the cabin in winter, she builds a fire in the kitchen only. The room she sleeps in is upstairs directly above the kitchen. So, no need in a fire at the living room."

Rick held his questions, allowing his wife to ramble on about the cabin.

"There is a well right outside the kitchen door on the back porch," she went on. "Recently, Liz and her husband closed in the porch, adding a bathroom with indoor plumbing."

"Well, it's sounding better," Rick squeezed in his first comment.

Madison continued talking and planning their stay as she thought of things they'd need. "We'll have to stop at a grocery store for food. Liz doesn't leave much in the cabin, so as not to tempt the bears or people, I suppose."

"Paved or gravel road?" Rick asked.

"Gravel most of the way. But a good road. It doesn't get a lot of traffic." She held any more comments.

"Maybe we can talk Henry into bringing Bud over to stay with us?" Rick asked.

"That's a great idea. Why don't you call him?" Maddie dared sounding excited again.

"Wait for a while. I plan on returning to my apartment straight from here. I'll have to return for a ten-day check-up. No point in rushing out there."

Maddie tried not showing her disappointment. She nodded her head but said nothing.

Rick pushed at his tray table, nearly turning it over as an aide came to remove the dinner tray. The young woman didn't say anything to them; she just took the tray and left.

Rick fiddled with the TV remote, trying to find a suitable program. He and Maddie sat silent for more than an hour, with Rick switching channels. Finally, she told him she was getting sleepy and she'd return to his apartment for the night.

"Good idea," he said, still looking at the TV. "See you tomorrow, I suppose?"

"Yeah, call me if you think of something I need to get for you?" She was quiet for a minute. "This is going to be good, Rick. You'll see."

She thought, *Liz wouldn't stay there alone if it wasn't comfortable.*

"There's a great flowing creek on the property, originating in a spring at the top of the mountain," she said. "And it connects to another creek down below the front of the cabin. We can always bathe in the creek." She added this final note to rattle Rick.

"So, they added a bathroom, but no tub or shower?" he asked.

She laughed at his reaction. "There is a small shower next to the toilet."

Maddie walked to her SUV just as the sun was setting. She watched until it dropped out of sight. On the way to the apartment, she heard a text message come in. As soon as she parked, she looked to see if it was from Rick. But it was a short message from Nell.

Call me when you're not with Rick, it read.

Maddie climbed the stairs, unlocked the door, and went inside. First thing she did was open two windows on the back side of the unit. The fresh paint smell was still strong, and she needed it to air out.

She called Nell.

"Hello, Maddie, thanks for calling back," Nell said. "Drew learned that

Buck is loose again. He overtook a guard and escaped this afternoon. He'd been transferred to Jonesborough for better security in the Washington County Jail. Not sure how this happened, but Drew wanted you to know."

"Oh no! I just got back to the apartment," Maddie said. "Guess I'll shower, change, and go back to the hospital. I can't take the chance of him finding Rick again."

"Drew said if you want to come here and stay with us, he'll be on his best behavior. DJ is still looking for you in the basement and closets. I miss you too," Nell added.

"I think I need to stay close to Rick. Thanks for the offer."

"Drew also said he'd arrange for security for Rick. Do you want me to call him?"

"Is he working the night shift?"

"No, but he doesn't get home for another hour, at least."

"This apartment smells of fresh paint anyway. I'll get a shower and then come up to your house. Go ahead and let Drew know I appreciate him sending security. And I will stay with you and the kids tonight."

The drive up the mountain went quickly from where the apartment was located. As she passed by Holly's Hair Salon, she made a mental note of the phone number. She'd call in the morning and make an appointment. The red hair had to go.

DJ's little bare feet patted across the floor, meeting Maddie at the door. He leaped into Maddie's arms, saying, "Where you go?"

She hugged him and carried him to the kitchen. "I had work to do. I'm here now. Want to play?"

"Play on swings?" he asked. The tiny little fellow wriggled out of her grasp. He ran to front door, where Nell stood.

"Not tonight, sweetheart," Nell said. "Remember, Daddy told you the playroom isn't ready to play."

"Bedtime?" DJ started to cry.

"No, you don't have to go to bed yet. Do you want to read to Maddie?"

"My room!" He grabbed Maddie's hand and pulled her toward the stairs.

"Okay, but let me get something to drink first," Maddie said. She went to the fridge. "I hope you have some lemonade?"

"Help yourself," Nell said. "I'm going to run the bath for Rosie." She lifted her little girl from the baby swing in the living room and headed up the stairs.

DJ followed her, and Maddie followed with a large glass of lemonade.

Drew arrived home shortly after Maddie. He joined them in DJ's room. Rose was already sleeping in her crib in the nursery.

"How is Rick getting along?" Drew asked, sitting on the rug next to her and DJ.

"He's doing well, but his moods are like a roller coaster. I can't do anything to please him."

"What does the doctor say about that?" Drew asked.

"She told us it might happen," Maddie said. "But I didn't expect him to become so indifferent." She choked back tears. "He doesn't even know what he likes watching on TV. We can't communicate at all. He has never talked to me the way he did today. He pretty much told me to get out of his room."

The pressure became too much for Maddie to hold back. She buried her face in her hands and bawled like a baby. Drew wrapped his arms around her, holding her tightly. Nell dropped to her knees and joined the hug, crying along with Maddie.

"Hey, you're going to make me cry," Nell said. "Let's not do this. I think you're scaring DJ."

DJ climbed into his bed, begging for hugs from all. And he put himself to sleep.

The next morning, Maddie got up as soon as she smelled coffee brewing. She dressed and carried her overnight bag downstairs as she went. Drew met her with a mug in hand.

"What's this?" he asked, handing Maddie the mug. "You aren't going back to the hospital, are you?"

"I need to be with my husband," Maddie said.

"I get that, but you are in danger too. Buck has it in for you; you caught him. He will come for you as quickly as Rick. Maybe quicker. He knows Rick had surgery. They mentioned that when he was arraigned in court." Drew was holding back. "You crossed him, and now you are his focus. You need to just stay here. There is no way he's going to find this place."

"I don't believe that," Maddie said. "You want me to stay with Nell. I'm not falling for that again, Drew."

Nell walked in as she set the mug of coffee in the sink. "So, you are leaving again?"

"I have to. Rick needs me. He might not know it right now, but he needs me to protect him. You can take care of yourself, Nell. I am trained to kill if need be. And I don't want the killing to take place around you and your children."

Maddie hugged Nell tightly and left.

Drew followed her outside. "Don't be so stubborn, Madison. Look what it got for you in Alaska. You might not be so lucky this time."

Thoughts of the Alaskan plane crash pierced Maddie's memory. Thinking her pilot and friend had been killed, she found herself hog-tied in her aunt's wall tent. She swallowed hard, gritting her teeth. "I held my own then, and I can again," she said. "I've never killed a man, but I could after what my Rick went through. Don't stand in my way, Drew."

Madison felt chills run down her back. She'd never spoken so rudely to anyone. What was going on in her mind? Or was it the look Drew Perry gave her at this moment?

"Buck is insanely cruel and out for blood. He'll find you, and I don't think you can beat him when he's the attacker."

"Take care of your own family, Drew. I love them, but I still love Rick more."

Maddie got into her SUV and drove away. By the time she reached

Holly's Hair Salon, she'd calmed down and thought to look at the sign to see if Ms. Holly was open. She was standing at the door, so Maddie pulled into the parking lot.

"I'd like to make an appointment to change this red back to my natural color," Maddie said. She stepped from the vehicle and walked in the salon behind Ms. Holly.

"My first patron isn't coming until later this morning...Want to do it now?" Holly asked.

"I sure do. Is there someplace around back I can hide my SUV?"

"Yes, go ahead and park it in the carport next to mine back there. A tree blocks the view from the road, if that's what you're worried about."

Maddie retuned, and Ms. Holly was already mixing the color for her application. "Put that cape around you and have a seat," she said. "We'll get this goop on, and then we can talk."

As the color was developing, Maddie told Holly why she needed to hide her SUV.

"I knew it!" Holly said. "That fellow who picked you up. I knew you were not comfortable with him. I wanted to help you. I knew it was him."

"No, Drew is the chief of police in Sevierville," Maddie clarified. "He's married to my best friend. He is trying to get me to hide out at his house with his wife and children. He's not the enemy. But *that* one broke out of jail yesterday, so I want to be at the hospital to protect my husband. That's who he's looking for, not me."

"Just when I had it all figured out," Ms. Holly said, sitting in the dryer chair. "So, your husband didn't like your new look?"

"No, and I really don't fit the redhead look. I love my dark chocolate color. And I really do like this cut. I've never had it this short. It's so easy to fix."

"I would recommend you come back in three weeks to let me evaluate the color. It might need another application. This red is vivid. It might be a bit harder to erase than I thought. I told you it's a good color"

"Thanks, go ahead and make the appointment three weeks out so I won't forget."

Seeing the color solution rinsed out, Maddie was happy her natural col-or showed through. Ms. Holly blow-dried it, and she too was pleased.

"We might have done it, girl. This is looking very good. You are lucky having such thick, healthy hair."

Maddie was so excited that she hugged the hairdresser. She noted the next appointment on her phone calendar and slipped out the back door to her SUV. She felt more in control of her life. Now, if only she could get control of Rick. His attitude was worrying her. What if he never came out of this?

16

Maddie got lots of looks as she walked the hallway leading to Rick's room. Joy stopped in her tracks, nearly dropping the tablet she carried in her hand.

"Maddie? What's this?"

"The real me," Maddie said. "I know bulls are attracted to red. But my bull-headed husband isn't one of them. How's he doing?"

"He's still grumpy," Joy said. "Dr. Simms is coming in to see him today. She thinks there's something else bothering him. We shall see!" Joy continued on her mission, and Maddie slowed her stride toward the room she feared had not changed the forecast.

"Hey, Rick. I'm back," she said, tilting her head and offering her sweetest smile. "How's your day going?"

"Your hair," Rick said. "I'm glad you changed it back. This suits you better." He turned back to the TV.

"Yeah, I didn't care for the red either, but it will take a while for it to grow out again," Maddie said. Her sigh told her she missed her long hair. This was only the second time she'd had it cut. She felt saddened.

"Why do you want it long again? This style looks good on you, and I'm sure it takes less time fixing." Rick glanced at her and then back to the TV.

"Thank you. It is much easier to manage. I appreciate your opinion," she said softly.

An hour went by, and no more words from her husband. Dr. Simms arrived promptly at eleven and complimented Maddie on her new look. Then, she politely requested that Maddie go for a walk.

Rick's head snapped toward his wife and back to Dr. Simms. "Why?" he asked. "Whatever you have to say can be said to both of us."

"No, not this time, Rick," Dr. Simms said. "I feel this is between you and me."

Dr. Simms watched Maddie leave the room with puzzlement on her face. She continued, "I'm sorry about being so blunt. Your wife is suffering, whether you are or not. So, we are having a heart to heart, Sheriff."

Meanwhile, Maddie made it to the patient and family break room. She couldn't hold back the emotion she'd just become overwhelmed with. Luckily, Joy walked in right behind her.

"What's going on?" Maddie burst out.

"It's not as bad as it seems, I promise you," Joy said.

"You were here yesterday when they assigned security for Rick, right?" Maddie asked.

"Yes, I spoke to the officer myself. Dr. Simms didn't want Rick to know, so I met him immediately to be sure he didn't talk to anyone, especially Rick."

"Okay, so what then?" Maddie was impatient. "Tell me what's going on."

"Someone slipped a burner phone into Rick's room," Joy said. "I caught him talking on it last night. I'd forgotten to reset his IV drip to the night setting, so I went in, thinking he should be sleeping. He wasn't."

"So, you heard him talking to someone and he got the deer in the headlight look," Maddie said.

"And he was not happy to see me." Joy raised her eyebrows. "Does that sound like your Rick?"

"Yeah," Maddie said and wiped her face with a paper towel. "But why, and who was he talking to? Did you take the phone?"

"No, it was not my business, but I told Dr. Simms, and she became very curious. Curious enough to confront him."

"Oh, boy, this might not be a good day to tell him my news." Maddie sat on a soft wingback chair. "So, I'll wait here for Dr. Simms's report?" She looked up at Joy.

"I would, if he was my husband," Joy said, winking at Maddie and turning to leave the room. "Oh, there's a fresh bowl of fruit in the fridge. Help yourself."

Maddie munched on a red delicious apple while she waited for Dr. Simms. The apple was long gone before the doctor entered the room.

"Thanks for waiting for me," Simms said. She took a seat at the table in front of the window. "Who do you think Rick might have been talking to?"

"Maybe Drew, the chief of police in Sevierville," Maddie said. "That would be my first thought. Drew had me using a burner when I was staying out of touch before we found Rick. What did he say to you?"

"First, he blew me off. That's when I told him that he was not out of the woods yet. And he apologized. He said he felt safer using that phone rather than one the TBI could have bugged. I'm not a good judge, but it sounded reasonable to me. He isn't giving up anything. If you want to let him know about the security guard stationed outside his door, that's your call. You know him; I don't. Do what you're comfortable with." Dr. Simms stood up and asked, "How are you doing?"

"I'm okay," Maddie said. "I trust my husband. He's trying to protect me. He blames himself for everything. And as it turns out, he was right. The escaped prisoner needs Rick to testify for him in court. He doesn't remember the event, or me, or what happened last week. But his engrained nature is still in place. He will do what he feels is right and justified." Maddie stood. "I'm going to let him tell me what he wants me to know."

Dr. Simms nodded as she walked out of the room

On her way back to Rick's room, Maddie noticed the security guard sitting in the room across the hallway. "Hey...Drew sent you?"

The officer nodded and tipped his hat. Maddie smiled and pushed open Rick's door.

"You again?" Rick smiled for a moment as he looked toward her.

"I have something I want to discuss with you," Maddie said. "Is this a good time?" She sat on the sofa across the room from the man she wanted to throw her arms around and smother with kisses. But she resisted.

"Dr. Simms just wants me to understand that my attitude is temporary," Rick said. "As my memory returns, my kind nature will too."

He winked at her. A wink that caused her insides to flip flop. Her hopes rose in her throat. But that's all he said, and she waited, not wanting to rush his actions. *Let him come to you.* There was a nerve-racking silence hanging in the air. Maddie breathed deeply, trying to stop her heart from racing. She breathed out slowly like air escaping from a tire. She was suddenly aware of the way Rick looked at her. It gave her thoughts that he recognized one of her telling signs. One that he'd warned her needed dropping. But she hoped his memory was returning, and she let her "tell" show. She was nervous. Had he really remembered something between them? Did she dare pray it was the old Rick?

"What was it you wanted to discuss with me?" Rick kept his face turned toward the TV and the golfing sports report on its screen.

"You don't even like golf—oh, never mind." Maddie stood and walked to the window, to be sure her back was toward him. "As I was driving here, I had a call from Liz, the woman with the cabin in the Cove—"

"About that cabin—" he interrupted.

"I'm not finished!" She turned to face him. "She gave me a number to call. It was the ranger office in the Cove. Captain Jonas Ford, I learned, is looking for an officer to patrol the Cove. The crowds are out of hand, as we already know. And they offered me the position to help enforce the rules."

"Traffic control for the bears?" Rick asked, and his look crushed Madison's heart.

He made fun of the job offer without even thinking how much she'd love the work. It was perfect for her. The crowds were the very reason Rick refused to return to the Cove. She'd walked a mile line of traffic to investigate what the holdup was, and he laughed at her? This was not her Rick. Someone was playing a cruel joke on her. She felt the tears welling up. Crying in front of him would be humiliating. No, she would not give him the pleasure. She walked past the foot of his bed without turning to say a word.

The officer across the hall stood up. Maddie held her hand up to stop him and continued down the hall to the elevator and to her SUV before she choked.

She drove south again toward the Great Smoky Mountains. Darkness was not only the mood in the vehicle but also in the clouds looming over Gatlinburg. She pulled to the side of the road and called Liz.

"Hey, Liz. It's Maddie. I'm in Gatlinburg and wondered if we could meet for supper?"

"Hello, Maddie," Liz answered. "I'm so glad you called. Randy and his brother left this afternoon to drive to Atlanta. Come to our house, I'm making vegetable soup. You do like soup?"

"Sure. Especially on a rainy night." Maddie programed the address into her GPS and headed toward a warm meal and a good friend. She needed this tonight.

Liz's home was simple and cozy, just the way Maddie had pictured it. They sat at the bar in her kitchen and feasted on fresh-off-the-stove vegetable soup and crusty bread. Liz served a simple red blend wine, and they laughed like old friends. Maddie allowed Liz to talk as much as she wanted. She knew if Rick's name came up in the conversation, the dam would break.

Liz quickly stowed the soup away in the fridge while Maddie cleared the bowls and utensils, adding them to the nearly full dishwasher.

"You want me to start this?" Maddie closed the door.

"Yes, I've already put in the detergent!" Liz called from the living room. "It's set and ready."

Maddie joined her, carrying her wine glass. "Your home is lovely. I feel comfortable here."

"Comfortable enough to sit here and tell me why your eyes are swollen from crying?" Liz asked.

"Maybe if I finish my wine first. Tell me more about how you and Randy met."

Liz talked for another half hour. Then, she got up and opened another bottle of wine. "I love this wine. And it will help both of us sleep."

"Oh, I should find a hotel and reserve a room, while I still can." Maddie started to get up.

"No, stay right where you are. Your bed is in my guest room. I just put new sheets on it this morning, hoping you might stop by." Liz refilled Maddie's glass and her own. She sat on the floor in front of the gas fireplace. "Nothing better than a warm fire on a rainy night."

"With a friend," Maddie said, offering a toast. "Here's to newfound friends."

Maddie unloaded her story of heartbreak and dashed hopes of her husband ever going for the idea of staying at the cabin. But since she'd decided to accept the job offer as a traffic ranger, she'd still keep her plan of staying at the cabin, if that was still an option. Liz absolutely agreed and promised to come by at least once a week and possibly even stay overnight with her. The rain was still strumming on the metal roof when the wine was gone, and the girls called it quits on talking any longer. With tomorrow being Saturday, Liz apologized for having to open the shop at 10:00 a.m.

"That's okay, I can go with you. At some time, I can call the ranger station, and they can tell me when I start."

"Okay," Liz said. "I'll call you when my alarm wakes me, and we can stop for breakfast on the way."

"Sounds good. See you in the morning." Maddie looked at her phone, hoping she might have a text from Rick, but why did she bother? Now, she was put into a dark mood again.

Maddie's phone woke her before she heard from Liz. It was Holly, so she answered it. They talked for a while, gathering news from each other. The call ended with Maddie promising to call as soon as she learns about her new job.

Liz leaned against the open door while Maddie disconnected the call. "Rick?" she asked. The expression on Maddie's face made her wish she hadn't asked.

"We still up for breakfast?" Maddie asked.

"You bet!" Liz turned to go back to her room. "I'm wearing jeans and a T-shirt."

"Okay, me too...That's about all I ever wear!" Maddie called out.

Maddie followed Liz to her shop. She was surprised at how large her photo studio was. Besides a framing department, they carried books by local authors, small gift items made by local craftsmen, and a few larger unique ones. The back corner of the building was a glass blowing operation her brother-in-law used for making jewelry. Maddie browsed the small colorful pieces as Liz turned on lights and made the store ready for customers.

"That's Mark's little corner of the world. He makes those himself. Each one is different. They're blown Pyrex glass. Customers enjoy watching him make the pieces, and they often purchase them."

"You have a very nice business here," Maddie said. "I like it!"

"Thank you. Randy and I didn't want to work for someone else. So, we started with nothing, and it's grown into a good living. I like having the freedom to come and go as I please, shooting photos, and us choosing which make the best prints. Randy makes the frames himself."

"I wish Rick and I could do something like this. But I might not even have a future with him. I don't even know if he'll ever be my Rick again." Maddie turned away to admire the prints hanging along the walls.

"Maddie, give him more time. I've never met Rick, of course, but from what I feel from the way you talk about him, I can't help but think you're wrong to worry like that. He'll come back. He has to find out who he is now. After all, he came really close to death."

Maddie thought about what Liz just said. "You're probably right. I'm being selfish. I don't know what he's been through. Maybe, I've lost his respect. After all, I am the one who captured the monster who took him. He didn't have an opportunity to escape. He was injured. I knew I could save him. One of the last conversations we had—he told me he needed the old Madison, that I'd become soft, and he wanted the old Maddie back." She turned away again to hide the tears.

"I understand, you're hurt too, not physically, but the pain is just as bad. It's still pain! You two need this time apart. I don't know how to explain this, but that's what I feel." Liz stared at Maddie.

"He needs me," Maddie started to say.

"Then let him show it." Liz went to unlock the front door. "I have customers coming in. You are welcome to go into the back for a while until you compose yourself."

Maddie nodded.

Meanwhile, at the hospital, Joy discovered a friendly Rick.

"Are you feeling better today?" she asked while she checked his vitals. "Things are looking good. I'd say Dr. Simms will release you by week's end." She started out the door.

"Joy," Rick called. "Do you know where Madison is? I tried reaching her last night, but she didn't answer."

"You seem surprised," Joy said. She didn't turn to look at him. She just walked out, and the door shut.

Rick leaned back on the bed and thought about what she'd said. "If she only knew."

Just at that moment, the burner phone rang. He hesitated to answer it. But then, after several rings, he answered.

"Hello?"

As Maddie sat in the private room by the back entrance of the shop, she looked at her phone. She had not seen the missed call from her husband. But he left no message. So, she deleted it.

She punched in the ranger's phone number and listened to several rings. Then, a gruff voice answered, "Cades Cove ranger station."

"Hello, my name is Madison McKenzie Malone. I am trying to reach Captain...?"

"Yes, yes, this is he. I'm happy hearing from you, Ms. Malone. I read your resume. Quite impressive. I'm thinking you might be well above our needs in this job. You realize this is a trial period position, don't you?"

"Yes, sir. And I am perfectly happy to give your offer a try. I'm not looking for a full-time job right now. I'd really do a good job I promise. I've said for years that the Cove needed traffic control. I even put that in a suggestion box one time. I was thinking maybe on horseback or even motorcycle."

The captain laughed. "Mounted police, huh? That might get uncomfortable all day in the saddle. I have considered a motorcycle. But I've got a better vehicle. When can you come in to talk with me?"

"Whenever you say. I'm available this minute. Well, I'd need to travel from Gatlinburg."

"Okay, that's fine. It might be a good day. We're sometimes slow on Mondays, so come on out."

"Thank you, sir," Maddie said. "I really appreciate your consideration. I need something to do to keep me out of trouble." She laughed. "With my husband, that is. He's still in the hospital in Knoxville, and he's pretty grouchy."

"Very good. I'll see you within the hour." He cut off the call.

Maddie hurried to tell Liz. As she stepped out into the small hallway, she noticed Liz stood with her hands in the air. A masked man stood with his back to her. She saw he was holding a pistol. Liz looked scared, but she didn't say a word. Maddie held her finger to her lips and ducked down behind a display case.

"Get that money box, now!" the masked man demanded.

"I have to go to the back room," Liz said. "We don't keep it out in the front." Her voice sounded shaky.

Maddie slipped backwards and around the corner as the man turned and motioned for Liz to move toward the back room. He let Liz pass and then walked behind her, his gun nearly touching her back.

Maddie waited until he passed the aisle she was crouched in. As luck would have it, she got a good look at the gun. It was a small .22 caliber, with a very inaccurate reputation. So, she felt Liz was not in real danger. But to be sure, she slipped to the end of the aisle and stood up. Slowly, she approached the small figure of a young man or boy. Liz stepped out of sight into the back room. Maddie lunged from the left side, knocking the pistol from his hand. She quickly grasped his hand, twisting it behind him. He fell to one knee, completely off balance. She used his position to shove him all the way to the floor. In a matter of seconds, she had both hands behind him and a plastic tie wrap around both wrists. Liz stepped out and quickly retrieved the .22 handgun.

"What a way to start the week," Maddie laughed, letting the stress flow out.

"Not for me," the robber said. He hung his head, and the mask he wore dropped to his chin, exposing a young face with tears on his cheek.

"How old are you?" Liz asked.

"I'm fifteen. Please don't shoot me, miss." He was looking at Madison.

"I wouldn't shoot you," she said. "I just didn't want you to shoot Liz. What did you expect?"

"I-I just...I gotta have money to pay for my mom to go to the hospital. She's real bad sick." He continued crying.

"What is your name?" Maddie asked. "Do you live around here?"

The poor boy nodded his head and then tried speaking, "I'm José. We live in those condos."

"I thought you looked familiar," Liz said. "What's wrong with your mom?"

"I don't know. She's got an awful high fever, and she's going to have a baby. I need to get her to a hospital, but we don't have any money. I'm sorry, ma'am, I wouldn't have hurt you. I've seen you come and go from the store.

I know your husband and brother are out of town. So, all I could think of was to take your cash. I'm so sorry."

"Come in here and sit down, José." Maddie reached for the boy's arm and led him to a chair at the desk. "Don't you dare run. I'll take these restraints off if you'll stay right there."

Maddie pulled one arm down next to the arms of the chair and fastened the restraint around only one wrist. If he made a break for it, he'd have to take the chair with him.

Liz stepped into the hall, and Maddie joined her. "I'm not calling the police on him," Liz whispered. "I'd like to give him the money to take his mom to a hospital. Or actually, I'll take her and give her the money."

"That's up to you," Maddie said. "I'd like to take him home and meet his mother. He could be telling us a whopper."

"Okay, I'll lock up, put a note on the door, and we'll take him home," Liz said.

Madison drove them in her SUV, just a block to the condos. She and Liz walked with the boy to his unit he mentioned. Maddie knocked, and a very pregnant woman opened the door, just a small amount. She looked to be sweating with the fever.

"Hello, I'm Liz, and this is Madison," Liz began. "Is this your son?" She pushed the door open a bit farther.

"José, what have you done?" the woman said. The accent was strong, but she was easy to understand. At least she knew English. The woman said, "I'm Juanita. What did he do?""

"He is worried about you, Juanita. When is your baby due?" Maddie asked.

"Pronto, soon." The woman bent at the waste in pain. "Now?"

"Come on, we'll take you to a hospital," Maddie said. "You need help."

"No, I can't, please, no," Juanita begged.

"Are you an illegal?" Maddie asked her.

She nodded, in obvious pain.

"Do you have any other family?" Maddie asked.

"No, my husband did not make it through the border. They took him away."

"How did you get here?" Liz asked. "Well, that isn't important. Your health and the baby's is most important at the moment."

"Come with us," Maddie said. "You too, José." She took the ailing woman's arm. She and José got in the front, and Liz sat in the back with Juanita. "Guide me to the hospital, Liz."

The ER nurse took Juanita back, leaving José to answer the receptionist's questions as best he could. Maddie gave her credit card and phone number, along with the cash Liz had gotten from her store.

"Can you treat her with this and my card?" Maddie asked.

"Yes, we'll do it," the receptionist said. "She's in the hands of our government. I'll talk to you before I put anything on your credit card. It's nice of you to help her. She's really sick."

José and Maddie went into the waiting area. Madison began, "I know you only wanted to help your mom. Have you ever been in trouble?"

"No, ma'am, I was scared she'd die."

"I know." Maddie sat down, pulling José's arm, "Sit down, please. Can you tell me where they took your dad?"

"I can try to explain," José said and began at the point he and Juanita were handed off to the American authorities.

He didn't know where his dad was taken, but they promised he could stay with his mom because of her condition. So far, they kept their word, and after a three-day drive, they ended up in Gatlinburg at the condo and $150 in cash. No one checked on them again. They were on their own. The money was gone, and Juanita was in labor. The man who put them in the condo was called "White Hat." And they never saw him again.

"I didn't know what to do," José said, burying his face in his hands.

"Okay," Maddie continued. "Tell me about your dad and when this took place. I'll try and find him. At least your mom is safe now. You should stay here with her, and Liz will come back to get you. I have to go somewhere. I'm beginning a new job today and I am already late. Can I trust you not to get in any more trouble? Your mom needs you, and I'll do my best to locate your dad. Keep my card, and call me as soon as you know how your mom and the baby are. I could have taken you in to the police. I am an officer of the law; I can arrest you. But Liz chose not to. You are very lucky we were the ones you tried to rob. Take this as a lesson, and don't break any more laws. Unless you want to spend time behind bars. Do you understand?"

"Yes, Officer Maddie, I do, and I am thankful for you not taking me in," the boy said.

"Where did you get that gun anyway?" Maddie remembered she'd put it in her pocket.

"I found it in a ditch behind the condos. It has no bullets. I don't have any at home either."

"You could have been killed. Do you know how lucky you are?" Maddie put the .22 back in her pocket. "You don't ever touch another gun. At least not till you're older and get a license. In our country, that's the way we do it. Not the way you started out."

"Yes, ma'am, I will follow your rules, I promise," José said. "And I'll take care of Momma. Will you please find my dad?"

"I'll do my best, I give you my promise." Maddie put her arm around the young boy. "Let's go find Liz and Juanita."

Liz was coming out to the waiting room when they got to the hallway. She said, "José, you're going to have a baby brother or sister right now. Juanita is ready. They took her to delivery. You and I are going to the cafeteria for some food. This will take a little while, and I know you're hungry. Deal?"

"Yes, ma'am, I promised Miss Maddie. I'm going to be good, and she's going to find my dad. He was police in Puerto Rico."

Maddie and Liz looked at each other with astonishment. "He ought to be easy enough to find," Liz said.

"Let's hope so," Maddie agreed. "But now, I need to get to the Cove. Shouldn't I drop you off at your shop?"

"That's okay, I'm staying. The store can mind itself. This is way more exciting. Besides, I want to show José how to use the shuttle busses, so he can get his mom home when she's ready. I'm doing my public service today."

Maddie smiled at Liz and José. She said, "You two have fun. Call me later to update me?"

And then Maddie left.

17

Maddie walked into the captain's office with a guilty grin on her face. "You won't believe what held me up," she said. She proceeded to tell him about the robbery attempt, the baby, and its very sick mother. And then, she added, "Juan Martinez is the dad. The boy says he was a policeman in Puerto Rico. He might not be one of the dangerous illegals. I'm going to try and locate him."

"You're right," the captain said. "That's a fantastic story. But from what I've read in your file, I think you deserve this job. I'm glad to have you with us, Officer Malone." He handed her a dark green T-shirt and asked if the size would fit.

"Oh, my very own Cades Cove T-shirt!" Maddie said. "Yes, just my size. What type of pants do you require?"

"Jeans are fine for what you'll be doing," the captain said and led the way to the vehicles.

There sat a couple of side-by-side 4-wheelers with top, windshield, and doors. The captain walked up to one and indicated for her to climb aboard. "You ever driven one?" he asked.

"No, not like this. What can you tell me?"

"Let's just take a spin." He sat in the right seat, leaving the driver's side for Maddie.

"Okay, if you're sure. Hang on." She looked around at the controls and the instruments on the dash. "This thing is fancy," Maddie added, locating the proper reverse to get started.

The idea was to look efficient and not cocky. She knew from riding on Henry's side-by-side with the boys that they were not complicated. However, this one had more power. She'd already noted that.

"Where to?" Maddie asked.

"Take me down to the stables," he said, settling back into the seat, holding on with one hand.

Backing out of the carport area was easily mastered, and finding the gear to pull out was the next decision. Only when you needed four wheels to climb out of something did you use the low first gear. Since they were on concrete, Maddie slipped straight to second gear. The vehicle moved smoothly into a cruising gear. It was basically automatic, as she discovered.

"Now, if you feel comfortable, go for a round in the loop," the captain said. "I'll be in touch by radio." He handed her a walkie talkie. "It has a range all the way to the end at the park's gift shop. Now, there are areas on the trails that you'll lose signal, but basically anywhere in the park, we can connect. Because as you may know, phones don't work in here."

Maddie nodded her head. "See you back at your office at what time?"

"Today, I'm leaving at 5:00. If you don't make it by then, Jones will be here for the night shift."

"Okay...So, am I to come back again tomorrow?" Maddie asked.

"Unless you decide you don't want this job." He patted her shoulder. "Welcome aboard, Maddie."

"Thank you." She didn't have any questions. But she had lots to learn—that she felt sure of.

Back in Knoxville, Rick became concerned when he called Madison's phone all day and never got an answer. He called Holly. She didn't answer either. But he marked that up to the fact that she could be busy with Little Mattie. So, he left her a message.

Next, he tried calling Nell.

"Hello, Rick," Nell answered. "How are you feeling?" She recognized his voice.

"I'm feeling good, Nell, thanks for asking. I'm calling to see if Madison is with you?"

"No, I haven't talked to her in a couple days. I thought she was in Knoxville with you."

"She was, but I messed up," he explained. "I haven't been very tolerant of her. I'm sure I've hurt her feelings. That was not my intention. But it's been awkward."

"I'm sure you'll figure it out." Nell wasn't rude, but she was clearly on Maddie's side in this scenario.

"Thank you," Rick said.

"Anytime, Rick. We still love you. Even though you don't remember it." With that, she disconnected the call.

Rick felt empty. He had been too harsh with Maddie. He was learning the hard way what it's like to be alone.

Meanwhile, in the Cove, Maddie was finding a slow Monday to be a great first day on a new job. She easily managed the snarls of traffic when drivers slowed to watch or photograph the deer. So far, there had been no bears to complicate the scenery. However, as the sun dropped lower in the sky, that was about to change.

She drove back on the Loop Road, headed toward the back side of the eleven-mile loop. Woods were thick in this area, making dark shadows. Up ahead, she watched taillights disappear in the sharp curve. Before she could get to the curve, taillights were backing up. Something brought the line of traffic to a stand-still; this was what she was there to prevent. She'd discovered her little flashing light on the top of the four-by-four. So, she turned it on and proceeded around the parked cars with two left wheels off the asphalt as she passed. Some cars had their door swung open wide, so she had to drop all wheels off the paved road. She rounded the curve, completely off the narrow road, but she stayed in constant motion, looking for the head of the line.

Finally, she saw a car with a dozen people standing in the middle of the road. As she pulled up, they moved away, allowing her through to the lead car.

"Who's driving this car?" Maddie asked, looking at the people now moving away from her. No one answered. She reached in to see that the keys were in the switch. She blew the horn, and a couple standing way down in the field waved their arms. But no one came to the car. So, she started the vehicle and drove no more than 25 feet to a pull-off area so that the cars could move past. The car directly behind the offensive blocking car pulled off the pavement and also parked in the wide area.

"We tried getting him to move the car out of the road," the man from the second car explained. "There was no one else here at that time, but he laughed, saying he'd be right back."

"This is one of the narrowest areas, as you can see. And right there, just another 25 feet is a pull-off. What's so difficult to understand about this?" Maddie was frustrated. "What was he looking at anyway?"

"He said a bear and three cubs ran across in front of him, and he wanted to catch up to get a picture," said the second driver.

Meanwhile, the line of cars dispersed. Nothing to hold them up. Maddie drove the four-by-four into the field close to where the man and his wife stood.

"Do you even realize how dangerous this stunt is?" Maddie asked them. "Not to mention you caused traffic to back up over a mile. Come and get on here with me, and let's see if we can get out of here before that momma bear turns on you and claws your face off."

The man laughed, continuing to video the cubs playing. The mother bear was very patient at this point, but that could change at any moment. The man's wife pulled on his arm to get him to come away. He pulled his arm away to step closer. The momma bear lunged just far enough to say, *That's it, and you've been warned.*

Maddie pulled her sidearm from its holster.

"I don't intend to shoot the bear, but I won't hesitate to cut you down at the knee if it means removing you from the premises," Maddie said. "Get on this side-by-side now." She aimed her pistol straight at the man's leg.

The man's eyes were wide open, and his feet moved as he said, "I'm going to report you."

"Oh, good, then I won't have to tell the story. I can't wait to hear your side of this to the captain." Maddie tapped the camera mounted on her vehicle. "I think my captain will side with the video I recorded for the last twenty minutes or so."

She made sure the man and woman were settled onto the back seat and holding on. Then, she drove without a word back to his car. "Just have a seat in your vehicle, while I write out all the necessary tickets," she said. "And then I'll escort you to the ranger station."

"You can't do anything to me." The man stood close to Maddie.

She calmly reached into the glove compartment of the side-by-side and pulled out a pair of hand cuffs. "You want to make this harder on yourself?" She stepped closer to him, and he backed away.

The sun was nearly gone. She pulled onto the road, motioning for him to follow. They drove without stopping all the way to the ranger station. When she parked and went inside, she led the man in by one arm. He took one look at the night shift ranger and began stammering that he was sorry for the miscommunication. A six-foot-two, 300-pound ranger stood looking down at the man.

"I'll just watch the video if you'll shut your mouth for a while," the ranger said. He winked at Maddie, taking the video from her. She showed the beginning of the traffic line, and then fast forwarded to the end and the man's car in the middle of the road. He paid particular attention to the video where she drove down in the field to get the couple, listening closely to all the man had said.

"Let me see what your tickets say." The ranger thumbed through four ticket she'd made out with charges against the rude man. "I agree with these, but you missed a couple that I'll add. Thanks, Deputy Malone, you did a great job. Just leave this with me, and we'll see you again tomorrow. Goodnight."

"My pleasure, sir," Maddie said. She went outside, parked the side-by-side under the carport, and left in her SUV. As soon as she had a cell signal, she called Liz.

"I'm just coming through Townsend. Are you at home?" Maddie asked.

"Yes, come on to my house, and we'll finish off that soup. I'll tell you about my day. I hope you were planning to stay again tonight?" Liz offered.

"That would be nice, if you're okay with it."

Maddie turned right at the split and drove toward Gatlinburg. With a smile on her face and a very hungry growl in her stomach, she was grateful for her new friend Liz.

She turned onto Liz's street, the last house at the top of the hill—no neighbors, no noise. "I could live here," Maddie said aloud.

Liz met her on the driveway. "How was it?"

"Oh, it's going to be great. I'll tell you all about it. How are José and the baby and his mom?"

"I'll tell you all about it, but let's eat. I'm starving." With that, Liz led the way into the house.

Helping clear away the supper dishes, Maddie said, "Tell me how the hospital turned out."

"That baby is one of the prettiest I've ever seen," Liz said. "Sha'rie, that's what Juanita named her. She says it's French. She weighed eight pounds, six ounces. And the pediatrician says she's healthy. It's amazing. José was proud of her and carried her to show all the other babies in the nursery. He's a good boy. You don't think I made a mistake not reporting him, do you? He knew better; that's why he didn't have any ammo. He doesn't deserve to get a prison education."

"I agree. I've saved my share of kids, boys and girls." Maddie smiled. "There's one girl at home. I hope I've left a good impression. She's an artist. But she has no encouragement. Her mom is doing time now for selling drugs. And I learned that she only did it to get enough money to pay off her house, her bills, and have money to send her daughter to an art school.

"I interviewed her, and she made sense. She told me she never sold to a new buyer. Every one of her buyers had been on drugs for years. They had no interest in getting clean. She even told me her speech she insisted they each listen to. If they didn't buy from her, they'd buy from someone else. She never used drugs. She was judged on her first offense, and the judge threw the book at her." Maddie turned to Liz, continuing, "I think she should have had a second chance. The sale that got her caught was her last stock. She should have gotten away. I think someone set her up. And I believe I know who that was."

On Tuesday, Maddie drove to the Cove for the 8:00 o'clock opening. Randy and his brother were home to open the store, so Liz prepared her camera equipment and followed shortly behind Maddie. She'd make her normal rounds photographing select bears and a few coyotes, and a family of foxes with six pups. She and Maddie planned to meet up for lunch at Sparks Lane, a cut-through dirt road from one side of the loop to the other.

Liz passed time filming a pair of spotted twin fawns playing in the creek while the mother munched lazily on new spring grass. She'd never met this trio before. They were giving her some of her best shots of the day. But with the side-by-side's approach, Momma Doe gathered up the kids and faded into the depth of the forest.

"Good, you're just in time. Look what I've been doing." Liz played the shots of the deer back to show Maddie.

"Oh, that's so adorable!" Maddie said. "I scared them away when I drove up here. I'm sorry."

"No, they would have left soon anyway. I'm just happy I was early and got these. I'm even surprised at my own luck. Randy usually gets the best dear exposures."

The two friends settled onto a patch of thick grass, eating pimento cheese sandwiches and munching on golden delicious apples. Maddie's radio lit up and she heard the captain's voice say, "Any ranger in the area of Sparks Lane?"

"I am, Captain," Maddie answered. "What's the trouble?"

"Somebody's lost their children. I'll meet you in the parking lot of the cabin. You're looking for a Mrs. Phillips."

"On my way," Maddie said. "So, we're meeting at Rich Mountain Road at 5:00-ish." She laughed. "It will depend on whether I find these children, I suppose."

"Can I join you?" Liz asked. "I know that territory like the back of my hand."

"When looking for kids, I guess we need all the help we can get. Meet you there."

Liz hurried to put things back in her vehicle and followed Maddie.

The drive was less than a mile, and when they arrived, the children's mother was sitting on the steps of the cabin, crying inconsolably. People who had heard her story were already looking in the woods and down by the creek. Maddie quickly took charge. She listened to the woman's story and told her to stay by her car and stop crying. Hysterics only make a situation worse. The woman with her explained that the children ran off after a deer, and the younger child followed the two older ones. She pointed out the direction they'd gone.

Maddie asked the lady, who identified herself as a concerned citizen, if she'd mind staying with the mother to try keeping her from going looking herself. All they needed was for the distraught mother to get lost.

The lady accepted the challenge. So, Maddie and Liz climbed on the side-by-side, attempting to follow the trampled grass toward the woods.

Liz noticed a game trail veering off to the right and pointed out to Maddie, "This trail goes to the creek and is most likely the direction the deer would have gone. If we stay straight on this trail, it gets steep and rocky. I think the children would have stayed with the deer, don't you?"

Maddie agreed. "And hopefully along the creek, they'd leave footprints."

The trail led through a swampy area, and due to recent rains, the creek overflowed its banks, leaving pools behind all around the grassy wetlands. Maddie and Liz got off the vehicle and looked for any telltale signs of fresh deer or children's tracks.

"Over here," Liz called out. "I see lots of deer tracks, and they are fresh. These might be tracks left by the kids." She examined scuff marks, looking like shoes, possibly.

Maddie joined her. "Look, there." She stepped across the mud. "This is definitely a shoe print."

Liz stepped beside the print. "It's smaller than mine, and look, it's deeper. The older girl might have been carrying her little sister."

The two women continued looking closely at the wet trail. Reaching the main creek, they found more prints which followed the creek.

"Maybe they realized the water ran toward the road. Let's go that way," Maddie said.

"I'll stay on foot, while you choose the best route for the four-wheeler," Liz said. "The underbrush is getting thicker."

"Okay, but I'll keep you in sight," Maddie laughed. "I don't want you getting lost, or I won't have a place to sleep tonight."

"Oh, you mean you won't go on to my cabin if I disappear?" Liz laughed. "That's comforting at least."

"No, I don't know that I can find it from this side of the mountain. I plan on keeping up with you." Maddie moved the four-wheel vehicle along the rough terrane, dropping off into holes and climbing out slinging mud. "I'll have to drive back to the creek crossing on Sparks Road to wash this thing. I'm making a mess of it."

"Here is a set of three tracks in the sand. The girls definitely went this way." Liz had an upbeat sound to her voice.

"Good! Do you want to climb back on here, and let's move a little faster?"

"Be right there." Liz jumped the last muddy pool and caught up with the vehicle. "We are almost back to the Cove Loop Road."

Maddie drove, keeping the creek in sight just in case the girls were still in the woods, and it was a good call. She saw brightly colored movement on the opposite side of the creek. At that moment, the girls heard the four-wheeler approaching.

"Hey...Hey there," one of the girls called out. "Help, we're lost."

Maddie crossed the creek, moving straight to the frightened girls. "We're looking for you!"

"Climb aboard, your mother is worried sick," Liz said. "This is Ranger Maddie, and I'm Liz. We're really happy to find you."

"And I'm glad seeing you cared for your little sister," Maddie said.

"She followed us, and we didn't realize it until we got to the muddy area. She was so scared. I had to carry her to keep her out of the water," the older girl reported.

"And I'm glad you did. That was very loving of you," Maddie said, smiling at the older sister. "But you should never have run after the deer. There are bears in these woods, and if you startled a momma bear with cubs, she might hurt you. Please don't ever run away like that again. It is not fair to your mother. Now is it?"

"No, ma'am. We'd never seen a real deer before," the middle girl spoke, finally. "It was my fault. I wanted to touch the baby deer. But the mother took it away."

"She was scared of you. I'm glad you didn't see a bear!" Liz laughed, and all the girls laughed too.

The muddy four-wheeler with five passengers rolled into the parking lot of the cabin. The mother ran to her girls, crying happy tears this time.

Maddie saw her captain leaning against his vehicle with his arms crossed. She parked her side-by-side and walked to him with Liz in toe.

"I think you might already know this lady," Maddie said. She stopped in front of him. "Liz helped me track the girls. She was taking pictures on Sparks Lane when I heard you on the radio."

"It's nice seeing you, Liz," the captain said. "And thank you for your help. I'm sure you know every trail in the park. Great job, girls. This could have been a disaster. Thank you for taking charge." The captain tilted his head, looking toward Maddie. "How did you two meet?"

"We met out here on a trial one day a few weeks ago. We're both fans of a certain bear," Maddie said.

"Well, it's comforting to know our park has such capable ladies. I might need to add you to our list of employees, Liz." He turned and walked to his car. "Maddie, I got all the necessary information from Mrs. Phillips. You can stop by the office and write up your impression of the account after you untangle another bear encounter traffic jam in the same place as yesterday. Take a few moments to survey the situation and submit your theory of what's happening there. Will you?"

Then, the captain got in his vehicle and drove toward headquarters.

Maddie looked at her watch. "It's after three now. By the time I deal with the traffic jam, I'll go straight back to the office and get the paperwork done. Then, I'll get to Rich Mountain Road as quickly as I can."

"I'll be there," Liz said. "And don't worry if you're a little late." She stopped for a second. "Say, would you mind using the ranger's landline and calling Randy?"

"Not at all. What should I tell him?" Maddie asked.

"Say that I'm staying at the cabin tonight, and I'll see him tomorrow night." Liz winked. "Why shouldn't I get a night out? He and his brother were in Atlanta two nights." She laughed.

"Oh, good. I'll be a lot more comfortable spending the first night in your cabin if you're there too. Thank you."

Maddie got on the four-wheeler and zipped in the direction of the traffic jam.

By the time she caught up with the backed-up traffic, it had begun moving. She left the roadway and passed the long line of cars. As it had been the day before, one or two cars sat in the middle of the road at that same narrow location.

Maddie talked to passengers in the first car to discover where the driver was. He was not so far away this time, but Maddie drove to his location. "Mr. Spears, you'll have to move your vehicle so this traffic can pass," she said. "There is a pull-off just a few feet away."

Then, she continued, "I need all of you to return to the road; this is the bear's private domain. You cannot invade them, especially a momma with cubs. These are not tame. They might turn on you, or if they become accustomed to humans, the rangers might need to relocate them and remove the cubs from her. That can result in the death of the cubs. So now, all of you trespassers go back to your vehicles. I don't like writing tickets, but I'm forced to when you endanger yourselves and others."

Maddie pulled the four-wheeler to the edge of the wood line to watch.

The people began moving back toward the road. She waited for the line to move. A new car approached and stopped in the same spot. This one took out a pair of binoculars. She drove toward him, and he moved on his own.

She parked the four-wheeler and took some photos. It was apparent that the asphalt had been narrowed at this point due to a large tree almost in the road. Checking the opposite side, she saw there was a pile of rocks. She took close-ups from different angles. *Why has this pile of rocks been placed right here?* It would be simple to remove them and widen the road. Even a truck load of gravel could give cars a place to pull off. This situation was just asking for people to disobey the rules. All the way back to the ranger station, she entertained thoughts of why that was done. It made no sense. And there was a simple fix.

Maddie stopped at a creek crossing. She drove through back and forth, washing mud off the tires. *I need to ask who is in charge of cleaning up this mess. I might start the day tomorrow in the car washing business.*

Back in the ranger office, she quickly wrote out her report of the missing children and locating them safely. Glancing at her watch, she put the original report on the captain's deck and filed two copies in the proper folders.

Having her former position in the sheriff's office gave her an understanding of the paperwork, and how important it is.

She looked for the captain but was anxious to leave. Hopefully, driving back through the park to meet Liz wouldn't take too long. Most of the traffic remaining were parked off the road to view animals coming out as the sun set. She would have just enough time if there was no holdups.

She used the landline to call Randy. He answered, "L&R Photography."

"Hi, Randy. This is Maddie. Liz asked me to call you to say she's staying with me at the cabin tonight. And I'm glad she is. I hope you don't mind?"

"Not at all," Randy said. "I was surprised when she left this morning that she didn't tell me then."

"She didn't get as much time in for photography today," Maddie said. "She helped me track some lost children and get them back to their mother safely. I was happy having her assistance because of her knowledge of the woods and these trails. I'm leaving the ranger station as soon as I hang up."

"I look forward to meeting your husband. Will he join you soon?" Randy asked.

"I'm not sure. Even after he's released from the hospital, he'll have to stay close. He has an apartment only a mile or so from UT Hospital. That way, he can return until Dr. Simms releases him completely." Maddie neglected to mention that he wanted away from her too. Randy did not need to know about that part of Rick.

"You girls stay safe. I might surprise Liz and show up in the afternoon tomorrow. In the morning, only bicycles are allowed. Will you still have a route, even with the bikes?"

"Oh, I hadn't thought of that. Well, I'll have time to wash my mud buggy. We tracked the girls through a swamp and down a creek all the way back to the road. She's really a mess."

"Thanks for calling, Maddie. We'll see you soon."

"You're welcome. Thanks for your wife's company. And yes, I hope you can meet with Rick soon."

Maddie drove straight through the park without any holdups. She spotted Liz in the church yard, still taking photos.

'Liz waved. She crossed the road to her vehicle and joined Maddie on Rich Mountain Road.

"Just follow me," Liz said. She threw her arm out the window, motioning as she spoke.

18

The gravel road was seldom traveled. So, it was well kept, at least for the first stretch. When Liz stopped on top of the first ridge, she walked to Maddie's SUV.

"Did you remember to call Randy?" she asked.

"Yes, and he said he was not surprised. I let him know that you helped me track and return the lost girls."

"I'm sure he feels better with me being there with you, rather than you alone. Besides, he knows how much I like staying there."

Back in their vehicles, they drove on and on till Maddie recognized the left turn, opposite of the direction they came before. Now, she'd made the complete circle and felt better seeing how easy it was to find. There weren't many other roads to take, and this main one obviously was the most traveled.

A small amount of dread and excitement caused a twinge in her gut. But she felt an emotional attraction to this antique house. And it was a relief that she wouldn't be alone this first night.

Liz parked in front of the cabin on the grassy overgrown drive. Maddie pulled up beside her. She carried a small suitcase with her as she walked into the living room.

"I want to open the upstairs windows, so air can circulate," Liz said and took the stairs two at a time. "Bring your bag up here. I want you staying in the master bedroom. I usually stay in the room where the twin beds are."

Maddie opened the window at the head of the bed. A nice gentle breeze blew the lace curtains up. "I love the breeze coming through this window," she said and joined Liz in opening the ones in the other two rooms on the same side.

"I want to make this room into a bathroom, eventually," Liz said. "For tonight, I'll give you a chamber pot. I hate going downstairs to the bathroom in the middle of the night."

"I have not seen one of these in a long time," Maddie laughed.

"Apparently, a house with two chamber pots in the main bedroom was a sign of status," Liz said. "These two are originals with the house. My ancestors took good care of their things."

"They sure did. These don't even look used. I've seen them for sale in the Jonesborough antique shops with more dents and scratches. These are amazingly well preserved."

Maddie took her "pot" into the room where she was to stay.

When she returned, Liz had pulled the bedspread off one of the twin beds. "I don't leave the sheets on these, only the spreads."

Maddie saw that she'd carried a canvas bag up with her. She pulled out the bottom sheet and shook it out, spreading it across the clean mattress. Together they made the bed for Liz. The second twin bed held towels and washcloths stacked neatly in matching sets.

"Choose your color, and that will be your towel," Liz said. "There's plenty of space to hang them in the laundry room after you use them." Liz pulled a ladder-back chair from the far corner, putting it next to her bed, and sat down to remove her hiking boots. "I keep a couple pairs of house slippers in the armoire. I don't run around barefoot, so we can share them if you can wear my size."

"I brought a pair, size 8," Maddie laughed.

"Oh, mine are smaller," Liz said. They both laughed.

Returning to her SUV, Maddie brought in a box of things she'd brought from the apartment. She put them in the kitchen. "What should we open for supper?" she asked. "I brought lots of canned foods. Most are soups, but I do have a few canned pastas."

"I forgot; I have a cooler full of groceries," Liz said. She went to get them, and soon the smell of ravioli and toasted Italian bread spread throughout the house. The women sat at the dining room table by candlelight. Two chairs closest to the kitchen and an additional eight feet of space filled the rest of the room.

"This was made for a large gathering of family," Liz spoke as though she's seen the room full of people. "It's been about ten years since everyone was here. Those were happier times. But I'm happy even when I'm here by myself. I've never been scared. And I've never had any strange happenings. I come from a long line of happy people."

"I feel right at home. It's so very nice of you allowing me to stay. Maybe Rick will come to his senses soon. But he probable hasn't even missed me." Maddie sat quietly for a few minutes. Then, she said, "Do we draw straws to see who is first to shower?"

Early the next morning, Maddie was up, dressed, and putting together a lunch for Liz and her.

Liz bounced down the steps, fully dressed and looking well rested. "Good morning. How was your first night in the cabin?"

"I slept great! And didn't even have to use the chamber pot," Maddie laughed. "I'm fixing lunch. Are you going to eat breakfast?"

"I usually have a couple soft boiled eggs and a bagel. How about you?" Liz asked.

"Sounds good to me. I'm putting our lunches separate. In case I get stuck at the office. Where do you park on these mornings that bikes only are allowed?"

"There, at the gate to Rich Mountain Road. Then I'll move to Sparks Lane after the bikes are done." Liz pulled the eggs from the cooler, placing them into a pot of water steaming on a small, single burner. "I boil mine three to five minutes."

"That's fine for mine, too," Maddie said as she put the two bagged lunches by the cooler. She joined Liz at the huge table to eat.

"I'm going to try calling Rick today," Maddie said. "Maybe he knows by now when he'll be released."

"That's a good idea," Liz said, smiling. "I'm betting he's missed you."

The two women retraced their path back to the Cove and parted at the church. Maddie drove the cutoff lanes to get back to the office shortest route. She parked and went straight for the muddy four-wheeler. To her surprise, it was already cleaned up. She went inside to find out her role today.

"Who cleaned up the four-wheeler?" she asked. "I was going to do it this morning."

"You don't have to; that's why we have maintenance guys," the captain said, joining her from his back office. "That report you wrote last night was spot on. You covered every angle and explained thoroughly. Good work, Maddie."

"Thank you, Captain." She waited to see if he had any instructions for her this morning.

The captain went into his office and sat down. Maddie walked to his door. She asked, "Am I to work the loop while the bicycles are out?"

"Oh, I neglected to mention this didn't I?"

Maddie stood quietly, waiting.

"You might as well," he continued. "You'll be the only person with a motor, but it'll be nice in case someone needs assistance. We've had times when individuals crashed and lay undiscovered for hours. We discourage single riders, but we can't stop it. Maybe this is a good test today. You should pick up a case of water at the camp store. Take a cooler from the storage area. At least handing out water is a good way of keeping tabs on our bikers. Don't you think?"

"Yes, sir," Maddie said. "I believe you might be right." She smiled. "Before I begin, can I call Rick on your landline?"

"By all means. You don't ever need to ask." With that, Captain Ford walked toward his truck.

Maddie was growing to love her new job. This morning was surely different from the previous two. In the beginning, she passed up the bikers—slow family riders, mostly. She waved to the children and called out encouraging comments to the parents. After cruising up the first hill, she caught up with the hardier bikers. Surprisingly, none were pushing the bikes. These must be regulars who've acquired stamina over time to pedal these hills. Moving on to another low-level section, she came across the first group taking a rest break. Maddie asked if anyone needed water. It seemed they all had plenty at this point.

"Stay safe and enjoy your ride," she said and motored on.

Approaching the steepest hill on the loop, she finally caught up with the hardcore riders. Some stood up to pedaled, mostly leaning forward on the handlebars. Maddie watched the muscles in their calves as they pushed up the hill. *That's a lot of training,* she thought. *The best I've ever managed was running up hill with Bud.*

Suddenly, she was overwhelmed with sadness. Bud should be with her. At that very moment, she declared, "I'm going to get my Bud on the first day I have off." And then, she looked around, making sure no one heard her talking to herself.

Going down this hill was a different story. The riders on geared bicycles had to use a lower setting and depended on the hand brakes. Maddie parked off the road at the bottom, watching how fast they could ride downhill.

Several had already passed, but more were coming. As they swished past, she observed they were obviously speeding, but she said nothing. As long as they remain in control, not running over each other. This group were advanced riders, to say the least. She motored past them, waving and smiling.

By the time Maddie made the complete circle, she found the ranger office empty. She hurriedly called Rick's cell number. As he answered, she realized her heart was pounding. She was nervous from just dialing his phone.

"Hello?" Rick answered.

"Hey, how are you doing?" Maddie could barely breathe.

"Madison?" he asked.

"Yes, it's me. I'm using the landline in the ranger office, where I'm working now."

"So, what do you think of your new job?"

"Tell me about you, first," she said. "I thought you might know more by now, when they will discharge you?" Maddie felt lightheaded, and her stomach was exceptionally nervous.

"I can leave any time after today," Rick said. "Are you my driver?" He sounded hopeful.

"If you want me, I'll come," Maddie said.

"Will you take me to my apartment?" Rick tested.

Maddie stayed quiet for a moment, and then she agreed. "If that's the way you want it."

"Then I'll see you about 9:00?" he asked her with confidence.

"9:00, okay, see you then."

Maddie quickly hung up the call. Her hands shook, her face burned, and she felt sad. Why had she thought five days could change her husband's mind?

Maddie went outside and back to her four-wheeler. She started the Loop Road again. *The Loop*, she thought. *That's my life. I'm going in circles between a couple of happy years, then the dreaded circle of sadness returns.*

At the end of her shift, she parked the four-wheeler in the storage barn and went to find the captain.

"So, Maddie, how did your day go?" he asked her.

"Another good day at the outside office," she tried sounding convincing.

"We will be really busy over the weekend," the captain said. "Why don't you take tomorrow off? Then, if you'll cover Saturday and Sunday?"

"Perfect," Maddie said, then asked, "I've wondered about my Bud, a blue heeler. He's always been with me in the woods, very well behaved, and I wondered if you'd be okay with him riding with me?"

"What about the bears? Will he bark at them? That might cause an attack," the captain said.

"He doesn't bark at anything unless it is a threat, or he's excited to see you. We've encountered bears on our run, and once, he got slapped. I think there was a cub involved then, and he wasn't a year old."

"You're staying in the big cabin of Liz's, aren't you?" he asked.

Maddie nodded her head. "Alone, and Bud would be alone during the day, in a strange place. But I can keep him on the four-wheeler. That's not a problem. He's with me all the time back home."

"Okay, we'll give him a try. Plenty of tourists have dogs in their cars. I guess it will be okay. He'll be good company for you." The captain turned and walked back into his office. "Oh, Mat, you had a phone call earlier. Some guy asked where this phone was located. You know a guy named Buck?"

Maddie choked, "What? Buck called here? What did you say to him?"

"I told him it was a private phone, and I didn't give out information. You want to explain who he is?"

"He's a prisoner, an escapee. The last person I arrested before I came here, and he managed to escape again. He's a dangerous man. How could he have guessed where I am?"

"The number he called from was blocked, but I can get it unblocked pretty easily. We'll take care of you, don't worry." Captain Ford placed a large hand on Maddie's shoulder. "We take care of our own."

"No one else here knows about Liz's cabin, do they?" Maddie asked, beginning to question her decision.

"No, and I'll never tell. You be careful. See you on Friday."

19

Maddie drove to the cabin as quickly as she could. She threw a few things in a bag and took off toward Knoxville. Stopping by Rick's apartment, she grabbed more clothes. Seeing everything the way she left it, she got on I-81 and drove with the fast-moving traffic to the Greenville exit. It was slow going through town, but hitting 107, she made up time and was able to arrive at the Jacobs Farm before dark. Holly ran out to meet her.

"Why didn't you tell me you were coming?" she said.

The two friends hugged until the dogs arrived from up at the barn. Bud was all over the place with excitement. He jumped into the open door of her SUV, signaling he was ready to go.

"Come in, we were just about to eat," Holly said. "I know you'll eat with us. You probably have not even had lunch."

"You're right, I didn't eat lunch," Maddie said. "What are we having?"

"Fried chicken and fresh garden vegetables from my greenhouse," Holly announced.

"You better believe I'll eat with you."

Maddie encouraged Bud to get out of the vehicle and promised he could get back in when she's ready to go.

That sparked Holly's radar. "You're taking him back with you?"

"Yes," Maddie said. "He can ride on the side-by-side with me while I work, and then he'll sleep in my bed in the cabin. Say, do you still plan to move the boys out of the bunk beds?"

"We did that this week. Why? Do you want the bunk bed?"

"I do. I'll buy it from you and put it up at the cabin. And any other stray beds you have laying around."

"That must be a big cabin," Holly said.

"Why don't you come over and see for yourself?" Maddie said. "I want to make beds for all the kids. But I also hope to talk Henry into helping me put a bathroom upstairs. Liz has only a small one in the laundry room, the back porch space. It has a toilet and small shower."

"Henry will do anything for you, you know that!"

Henry grabbed Maddie as soon as she walked into the kitchen. "What's upstairs now?" he asked.

"There are four rooms beside the master, which is the only big room," Maddie said. "I thought I could pay to have the bathroom done, because Liz isn't charging me to stay there. I have to work Saturday and Sunday. Tomorrow, I'm off. So maybe I will be off next Wednesday and Thursday. Do you think we can do all this in two days?"

"We'll see," Henry said and pulled her to a chair. "Let's eat supper first, though."

Maddie apologized for the short visit as soon as supper was over. She wanted to see her folks and drive back to Knoxville. She said she'd have to pick Rick up in the morning and leave him at his apartment. At that point, her tears returned. "At least I won't be alone at night now, because Bud will be with me," she said.

Henry looked at Holly, then back to Maddie. "You know Buck escaped again."

Maddie nodded. "I called Rick earlier today from my captain's landline, and shortly after, Buck called and asked for me."

"Did you tell the captain who Buck is?"

Maddie nodded. "What I can't figure out is how'd he get the number? Rick was the only call I made. We both know he didn't give the number to Buck."

"That's strange. So, do you think he knows where you were?" Henry asked.

"I don't know."

"I'll load up as many beds as I can, and any supplies for pluming. What will you do about mattresses?"

"I'll get those. Liz's husband has a truck. He'd haul them for me."

"Sounds like you've got things under control. Call us to check in when you get Rick back to the apartment?" Henry hugged her. "Be careful, Maddie."

Holly walked to the vehicle with her friend. "I miss you and worry about you," she said. "Take care of yourself."

"I know, and I love you, too. I'll call when I can," Maddie said.

She didn't need to call for Bud; he'd already beat her to the SUV and waited for the door to open.

Maddie and Bud stopped in Cold Creek for another short visit, then left for Knoxville.

Rick called her cell phone. "You sure it's not too much trouble for you to take off tomorrow to give me a ride?" he asked.

"No, I'm off tomorrow," Maddie said. "I'll be there at 9:00. Rick, a strange thing happened after I called you from my captain's landline. Buck called later asking for me."

"How? Wait a minute. You called from a landline to my cell, so how did he track the number?"

"I don't know, unless he has a tracker on your cell," Maddie suggested.

"I don't have that burner anymore," Rick said. "I gave it back to Drew. But I never talked to you on it anyway. You don't think Drew—" Rick stopped mid-sentence. "I thought we could trust him; now I'm not sure."

"That's probably why Drew gave you the burner," Maddie said. "I don't know what hold Buck has over you, but he's one pushy SOB! I'll see you in the morning."

When she reached the apartment, she carried her pistol and walked all around the building. The manager happened to come outside, who said someone stopped by to see if there was an empty apartment. From the description, Maddie thought it sounded like Buck. She got a description of the vehicle he drove. But knowing Buck, that didn't matter; he'd steal a different one every day.

"I'm staying in the apartment tonight, and Rick will be home tomorrow. I'd appreciate it if you'd call me, should you see that man again. Or, if you see anything unusual around Rick's apartment, call the police."

Maddie went back to the SUV and got Bud. She felt really nervous staying there tonight. But if anyone nosed around, Bud would let her know.

The next morning at 8:30, Maddie walked into the hospital. She saw Joy, and they spoke for a few minutes. Rick was up, dressed, and pacing the floor when she entered his room.

"Good, I was worried about you staying there alone last night," Rick said. "Buck won't stop till he has me in his clutches again."

"Why, Rick? What does he know about you? Or what do you know about him?"

"We'll talk about it," Rick said. "But I'm ready to get out of here!" He walked to the door. "You coming?"

"We are waiting for Joy with the wheelchair," Maddie said. "You know they don't let patients walk out on their own." She smiled at her annoyed husband. "See, there she is now."

Joy pushed Rick to the elevator in a wheelchair while Maddie went to bring the SUV up front. Bud jumped continuously once he caught sight of Rick. Maddie was afraid he'd cause and injury. Rick was in a fragile state right now. So, she scolded Bud and made him lay down while Rick got into the front seat. Then, he told her to let Bud come to him. Bud crawled between the seats and gently stepped onto Rick's lap. Joy watched in amazement at how well Bud obeyed. She walked around to Maddie's side and hugged her goodbye. She teased Rick, saying, "Good riddance to you." Then, she threw him a kiss.

Maddie circled the block as she approached the apartment. Things looked the same to her, so she pulled into the normal parking spot.

The manager stepped outside to greet Rick. "Nice having you back," she said. "I'll be here if you need me. Just buzz me. And if you need a driver when Maddie is working, I'd be happy to help out. Don't call an Uber." She patted Rick's arm and walked back toward the office.

"Well, looks like you'll be well taken care of," Maddie said and blinked back a tear. "Come on, let's get you upstairs."

Rick was all settled in and thanked Maddie for airing out the apartment. The fresh paint smell was pretty much gone. She'd placed a couple of fresh-scented room deodorizers around, leaving mild scents.

"Rick, is there anything I can move or rearrange for you? I don't want you trying to move things. You understand that?" She touched his hand, wanting so much to wrap her arms around her husband, her lover. But for now, she'd take what he allowed—he stopped fussing at her.

Rick stepped away, turning his back to her and peering out the back window. "Things seem fine to me. If I get the urge to mess with the furniture, I'll call the manager."

"Yeah, she seems very accommodating. What's her name?" Maddie asked, as though she'd forgotten.

"Frieda, I think," Rick said.

"Nice that you remember her and not your wife," Maddie said. "That really hurts, Rick."

"Remember, we just talked to her right before my surgery. Remember?" He turned and glared at her.

His eyes gave her chills. She ignored his comment and said, "I stocked the pantry with your favorite foods. And the refrigerator has anything you might need. Try keeping your strength up. I'm hoping for you to get back to the old Rick. Like you told me?"

Rick frowned. "When?"

"Never mind. I'll be back on Thursday, week after next, to take you to your appointment with Simms. It's noted on the calendar on the fridge. You can't reach my cell during the day. There's no service in the Cove. But call that office number I gave you. They'll get a message to me."

Maddie called Bud as she started down the stairs to her SUV. "Bud, come!"

"I thought he'd stay with me?" Rick said, following her out the door.

"No, he belongs to me, remember?" Maddie said. "Besides, he'll keep me company while I'm working and comfort me overnight at the cabin. What do you need him for? You've got Frieda!"

Without looking back, she walked down the steps to the SUV. Bud looked back at Rick, standing in the doorway. He whined and then jumped in.

Madison stopped in Maryville for a lunch-supper combo. She recalled that Bud's food bag was low, and since there was no pet store in Townsend, she stopped at Tractor Supply Company. "That ought to take care of feeding us for a while." She ran her hand across Bud's head and along his neck. "You'll love where we are staying. There's a nice creek, no fences, no traffic, just solitude and Mother Nature."

Bud cocked his head and whined.

"Yeah, and no Rick. I get your message, Bud."

She was quiet on the remainder of the drive.

The sun hung low in the horizon when she reached the high ridge. Maddie pulled out her phone to check for a signal. "Yes, I do have a signal here." There were no messages, so she drove on to the cabin.

Bud explored the area while she carried her things inside.

She brought her supper out to the porch, along with Bud's feeding bowl. They ate their meal and sat in the cooling evening air. Bud ran to the creek, wading for a while, then sniffed his way back to Maddie on the porch.

"You like this place, don't you?" Maddie said. Bud lay his head on her lap. "If only you could talk. I think I know what you'd say, and I agree. I want Rick back in our family circle."

As the last flicker of light faded, Maddie and Bud went inside. She toured the downstairs rooms to make sure all the windows and doors were locked. They climbed the staircase together, and Maddie turned the bed down. Bud settled on the cool hardwood floor under the open window. Maddie noticed the long sheer curtain brushed across his back, so she pulled it up and tied a loose knot to shorten the fabric.

She'd already opened the window at the end of the hall so as to make a nice cross breeze. Not only was it working to allow a nice breeze through the bedroom, but also the sounds of crickets and other night bugs drifted through. Maddie loved sounds of outdoors. They hummed her to sleep.

20

Bud woke her, wanting to go outside. She looked at her watch. It was almost 6:30 a.m., so she got up and ran downstairs to let him out. "Bud, stay close," she stressed, pointing her index finger. That was a signal she'd used since he was a tiny pup.

Bud replied by spinning in a circle and racing off the porch. She leaned against the door jam, watching him run toward the creek. He crossed to the other side, looking back at the cabin. Maddie raised her arm, motioning for him to come back. He waded the creek for a while and returned to the cabin side of the water. Maddie called out, "Good boy," and returned to the bedroom to get dressed.

She walked to the window to close it. Bud heard the sound and looked up, barking at her. "You're okay," she told him. "I'm not ready yet."

Maddie put her small cooler containing her lunch and a portion of kibble for Bud into the SUV, a trick she learned from Liz about not carrying food in open containers for bears to smell. Her water bottles were in a bucket cooler filled with ice. She thought to run back upstairs for a jacket, then she and Bud drove toward Rich Mountain.

Bud sat up tall, watching the unfamiliar landscape pass by the windows. Dropping over the final stretch toward Cades Cove Loop, they came across a heard of deer. Maddie counted at least twenty. Bud watched without barking, just enjoying the wildlife movement. He turned for a moment, glancing at Maddie, and then back to watching their white tails vanish into the dark depths of the forest.

"Good boy, not barking," Maddie said. She scratched his head between his ears. "I need my good boy all day."

When she parked her vehicle back of the ranger station, Bud was ready to jump out and explore new scents. She watched him for a few minutes and loaded him up on the seat of the ATV. She drove to the front as the captain walked out into the early sunlight.

"Captain Ford, this is Bud. Bud, meet my boss," Maddie said. Bud sat still but raised his right front paw to shake hands.

Captain Ford accepted the paw and shook gently. "Glad to meet you, Bud."

Bud sat quietly while Maddie spoke with her captain for a couple minutes, then she drove off toward the campground. Bud looked at her as though he realized what was expected of him. "Sure, you know what riding the ATV is about, don't you?" Maddie said.

He yapped a low sort of bark. Maddie felt like the old days when she and Bud patrolled together in her old Blazer. She still missed that SUV. But it rested in ashes and crumpled steel at the bottom of a ravine on the mountain below Sam's Gap—too far below the road to be seen on a hillside, and too steep to retrieve by wrecker. That part of the old days she didn't care to recall. She'd survived by hiding in a laurel thicket and was thankful Bud had not been with her that day.

The Friday traffic began slowly increasing as the sun rose higher. Maddie sat on the side of Loop Road waving at children who waved at Bud as they passed by. She rigged the passenger seatbelt to attach to Bud's collar so he couldn't be thrown off the seat. She had noticed his feet slid a few times when they went over a bump on the side of the pavement. So, she stretched a large towel across, tucking it into the crack of the seat where it met the backrest. She was going to make a seat cover for him to be safer.

Her captain called her on the radio. "Swing back by here when you can," he said. "I need to talk to you."

"Yes, Captain. I'll be there shortly. Anything wrong?" she asked.

"We'll talk over lunch," he said. He clicked the radio two times, indicating he was not saying more.

Maddie cut through the horse pasture and passed their stables, ending up at the back of the ranger station. She and Bud went inside. Captain Ford met her at the front counter and motioned for her to follow.

"You made a quick trip," he said and motioned toward the door.

She closed the door behind her. "You sounded serious on the radio."

"Remember I told you about that Buck fellow calling for you? He called again this morning. I asked who he was and what he wanted. I told him I was sure he had a wrong number. He told me that he knew you're here at some time of the day. And he wants you to call him." Ford paused and looked at her for a moment. "And then he told me that he's with Rick."

"Oh, no," Maddie said, shaking her head. "I should have never left him." She buried her face in her hands. Bud raised his front legs up onto her knees and whined with concern.

"Maddie, tell me what's going on," Ford said. "I know you're a private person, but you appear to need help with this matter."

"Will you let me try calling Rick's phone?" she asked, tears streaming down her cheeks.

"By all means," the captain said. He handed her the phone.

"Rick? Are you alone?" she asked. After a few seconds, she said, "Buck called me on my captain's phone again this morning. He said he was with you. Rick, tell me the truth!"

Rick breathed heavily into the phone, "He isn't here now. But he came early this morning. I'm going to appear in court for him tomorrow. Once I testify for him, he'll leave us alone. I didn't want you involved."

"Why do you have to testify for him? He's an escaped felon. You don't need have that kind of upset. Don't you remember what Dr. Simms said? Why do you think I wanted to bring you out here to the Cove? He'd never find you!"

"It will be over soon. I promise. Drew will pick me up and bring me back here. Buck is going to turn himself in after the judge hears my side of the story. Stay out of this, Madison. This was all long before I met you. Stay there; he doesn't know where you are. He's just fishing, looking for more pressure on me."

"Rick, you don't remember me," Maddie said. "How can you remember something that happened that long ago?"

"I don't know, but I do," he said. "Maybe it was pushed so far back in my memory that my injury couldn't reach. Maybe it's due to the nightmares reliving the memory every night. I don't know, but stay away until I contact you. Will you do that for me?"

She nodded her head and finally said, "Okay, I'll do what you ask if you'll come here with me when it's over."

"I always planned to. I don't want to give up on us. Promise me you'll stay where you're safe. Ask your captain to have a tracer put on his phone. And then he can block the call."

"He's calling from a blocked number," Maddie said.

"Well, ask him not to take the calls. That's the best he can do. That way, Buck can't find you. Don't call Holly or Henry. I'll call to tell them not to come this weekend. Can you carry your pistol with you while you work?"

"Yes, I have it at all times. But Rick, tomorrow is Saturday. There's no court on Saturdays."

"I'm meeting with the state attorney's office for a deposition...It's private," Rick told her.

"The night I arrested Buck, I overheard the conversation between two men—one from the state attorney's office, and another lawyer," Maddie said. "That's the one Buck met with a little while later. There's something screwy with that meeting. Are you sure you can trust Drew?"

"What? He's your friend," Rick said. "I thought he hung the moon in your eyes."

"No, Rick. You're wrong. Nell just happened to marry him. She's my friend. At least, I thought she was."

"I thought it was lucky how he got the chief of police position at the very time Buck was going to trial."

"Why don't you reach out to Donnelly? He helped me when you were kidnapped. He's trustworthy. Let me give you a direct number for him. He's going through a really rough patch right now. His wife is divorcing him. He's off for personal leave. I'm sure he'll help you."

"What's the number? I'll try to talk with him."

At this point, Captain Ford spoke up, "Rick, this is Captain Ford. You are welcome to use my number to contact or get a message to Maddie. I know where the cabin is if she's off duty. I'll keep a close eye on her on this end. Use this number whenever you want. No one gets the messages. I promise it's a secure line. I have no idea how Buck got it. It wasn't from this end of the line. I look forward to meeting you, son. I've heard enough to know you're a good fellow, and you're lucky to have this little lady. I'll guard her with my life."

With that, the captain got up and left the office, closing the door as he went out.

Maddie said, "Rick, we're alone now. Are you telling me everything?"

"I am," Rick said. "Are you okay? You and Bud will be alright for a few more days?"

"Yes, he loves the place we're staying. He enjoyed riding with me this morning, and as the traffic gets busier, he'll be able to help me. Rick, I love you, with all my heart. I want you to remember that."

"I want you to take care of yourself, Maddie," Rick said. "I'm looking forward to getting to know who I married."

Maddie and Bud walked out into the bright sunlight. She put her dark glasses on and went to the ATV, finding Captain Ford putting a tight-fitting, sheep-skin seat cover on it.

"There, that's a little better for our Ranger Bud," he said. "I got this special harness for him too. Up, Bud." He patted the seat cover. Bud jumped up as though he knew it was just for him. The captain put the harness on, leaving his collar on too. "How's that, Bud?"

Maddie sat on the driver's seat and checked the harness. She clicked the seat belt attachment, and they were ready to go. "Thank you, Captain Ford," she said. "I'm sorry to bring so much baggage. Maybe it will be over soon."

"Stay safe." He paused. "Say, we forgot to eat lunch."

"I'm not very hungry," she said.

Maddie smiled and drove away.

21

Traffic was backed up by the time Maddie reached the first curve. Passing on the left side where there was more room, she rounded the curve to see a bear in the middle of the road, just a short distance ahead.

"Oh, boy, Bud, what do we do now?" Maddie said as she approached the large black bear slowly with the ATV. He swung around to see what the noise was as she came about a car's length from him. Thankfully, no one was out of their cars. Maddie stopped for a minute to talk to the man driving the first car.

"Has he talked to you at all?" she laughed as the man put his window down.

"No, he was on that side when we got here, but he decided to move to the middle. But he's not talking. I wondered if 'he's' a 'she' and maybe has cubs in the tall grass."

"No, that's Bruits," Maddie said. "He's getting pretty old. I can't imagine what he's thinking. I'll try to have a conversation with him." She moved closer to Bruits and said, "Hey, big boy, what are you doing?"

The bear turned toward her and raised his paw. She stopped, holding tightly to Bud's harness. The old bear put his paw back on the ground but did not move toward the side of the road. He laid down again.

"Captain Ford, what's the secret to getting Bruits out of the middle of the road?" Maddie asked.

Over the radio, she heard the captain laughing. "You don't. He'll move after he rests a while."

"Oh, dear," Maddie replied. "Is he dangerous at all?"

"No, he's just old and tired. I'm on my way. How far are the cars backed up?"

"Just around the curve," Maddie said.

"I'm almost there," the captain said.

In a minute, she saw another four-wheeler coming up the side of the Loop Road. Captain Ford drove right up to the old bear, nearly bumping him. "Bruits, get out of the road!" he said.

The bear didn't move. He turned his head away from the captain.

"I guess this is a sit-in," Ford said. He pulled to the side of the pavement and got out a cattle prod.

"Oh, do you think that might make him angry?" Maddie spoke up.

"You got a better idea?" Captain Ford asked.

"What about if I walk Bud on the scene? Do you think he'd fear the dog or attack him?"

"I've never seen him attack anything. Go on and get Bud down. Maybe he can intimidate the old fellow."

Maddie snapped the leash on Bud's collar and signaled him off the seat. But seemed to understand. He followed her instructions. She walked toward the bear. He sniffed the air and turned to look at Bud coming toward him. He dropped his head as though surrendering. Then, he stood up and waddled toward the tall grass in the field beside the road. He sat down, looking back a Bud.

Bud raised his head and gave a low growl, then he barked one time. Old Bruits lumbered off out of sight without looking back. Bud stood as tall and proud as a short blue heeler could stand.

He and Maddie walked to the captain's ATV.

"I don't know what you said, Bud, but it sure worked," Captain Ford said as he smoothed the hair between Bud's ears.

They sat on the side of the road as ten cars passed slowly, each one looking to see what the holdup was. "I guess it's time we do something with Old Bruit," the captain said. "I'll have the team come from the rescue and get him."

"They won't put him down, will they?" Maddie asked with a cloudy expression.

"No, they'll take him and turn him loose way back in the mountain, far from roads."

"Good. Say, I know just the place." She smiled at the thought. "You know where I'm thinking?"

"I sure do!" Ford gave Maddie a high five.

Maddie and Bud resumed their patrol, and the captain headed back to the office. There was no more trouble out of the bears today, but the coyotes made an appearance at one of the cabins and scared some kids out of the woods.

Maddie and Bud found a den of copperheads where the kids were about to walk. She thanked the coyotes and asked them to come back after dark. Similar to the wolves of other areas, she'd been told coyotes have been known to kill poison snakes.

As her shift ended, she parked the ATV, and she and Bud walked to the store where she got a vanilla soft-serve ice cream cone. She sat on a bench to eat it, and Bud laid on the cool sidewalk watching for any drips.

Captain Ford walked up with a short cone of vanilla. "Do you mind if I feed this to my Bud?"

"I always give him the last of mine, but go ahead if you want," Maddie said. "He'll be your BFF, and he'll expect it every day."

"He did a good job today, and I want to reward him." The captain told Bud to come and then to sit. He fed the ice cream to the dog, who'd earned his admiration.

Bud ate slowly, only licking at first. Then, he took small bites of the cone. The captain held it for him until every morsel was gone and Bud had licked all the drips off his fingers.

"I think I'll go and wash my hands now," Ford said. "You sure are a good boy. You've trained him well, Maddie."

"Thank you," Maddie laughed. "I just treated him like family, and he had to learn rules just like a kid."

"Great job. See you tomorrow?"

She nodded her head but did not leave immediately. "Captain Ford, do you mind if I use your phone to call Rick before I leave?"

The captain turned around and smiled. "Of course, it's all yours. I'll give you some time alone."

"It won't take long. I'll hurry." She ran to his office and called Rick's cell.

He answered on the first ring, "Hello, Madison. I'm glad you called. You were right, Donnelly is on his way to Knoxville. He's going to stay with me until this ordeal is over. We may have been wrong about suspecting Drew. He gave me some information today that I really can use. I don't want to talk about it now. We'll get through this, kid."

"You haven't called me that for a long time," Maddie said. She was quiet for a minute. "Thank you. Yes, I believe we'll get through this. And I'll be happy when you're with Bud and I again. I work tomorrow, so if you learn anything, please call me?"

"I can't promise for sure, but I'll try," Rick said. "Take care, kid." And he disconnected the call.

Maddie stood in the office alone for an extra few minutes, then walked outside to find Bud. He had followed Captain Ford to his truck. "Come on, Bud. You go with me, you bum," she said. "No more ice cream today."

"Did you talk to him?" the captain asked.

"I did. Thank you so much." She couldn't help smiling. Rick was sounding like his old self again. "Come on, Bud. We gotta go."

Maddie climbed into her SUV and followed Ford out of the parking lot to the Loop Road. She went to the left, and he went to the right.

As soon as she got onto Rich Mountain Road, they saw a big bear in the road. "Oh, no, I hope that's not Bruits," Maddie said.

Bud stood on all four feet, intensely staring through the windshield. The hair on his neck raised and then on his back. He did not respond that way to Bruits. Was this a different bear? Maddie rolled all the windows up so that if he barked and the bear attacked, she'd drive on past and get out of his way.

"Quiet, Bud, good boy," Maddie said. "I don't think that's Bruits. Let's slip past and not rile him."

She drove far on the left around the large bear. He moved slowly out of road but did not appear in any hurry. She watched Bud as they passed; he obeyed and did not bark. "Good boy," Maddie praised. "That one was best left alone."

By the time they reached the cabin, the sun was dropping behind the mountain. Sunset wasn't for another forty-five minutes, but that would be in Knoxville, or any valley far enough from the higher mountain ridges. At the base of Rich Mountain, it was like a blanket blocking the sun's light. She let Bud run and play while she fixed her supper, a simple task of opening a can of soup. She chose potato for this evening. She fixed Bud's food bowl and walked out to the front porch.

"Come and eat, Bud." She sat in a ladder-back chair she'd brought from the back porch. "The first thing I want to do is find us a porch swing, Bud. Don't you think this porch is begging for a swing?"

After eating, she walked to the creek with Bud. There was enough light to see clearly, so they stayed out until the temperature dropped and Maddie felt a chill. Stars had begun sparkling against the darkening sky. A pale coral color silhouetted the high mountain peak. The trees gave off a sweet air of spring blossoms. Maddie loved the clean scents she breathed in. Suddenly, she caught the foul stench of a skunk.

"Oh, boy, come on, Bud. We better hurry. I don't want you smelling like a skunk." She ran to the porch, and Bud raced, thinking it was a game. "That's fine, I'll let you win this time." She laughed at her four-legged pal.

Maddie quickly cleared away her two utensils used to make her supper. She remembered Bud's food bowl was still on the porch, so she retrieved it. "We don't want a skunk getting a taste for your food, or we'll never be rid of him."

She turned the kitchen light out, and they went to the back porch shower. Bud lay on the floor in front of the shower curtain, waiting for her. And then, together, they climbed the stairs. The ritual of opening the two windows was completed, and Maddie turned her bed down. She'd put a three-way bulb in the small lamp so it was more like candlelight. Since she wasn't reading a book or writing, this was more appropriate.

"Just imagine, Bud. Back in the day when this cabin was built, they didn't have electric lights. All the light they used was either candles or oil lamps. They didn't put off a bright light. I'd guess people went to bed earlier. And they got up with the sun."

Bud looked at her for a minute, then lay his head down, closing his eyes.

"You haven't had even a short nap today," Maddie said. "I guess you are ready to sleep. You know, I think I am too." She turned the light out and listened to the rustle of a slight breeze blowing the curtains, still tied in a knot so as not to brush across Bud's back. Good thing the wind was out of the north, because the skunk had moved toward the creek to the east.

"Ceiling fan, that's what this room needs. I'll add that to the list and talk to Henry about adding a better electrical supply." She remembered Liz mentioning that when the horse stables had been built farther up the road, they ran a high powerline through for future expansion. By letting the line run across her property, Liz was allowed to tap in without a hook-up fee. Maddie wondered what kind of power they had access to. "Henry will know."

Bud hadn't moved. He was out for the night. And soon, Maddie was, too.

That next morning, Maddie was awakened by the sound of a car outside in the front yard. It was barely light enough to see the stairs. She quickly ran to the east facing window. It was Liz. Maddie felt excited, and Bud was already at the front, yapping to welcome her.

Maddie raced downstairs, unlocked the door and said, "Good morning. I'm so happy seeing you."

"I hope I didn't wake you," Liz said. "It is early. But I wanted to get to the Cove before the crowd."

"We went to bed so early, I'm ready to be moving about. Come in. I'll make us some coffee."

Maddie walked arm in arm with Liz.

"How's your week been?" Liz asked

"Oh, just fine. I really love the job and love this place even more."

"That's great. I wish we had phone lines out here. I wanted to talk to you and couldn't," Liz said.

"I know. I think about you all during the day and want to tell you things or ask you a question and...man, are we spoiled or what?"

The two women laughed.

"I took Rick to his apartment," Maddie said. "I didn't want him staying alone, but he's been terribly indifferent toward me. He is supposed to give a deposition today. I'm worried about him. He called me kid. He hasn't called me that in a while. I feel like he's starting to remember more."

Her excitement caused Liz to frown. "I hope you aren't getting your hopes up," Liz said.

"Me too," Maddie said. Moving to the coffee pot, she asked, "You want a cup?"

"Sure."

Maddie placed the percolator on the single eye electric burner. The water boiled quickly. "Do you have time to sit for a while?"

"Oh, sure." Liz sat at the table. "You know, I've been thinking about this huge table. What do you think it would take to cut it in half?"

Maddie poured the freshly perked coffee. "What? You mean, just saw it in half? That is probably a lot more difficult than you can imagine. But as soon as Henry is out here to look at it, I guarantee he can give us an idea. And he even has a sawmill on his property."

"Good. Let me know when he's going to be here. I want to talk about some other changes too."

"Liz, you've been thinking a lot, haven't you?"

"I have. I'm making a list," she laughed.

"We need to compare notes. I'm making a list, too," Maddie added.

Maddie and Bud followed Liz back across Rich Mountain and onto the Loop Road. They made plans to meet for lunch at the Primitive Church, and Maddie and Bud drove toward the office.

Someone had washed her ATV again, and the sheep-skin cover had been removed. She asked in the office if anyone had seen it. Captain Ford brought it out and secured it to the seat.

"The young kid that comes in late cleans things, and it was on my ATV," Captain Ford said.

"Aw, it's sweet that he washed them," Maddie said.

"Call it his penitence," Captain Ford said with a wink. "He's my grandson. Serving time for a misdemeanor."

"Oh, I see. Well, in that case, good for him," Maddie said, then she and Bud took off for another day in the mystery of the Cove.

Meanwhile, in Knoxville, Rick was awakened early by a disturbance on the street. He casually looked out on the street below. The only light shone from a streetlight, but the sun had not risen. Two men were walking toward a car that seemed to have plunged into a power pole. He watched as the two men opened the driver's side door and pulled the driver out. He didn't appear to be moving at all on his own. The larger of the two threw the driver over his shoulder and hurried back to their vehicle. They drove away.

"What the heck?" Rick said aloud as he grabbed his phone and snapped a photo, trying to zoom in on the license plate. He called 911 to report the crash and unexpected events.

The 911 operator kept him on the line so long, he advised her, "A unit just arrived, and I'm going out to meet them. I'm hanging up now." Rick laughed to himself.

Rick spoke to the officer and showed him the photo. He sent it to the officer's phone. In a minute, another unit pulled up, and an ambulance.

Then, a firetruck arrived at the scene. Each one had to listen to Rick's story.

Finally, he said, "I'm in that condo unit, room 223, if you have any more questions. But I need to get going."

Rick turned and started toward the condo. He saw Drew waiting by his police chief car.

"Got a little excitement going on this morning, Rick?" Drew asked.

"Craziest thing," Rick said and began his story for the umpteenth time. "Poor fellow. If the crash didn't kill him, the treatment probably did. I've never seen anything like it."

"Are you for real, man?" Drew stared in disbelief. "What time do we need to be there?"

"Nine thirty," he said and started up the stairs. "Come on up, and I'll fix us some coffee."

Drew joined him in the condo. "This is a nice place, Rick. Where's Maddie?"

Drew's question completely threw Rick for a moment, but he said, "Aw, she got herself a little job. She's working today." He thought it was odd. He knew Maddie and Nell talked about her going to work as a ranger. But why hadn't Nell confided in her husband? "How are Nell and the kids?"

"They're doing great," Drew said. "I can't wait for you to meet our Rosie. She's a beauty." He sat on the end of the couch next to the window.

Rick asked, "No sugar, just cream, right?" He'd known Drew for years, but had he actually remembered what he took in his coffee? Or was he just guessing?

"No, I take it black," Drew corrected him.

"Oh, yeah, I guess I didn't remember."

Rick sat across from Drew in a recliner. He continued, "I thought my old buddy Donnelly might come by this morning, joining us. Guess something came up." He sipped his coffee. "Tell me about this house you bought. Maddie said it's really high up on the mountain. Bet you've got a good view, huh?"

"Yes, and the sunsets are spectacular!" Drew said. "You and Maddie should come up. I'll throw steaks on the grill." He went into a drawn-out story about the construction of turning the basement into a garage. Rick glanced at his text messages as he listened to Drew's narrative of all the problems the crew encountered cutting a driveway on the steep mountainside.

Rick saw he had a message from Donnelly: *Running ahead of time, see you in about 30.* The time sent was 5:45 a.m.

"Wow, I lost track of time," Rick said. "I better hit the shower and get dressed." He tossed the TV remote to Drew and said, "You might find the local news or weather. I'll hurry."

Rick started the shower and called Donnelly's phone. It rang, then went to voicemail. Before he could leave a message, someone spoke, "Who is this?"

Rick knew it was not Donnelly's voice. He asked, "Who is this? I'm calling Greg Donnelly. Who are you?"

"This is Officer Watkins of the Knoxville PD. Tell me who you are."

"You're working the wreck of the car into the light pole, right?" Rick asked.

"That's right."

"This is Rick Malone. I'll be down in just a moment." He turned the shower off and walked back to where Drew sat, talking into his cell. "Be right back," he said to Drew and walked out the front door.

Officer Watkins met Rick with the phone in his hand. "Who did you say you were calling?" he asked.

"Greg Donnelly, Agent Greg Donnelly, my friend," Rick clarified. "And you found the phone in that car?" Rick had a realization and continued with a catch in his throat, "I watched my friend be carried off." He stopped. "He was meeting me this morning. I had no idea it was him. Those goons that took him are Buck's men. His life is in danger if they haven't already killed him."

Rick walked past Watkins, looking into the smashed car.

The wrecker pulled up on the scene. Watkins told the driver, "Hold off a minute. This was no accident. I need CSI going over the scene before you touch anything."

The driver returned to his truck. Watkins stepped closer to Rick and asked, "Is that the new chief from Sevierville? What's going on here, Malone?"

"I'm Sheriff of Cold Creek, in Unicoi County," Rick said. "I was kidnapped a few weeks ago—"

"You're that Malone? I am sorry, I didn't realize. And your wife, she's your deputy. That's why your name sounded familiar." Watkins signed. "Man, I'm really sorry."

"That's right," Rick said. "I was released from the UT hospital yesterday."

Watkins pulled out his radio and listened to an announcement that said the car had been spotted, and another unit was in pursuit.

Rick leaned in to listen closely. "Warn the officer that they should consider them armed and dangerous," he told Watkins.

Watkins nodded and relayed the message into the radio. Drew came down to remind Rick it was time to go to the courthouse. Watkins told Rick that he'd notify the officers, and he had Rick's phone number.

Drew and Rick made their way to the courthouse in complete silence. Was Drew the common denominator with Buck? How else could Buck stay one step ahead of Rick? True, he'd damaged his memory, at least short term. But those early years in D.C. with the FBI—were those memories still intact? Rick hoped so.

He'd reviewed the points of the deposition from where he'd looked it up online.

Be prepared...

Think before answering...

Never volunteer any information...

Make sure you understand the question...

You must tell the truth...

Stay relaxed, don't become rattled or upset...

Don't guess...

If you do not remember, say so.

How many times had he gone over these? Each time, he recalled the same story. That's all the law expected of him. *I can do this. I have to do this, and then get on with my life.*

As he waited, his thoughts returned to Donnelly. How badly was he hurt? Was he even still alive?

Meanwhile, in the Cove, Maddie and Bud made the second round on the Loop Road, when a lady came running out of the woods and flagged her down. Her hands were waving in the air, and she was yelling. Maddie approached the frantic woman.

"Ma'am, stop screaming and tell me what's going on," Maddie said. She got off the ATV. "Are you hurt?"

"No, it's a bear." The woman spun around, pointing up the hill toward a thick stand of trees. "My son, he's trapped. The bear is going to get him. Oh, you have to shoot it. Please hurry!" And she ran back the way she came.

Maddie followed on the ATV as far as possible. She ordered Bud, "Stay," and chased after the woman. When they got to the spot where a teenage boy sat on a limb about five feet off the ground, no bear in sight, Maddie instructed the boy to jump down.

"No, you stay up there. It might come back," the mother said. She picked up a large stick. "If it comes back, you have to shoot that beast," she added to Maddie.

"How big was the bear?" Maddie asked.

"It was huge," the woman said.

"Well, I don't see it now, and with all your noise, I'm sure it's long gone. So, come on down here, and I'll take you back to your car."

The teen started turning around to slide down the limb. His mother screamed a bloodcurdling scream and began hitting at a small bear cub who ventured out of the underbrush.

"Stop," Maddie said. "Don't hit the cub. You could hurt it, and then the mother will be back with a vengeance." She grabbed the stick away from the woman.

"That's the bear that chased him up the tree," the woman said. She tried kicking it.

"Ma'am, stop. That's a baby bear, no more than a couple months old. It can't hurt him." Maddie turned to the boy. "Come down here right now!" She was losing patience with the boy and his mother.

The boy jumped down, now standing behind Maddie. The cub raced up the tree, almost to the top. Another small cub came out of the bush, also running up the tree.

"Down that trail now," Maddie pointed the boy and his mom in the right direction. "Where are you parked?"

"That's our car, up that hill," the boy pointed farther down the road from where they were. "We've been looking for squirrels and rabbits, but those bears chased us."

Maddie got the city folks back to their car and told them not to get out anymore, and to follow the road until they left the park. "If you thought those cubs were huge bears, I hope you never run into a papaw bear!" she said.

Driving slowly to be sure the car with the woman and her boy made it out of the park, Maddie followed them to the exit gate. She and Bud stopped in at the ranger office. Captain Ford enjoyed her story of the huge bear cubs.

"Maddie, when I first came to work out here, I thought we had a good idea letting the general public drive among wild animals," he said. "But honestly, the more years I put behind me in this Cove, the less faith I have in the people who visit here. Sometimes I wonder if they shouldn't have to pass some type of test before they can be allowed to enter."

"I agree! That's why I followed them out of the park."

At that time, the phone on the captain's desk rang. He answered and handed the receiver to her. "It's Rick." Captain Ford left the room, closing the door behind him.

"Hello?" Maddie said hesitantly.

"Hey, kid. I wondered if you might come and have dinner with me this evening?" Rick asked.

"I guess we can. Do you want me to pick up something?"

"No, I want to take you and Bud somewhere, my treat," he said. "You know, like a date night."

"Oh—okay. I should stop by the cabin. We can be there by 6:30. How's that?

"That will be just about right." Then, Rick disconnected the call.

Maddie thought about the way Rick worded the conversation. Deep in thought, she walked right past her captain and Bud. She didn't even hear him talking to her.

"Madison," Ford called out. "Is everything alright?"

She stopped at the front door. "I'm not sure. Rick just doesn't sound like himself." She snapped her fingers and said, "Come, Bud, we need to get going."

"He didn't sound like Rick to me either," Captain Ford said. "But he said, 'This is Rick. I want to talk to my wife.' Maybe we should call that number back to make sure."

Maddie ignored the comment and walked to her vehicle.

22

Captain Ford pushed redial on his office phone. The thought that he didn't know Rick's voice well, but even Maddie questioned the conversation's legitimacy, kept weighing on his mind.

What if...There are so many voiceover tricks now, and that fellow, Buck, was such a villain. What would it hurt checking out the number?

"The call cannot be completed as dialed," sounded over the speaker phone, just as it would if the number had been blocked.

"Now, if Rick called from his cell phone, the call would have gone through," Ford said aloud.

Catching up with Maddie in the Cove could be a problem with the restricted speed limit. However, she would hurry every chance she could get away with, knowing there were no radars or persons watching the traffic. Ford reckoned he might catch up once she's on Rich Mountain Road.

Leaving the park's paved road also meant a dust trail ahead when he got close to her vehicle. He drove carelessly fast; still, he was not seeing any sign of her SUV.

Reaching the driveway to the cabin, he was shocked to see her vehicle was not there. That only meant she'd continued on the old Cove road instead of stopping. Could he possibly catch her before she reached the paved Alcoa Highway?

Ford slid into a ditch in the first curve. Luckily, he got out by using the four-wheel drive. He couldn't do anything to help Maddie if he crashed before catching her. So, he willed himself to maintain a safe speed. But if she reached Maryville ahead of him, he'd never find her in the Knoxville traffic, and he didn't know where Rick's apartment was located.

Flying through Maryville's yellow traffic lights made up some time, and yet Ford wasn't breaking too many rules. Finally, he spotted her SUV just ahead. He made sure to keep a car between them so that Maddie didn't see him following.

Once they were in Knoxville traffic, Ford had to stay close, and when Maddie changed to the left turn lane in mid-block, he saw it was an apartment complex. So, he made a right-hand turn into a Gas 'N Go parking lot. He backed into a spot, allowing full view of the parking lot across the street. He watched Maddie run up the steps and knock on a door. Bud remained behind in the SUV. He could not see the man clearly as the door opened. Maddie seemed hesitant to enter. After a few seconds, she went inside, and the door shut behind her.

Ford watched, waiting. There was no movement toward the SUV. Thirty minutes passed. Surely, she'd not intently leave Bud in the vehicle for this long, with the temperature as warm as it is. Ford grew curious enough to cross the road and parked his truck down close to the office. He waited. Another twenty minutes passed, and still no Maddie. He walked to her vehicle and checked the driver side door. Finding it unlocked, he opened it, and Bud jumped out, panting to get cooled.

"Come, Bud," Ford said. The dog followed him without hesitation. He started his truck to turn on the AC. Leaving Bud in the front seat, he walked into the office.

"Can I help you?" a young man said, standing up behind the desk.

"Can I get a dish of water for a dog I found in a hot car?" Captain Ford asked, approaching the desk.

"I can find something." The young man disappeared into another room. He returned with a paper cup. "Will this be big enough?"

Water dripped from around the rim. Ford took it and returned to the truck. The young man followed.

Bud lapped the cool water, and the man ran back to get another. Soon, they had Bud cooled down. Captain Ford asked the young man if he'd allow the dog to remain in the cool of the office while he went to question the driver who'd left him.

"Sure. I'll keep an eye on Bud. We're friends now."

"I'll be right back in just a minute," Ford said. He smiled and went outside. He thought better and stepped back in the door to say, "Say, have you seen the folks in the room at the top of the stairs today?"

"Sheriff Malone is up there," the young man said. "He's not able to drive yet; just had some surgery. But there's been a couple of guys coming to take him places. One of them is up there with him now. He's driving that silver Mercedes."

"Aw, good, thanks a lot," Ford said. "Buddy, I'll be right back." He went out into the warm evening air.

The door to Rick's apartment opened, and Maddie ran out. She started walking to her SUV but was stopped when an older man in a gray suit carrying a gun called to her from the doorway.

"Get the mutt and get back up here!" he said. The man stood in the doorway.

Ford stayed in the shadow of the balcony from upstairs. As soon as Maddie reached the SUV, she called Bud's name. She turned, looking to see where he might have gone to. That's when Captain Ford waved his hand to her. She spotted him and froze. He motioned toward the office. She spotted his truck and took a deep breath.

Maddie called out to the man, "Bud must have jumped out the window. I have to look for him. I'll come right back; I promise."

Buck leaned over the railing of the balcony. "You better hurry. I won't hesitate to whack Rick in the head, and with his recent surgery, that couldn't be good for him."

"Please, don't," Maddie said. "I'll just check in the office. They might have him in there." She walked toward Ford.

He pulled his service weapon from the shoulder holster and offered it to Maddie. With his index finger to his lips, he nodded his head, and she slipped the Glock into the back waistband under her shirt. Ford pulled a second smaller pistol from his pants pocket.

"Bud is in the office," Ford said. "He's safe. Let's go get this ass once and for all." He pointed to the second set of stairs at the north end of the building.

Maddie nodded and started up the southern set of stairs. Ford waited until she was at the door, then he hurried to the other stairs.

He heard her say, "The boy in the office has him. I didn't let Bud see me. He'll be better there."

Ford listened for the door to close. He had to formulate a plan. He called Maddie's cell. He noticed she had it in her hand when he gave her the pistol.

Maddie answered, "Hello, Nell. How are the kids?"

"Good girl. Is there anyone there besides Buck?"

"No, I just stopped by to see Rick."

"Good. I want you to unlock the door without being seen. And then try getting Buck into a room out of view of the door. I'm coming in. Do you think you can do that?" Captain Ford asked.

"Why, of course! I'd love seeing you and the kids. When is the best time?"

"ASAP," Ford answered.

"Okay, I'll do the best I can. Give them a hug for me."

The call ended.

Ford waited, watching for the door to move open just a bit. It seemed an eternity, and then finally it cracked, and he made his move. Slowly, he pushed far enough that he could see the room was empty. He snuck in and closed the door quietly. He darted to the kitchen and ducked behind the bar. This was a blind entry, not knowing the interior floor plan. But he'd guessed right. The basic plan was set up much like the office floorplan. In only a couple minutes, he heard footsteps back in the living room.

"What is your plan for us, Buck?"

"Now that Rick gave the deposition, I don't need him. And since he doesn't remember you, he won't miss you. But you, little lady. You caught me off guard, and I don't appreciate you arresting me. So, you've got to go. Rick will be better off without you. See, I have it all planned."

Ford heard the thud of the pistol laid on the bar. And he could hear a stool squeak as someone sat on it. He listened closely, hoping Maddie could make a move, and she did.

"Well, Mr. Buck, here's your chance—Rick tied up in the other room, no Bud around to bite your ankles," Maddie said. "If you're that bent on doing away with me, come on. You can't match me. Why not try? You still got it in you? I heard you use to beat women up often. Can you still do it?"

The stool squeaked again. Ford jumped up, and Maddie pulled the Glock. All of it took place in a split second. Buck stood frozen, staring at the Glock in her hands. And then, behind him, a click of a trigger pulled back. He started to turn.

Ford said, "I wouldn't move if I were you." He stepped around Buck carefully and stood beside Maddie. "You got any cuffs?"

"Rick does. I'll get them." She stepped into the kitchen and grabbed them from a drawer. She snapped one on Buck's wrist and twisted that arm behind his back. Buck moved slightly, as if he was going to turn on Maddie.

Ford shoved the pistol into Buck's groin. "This shot won't kill you, but you'll wish it had," he said.

Buck put his other arm behind him, and Maddie clamped the cuff on that wrist. She kicked him behind the knee, and he fell to the floor with a thud. She called 911 and asked for an escort to jail for her prisoner.

Ford held the gun on Buck, just itching for a chance to use it before the officers arrived.

In less than ten minutes, they heard a siren, and two Knoxville City Police Vehicles slid to a stop in the parking lot.

Maddie had Rick untied and examined him for any additional damage. He hugged her so tight she nearly lost her breath. Or maybe it was the kiss he gave her.

"If you can't avoid trouble, I don't care if you don't get your memory back," Maddie said. But the way she held onto him told him otherwise. Together, they went into the living room.

"Captain Ford, meet Rick, my wayward husband," Maddie said.

"Nice finding you in one piece, Malone," Ford said and extended his arm to grip Rick's hand.

"I don't know how you got in the picture, but I'm certainly happy to meet you, Captain," Rick said.

With Buck gone to the Knox County jail, one of the officers in the second car questioned Rick and Maddie. Captain Ford went down to the office to get Bud. He explained to the young man what was happening and thanked him for caring for the dog. They walked up the stairs to Rick and Maddie.

Bud jumped into Rick's arms and lay his head against his neck the way he had in the car a few days ago. He sensed the change in his master's health and began licking him in the face. Rick was back and in good health, according to Bud.

"Careful, Bud, don't hurt Rick," Maddie said.

"Aw, he's fine. I've missed his love bath."

"Malone, what have you gotten into this time?" Officer Watkins said, walking through the door. "Oh, I got some good news. We found your friend, the one who crashed out here. He's in Maryville Hospital now. He'll be okay, but from the looks of him, he had a rough time getting away from those fellows."

"Did they get away?" Maddie asked.

"For now, but we'll get them."

"I'm going to Maryville to see Donnelly. You want to go, Rick?" Maddie asked.

"Sure, after we eat. I've starved all day."

Maddie turned toward her husband, putting her hand on his arm. "You're in a much nicer mood since you got tied up. Maybe I should try that."

Watkins laughed, "That sounds like fun, and I assume you are Maddie McKenzie-Malone. I've read articles about you. It's a pleasure meeting you. I'm Bryce Watkins. I met this fellow the day Donnelly had his, um, accident?"

"She didn't know about that yet," Rick said. "Let's go to Calhoun's on our way. It's been a long time since we've eaten there." He placed his arm around her shoulder. "Do you need anything more from me?" He looked at Watkins.

"We're good," Watkins said. "If I learn anything more, I'll call you." He turned back to Maddie. "I'd like talking to you sometime. I've admired your career for a while. You're like a paperback hero. I've read all of Michelle's books. Some of them make me think she's a fiction writer. I'd like to know which stories are true adventures."

"Michelle? From the bookstore? How do you know her?" Maddie was completely surprised.

"We met in college, and we've dated for a couple years. She's your biggest fan. And naturally, I'm in agreement with her."

"I had no idea," Maddie said. "We lost touch. I drove by the store last year and it was closed down. I didn't know where she went."

"She moved to a new location, across the river. It's on the strip near the university. She and Claudia are doing a great business there." Watkins paused to pull a business card from his wallet. "Surprise her; call her. She'll be happy hearing from you."

"You bet I will." Maddie felt guilty about not keeping better connection with Michelle. She wanted to become a writer, and now it seemed she had succeeded.

"So, let's get going," Rick said. "Do you want to leave Bud here? Since we can't take him in either place?"

"I suppose we should," Maddie said.

Bud whined, and she knelt down to stoke his head. "We won't be that long. You can rest on Rick's bed, and he'll never even know it."

Captain Ford stepped into the room. He said, "Maddie, I'm heading home. Why don't you take the day off tomorrow? You've had enough excitement for one week."

"Yes, why don't you?" Rick said. "We need to spend a day together. I believe Bud misses me." He pulled her close and kissed her on her forehead.

"Thank you, Captain," Maddie said. "See you Monday." Her smile was an expression of true thankfulness.

The apartment soon emptied, and Maddie drove toward the river and Calhoun's famous barbecue restaurant. As she parked the SUV, it suddenly sunk in. Rick had said, "We haven't eaten there in a long time."

"Rick, how do you know it's been a long time since we've eaten at Calhoun's?" Maddie asked him.

"I just thought about it. I guess I remember eating there, and it could have only been you."

"Oh, okay, that makes sense." Her raised hopes collapsed.

After dinner, they drove to Maryville to the hospital. Donnelly looked to be sleeping, but Maddie wanted him to know they were there.

"Agent Donnelly," she whispered.

He opened his eyes, smiled, and said, "Didn't I tell you to call me by my first name?"

"Okay, Greg, Rick is here with me," Maddie said. "We both came as soon as we heard. Do you feel like talking?"

He nodded his head.

Rick slipped to the back of the bed. Looking at the broken and scared body, he asked, "How are you feeling? 'Cause you aren't looking all that great."

"Hurting, pretty much all over," Donnelly answered.

"What did they do to you?" Rick pushed for answers.

"They drug me out of my vehicle after they nudged me into the light pole. I knew they'd work me over or shoot me after we got out of town. So, as soon as I got the chance, I jumped out of the car. I rolled down a fifty-foot embankment. Thankfully, a deputy sheriff located me. Pretty soon, he had a couple of EMT medics and a stretcher on the spot. I couldn't have crawled back up that bank."

"From the looks of your truck, you were beat up bad enough by the pole. I didn't know it was you until I called, and Watkins answered your phone. I hadn't seen your last text. Man, I'm so sorry."

"Where's my phone now?" Donnelly asked with heavy breath. "I gotta call my kids."

"Knoxville PD has it," Maddie said. "You can use my cell, if you know their number."

Donnelly told her the number, and when it rang, she handed it to him.

Maddie stepped into the hall and asked a nurse of his condition. After Madison identified herself, the head nurse spoke with her for a while. Aside from a couple of fractured ribs, Donnelly was in surprisingly good condition.

"That's good news," Maddie said, "'cause he looks awful."

Maddie thanked the RN and returned to Donnelly's room.

"I left a message for my daughter to call the hospital phone," Donnelly said. "I hope it doesn't scare her to death."

"I took the liberty of talking with the RN, and she's optimistic about your recovery," Maddie said. "I'm sure you feel like death warmed over; you'll need a long rest."

"I'll get your phone back to you," Rick said. "When you're released, Maddie and I can take you home." He shook Donny's good hand. "Just don't rush it. Allowing time to heal is important."

Rick surprised Maddie as they drove back to Knoxville to his apartment. At first, she thought he had meant for Bud and her to stay with him. But he packed up his clothes and all the fresh foods stored in the refrigerator.

"We can pick up more ice on the way out of town tomorrow," Rick said.

"You're going with me? I didn't think you would ever—" Maddie started to say.

Rick hugged her. "I don't want to be away from you any longer. Besides, Bud missed me."

23

The next morning, Maddie and Rick were up early, the SUV was packed, and the family of three headed out of Knoxville on the Alcoa Highway.

"I thought I knew all these back roads," Rick said. "But you found one I've missed."

Maddie saw the sign pointing to Tuckaleechee Caverns. "We're almost to our turnoff. I'm pretty sure you won't know that road either."

About ten minutes into the drive, the paved road ended.

"Now's when the fun begins." Madison said. "I've been thinking about the Knoxville PD officer, Watkins? I was very surprised about Michelle's books. I need to check into that."

"If we'd have only thought in time, we could have run by there this morning, but I don't think she'd be open this early," Rick said. "For sure, our next trip. We will go and see her." He pulled a small notebook from his pocket. "I'm making notes to myself of things I want to remember to do."

"Yeah, sounds like a good plan." Maddie smiled at him. "I'm so happy you're feeling better. Maybe it was all the stress you were under, but you were a grouchy butt."

Rick quietly watched as they drove deeper into the wilderness. They had not passed any houses in at least fifteen miles. "This is exactly what the doctor ordered," he said.

"You think anyone can find us way out here?"

Before Rick could answer, they rounded a curve and dipped into a shallow creek. There on the hill ahead of them stood a two-story log house nestled into a clearing at the end of the driveway.

"Oh, wow," Rick exclaimed. Madison parked her SUV on the grass.

"Come inside and see how cozy it is. I love it here."

Maddie felt excitement in her gut. Rick would either love it or hate it. She prayed it would be love at first night.

Madison and Rick stepped inside the cabin and back in time. She watched his expression, remembering that he'd loved her cottage nearly as much as she did. He looked at the tall front windows encouraging the sun inside. Light hues of warm brown flagstones outlined the open fireplace, rising through the ceiling and beyond. The back wall displayed an artful stairwell disappearing through open beams in the high ceiling. A wide archway opened to the kitchen on the right side, and on the left a second archway exposed a long wooden table surrounded by hand-crafted, ladder-back chairs.

"This is historic. When was it built?" Rick asked.

"During the mid-eighteen hundreds, Liz's great grandparents began the construction, and her grandfather completed it around the turn of the century. The fireplace was built by her great grandmother. She worked with her hands making pottery and did this all by herself. The one in the kitchen is similar, but her grandfather built it about 1910. He copied his mother's pattern, but finding the same stones was impossible. Those came from the banks of Copper Creek out there in front of the property." Maddie told Liz's story as she'd heard it.

Carrying the food to the large kitchen, she added, "Liz's dad added the pump there on the sink. Until then, the well on the back porch supplied the water by buckets full." She turned to the fireplace. "Her dad grew up in this house. Her great grandma cooked on the fireplace during cold weather, and on warmer days, she built a fire in the firepit just off the back porch. Her dad went to work at the bank in Maryville after graduating high school. He bought that beautiful wood-burning cookstove for his mom."

"You and Liz must be very close now," Rick said. "I'm happy she was here for you, when I wasn't." He touched Maddie's face. "I'm sure you've been miserable. I'm so sorry."

"I don't blame you," Maddie said. "Dr. Simms said your personality could change. Don't worry about it. Love bridges the gap at times like that."

"I get it, but that's not how I want to be remembered. I mean, if anything ever happens again." Rick stumbled over his feelings, trying to make up for those bad days.

"Do you notice, this is a complete cooking setup? I've never seen one so well designed," Maddie said. "Liz's dad said his family believed in home cooking and big meals."

"And it's still usable. It's amazing." Rick beamed at Madison. "Wouldn't it be great having an old-fashioned Thanksgiving here?"

"I can just imagine all our family and friends here." Maddie smiled and nodded.

"Then, we should plan that. Not just Thanksgiving, but Christmas too!" Rick said, then added, "Show me the upstairs."

"Come on, I want you to see the future bathroom." Maddie followed Bud up the stairs. "Oh, by the way, these are the original stairs of the cabin. It took her great grandfather all winter building them. Isn't it beautiful?"

The bedroom at the top of the stairs was directly over the kitchen and held a smaller version of the downstairs fireplace. Other than a large bolster bed, the room had only a small round bedside table and a beautifully crafted armoire. Covering the hand-hewn hard wood floors, there was a light color Persian rug.

Madison suggested, "We don't dare walk on this with our shoes. We must remember to leave them downstairs."

"It's an heirloom; let's help take care of it." Rick slipped off his boat shoes. "I'll need slippers."

"I'll get us both some. First chance I get." She turned toward the armoire. "This is the room you'll sleep in, and you can put your things in there."

219

"You aren't sleeping with me?" The look on his face caused her heart to ache.

"We haven't been since your memory..." She stopped mid-sentence. "It was a mutual agreement."

"I don't remember agreeing to that." Rick reached out and asked, "Do you still love me?"

"Yes, of course," Maddie said. She turned her face away. "I mean, if you don't know me, are you sure you want to sleep in the same bed?" It was all she could do to keep her tears hidden.

"I loved you, didn't I?" Rick stepped closer to her. "But do you still love me?"

"I'm alive and breathing," she said. "That answers the question, doesn't it?" She stared into his emerald eyes. "I said I do. Nothing has changed in my mind."

For a long minute, they stood silence. Was that the answer Rick hoped for? It was the best answer Madison could say. "Let's look at the rest of the rooms," she said and walked to the hallway and into the empty room.

"Well, I guess Liz was here yesterday; the twin beds are moved." She went to the next bedroom. "Yeah, she's put them in here. That empty room is where she wants the bathroom. I think Henry will build it, and I'll pay for it. She isn't charging us any rent."

"Maddie, I need to know," Rick said. "Did I love you?" He grasped her by the elbow, turning her toward him.

"You said you did, but you have to feel it—not just take my word for it," she replied. Tears edged into her eyes, unable to hide her feelings. She bit her lip hoping it would stop quivering. "I just want you comfortable so you'll heal and so that your memory can return. Some of the things you've said the last couple of days sounds like the old you, and your kindness has returned. At first, I thought you, well, that maybe you wanted to forget me."

"I don't know what was going on with me at the hospital. It felt strange seeing you and not knowing our relationship. But I feel drawn to you. I've seen how everyone cares for you. And I know it will come back to me. I guess

I'm remembering a little at a time. Help me find you again. Help us. I know I need you. For now, I can say I really want to love you. Can you understand that?"

Maddie dropped her head. "All I want is you and our life back. I'm trying to do whatever I can to be normal again. This was my idea of having us regain what we had. Just you and me and Bud. That's all I ask."

"Then why did you leave me and go find a job?" Rick asked.

"You didn't want me around. Liz and I have a lot in common. She understands some of my special abilities. I needed a friend. You know I'm not great alone. Well, maybe you don't know, but you did. I thought if I had something to do, I could wait for you to find your way back. It's been good for me. I enjoy the work; it's not really even work. I'm getting paid to do what I love. And Bud was able to go along for the ride."

"Okay, then keep your job," Rick said. "I'm fine here alone. No one will ever find me if Buck sends them looking for us. And since he doesn't know where you are, maybe this is good for all concerned. Will you let Bud stay with me?"

"I think that's a good idea. Captain Ford has been so concerned for me and now you. I hate letting him down by walking off the job with only a couple weeks in. He's considering another person on my days off. Probably his young nephew. For now, I can help train him. I get to do all the fun stuff."

Bud ran down the steps, barking as though he heard something. Maddie followed to see who was in the driveway.

"It's Liz," she called out to Rick. "Come on down, so you can meet her."

"I hope I'm not intruding," Liz said as she got out of the car with a bag full of groceries. "Brought you some supplies. I thought Rick was with you, and I couldn't wait to meet him."

"Welcome, but you don't need to bring food for us," Maddie said. "We brought things from his apartment." She met Liz with a hug. "It's time for you and Rick to meet." She took the bag out of Liz's arms.

Rick stood on the porch. "Yeah, I need to see my competition." He opened the door for Maddie, and she went inside. "Liz, I feel like I already know you. Maddie and I were just talking about you. I'm sorry you did all the moving of beds by yourself."

Liz offered her handshake. "Oh, no, I had help. Randy, my husband, was with me. I couldn't move and set up those beds by myself. I'm not as much of a Wonder Woman as Maddie. I require help."

"Is Randy coming back today too?" Rick asked when they went inside.

"No, he has to be in the store today. You'll meet him soon." She knelt to hug Bud. "I bet you're happy having Daddy around the house, aren't you, Bud?"

Liz joined Maddie in the kitchen. She helped put the supplies in the cabinets. "So, what did Rick say about your hideout?"

"He loves it!" Maddie folded the grocery bag, putting it under the sink. "He's like me about old houses. We both love them."

"Did you tell Rick about the bathroom?" Liz started up the stairs with a tablet.

"That's what we were about to do when Bud announced your arrival," Maddie said.

Rick and Bud followed the girls up the stairs. Liz went to the small room right off the master bedroom. "This is supposed to be for the children, so it's smaller and had the twin beds," Liz said. "I bought new mattresses for it last winter. Randy and I moved them yesterday."

She led Rick to the other two rooms, which were empty of furniture except for some storage shelves with oil lamps and candles. "Eventually, I'd like filling these rooms with beds," Liz explained.

"I have bunk beds to donate if you're interested, no cost," Maddie said. "The mattresses have plastic zip-off covers. My friend's twins outgrew them, but they look just like new. They are heavy wood and practically indestructible!" Maddie looked for a sign that Liz would want them.

"Absolutely. My dream is to furnish these rooms with period bedroom suits. However, they are not cheap, and I'm rethinking that route anyway. Yes, we definitely can put them to good use." Liz giggled.

"I'd love staying here," Rick said. "I don't know what arrangements you and Maddie made, but I'll make you an offer." He wrapped his arm around his wife. "I'll build the bathroom with the help of our friends Henry and, hopefully, Jess. And I can promise you a good price on completing the electricity if you are interested. This is cozy, but I doubt it's up to code for insurance. You need insurance on a special place like this."

"I planned on getting that all done, but business has been slow since Covid-19," Liz said. "We have not recuperated from those couple of years. We opened our new store to give us a better location, and we're doing well, but not enough to put money out for my dream. My husband doesn't feel the family tugs like I do. He's from the city—New York to be exact. He doesn't get the country living vibes." Liz stared at the floor.

"I understand. I'll still uphold my end and turn that into an upstairs bath, just for you letting us remain here for whatever time Dr. Simms feels necessary. It most likely will be eight or nine weeks. Can you do that?" Rick smiled and turned to Madison. "That work for you?"

"Of course," she said. "Henry is really busy. How can you drag him away?"

"Just leave that to me," Rick said and started down the stairs. "Henry is the only person I know that can compare to the construction on this Home. The only person I trust this beauty to."

Once downstairs, the three of them walked through a doorway between the kitchen and dining room. There was the small bathroom with a shower and commode. In the remaining space stood a pedestal sink. On the opposite wall was an old ringer washing machine and a laundry tub beside it.

"Oh, how quaint! I love this!" Rick said. "I suppose out that door is the clothesline?"

Liz opened the door. "There you are, Rick." Next to the porch stood two strings of tightly strung wire between a couple sturdy posts.

"All we need now is the hay barn." Rick wrapped his arms around his wife. "I love this place."

"Unfortunately, we lost the barn a few years back," Liz said. "It was a forest fire. About the same time that one burned so much of Gatlinburg. We were so concerned about our shop and home that we didn't think of coming

223

out here. Some friends from the riding stables called to tell us about losing it. Thank God, the house was in a safe place. We've always kept underbrush cleared to keep that from happening." Liz put her tablet away. "I won't need to make plans for the bathroom. Sounds as though you have it covered, Rick. When do you think Henry might come out? I hope to meet him and have some input, too."

"They won't work tomorrow; it's Good Friday," Rick said. "And that makes for a three-day weekend. Maybe I can persuade him to come. Where do we have to go to get a cell signal?"

"Up on the Ridge Road," Liz said. "Maddie knows. The closest phone service is out near the riding stables you passed on the way in."

"I think we'll have to do that, Maddie."

"I already talked to Henry when I went to pick up Bud," Maddie said. "He's planning to make it. But Holly and the kids can't come this trip. She'll wait until there's no work for the kids to interrupt. Henry thinks there are a couple more bed frames with headboards stored in the barn. If any are salvageable, he'll bring them too. He said if we can't use them as beds, they will make good firewood."

"That is so exciting," Liz said. She planned on returning the next day. Her husband usually came to the Cove with her on Saturday. She was excited about Rick's offer and hoped her husband would agree. How could he not?

Maddie and Rick loaded Bud up in the SUV and retraced their route from earlier that morning. She drove to the main road. "Townsend is that way, and Maryville is this way," she said. "Which do you want?"

Rick answered, "Townsend. We only need the phone and some lunch."

The couple sat in a small barbecue restaurant on the river, drinking iced tea and pulled pork sandwiches, while Bud played in the edge of the river. Rick and Henry were on the phone for about an hour. Maddie talked to Jess and Shirley. They asked about driving their motorhome over for the weekend. Of course, that made Maddie happy. They'd bring their own beds. And Jess would be a big help.

Henry already had his truck and his brothers loaded. He discussed items

CABIN IN THE COVE

the brothers' company already had in stock and said that he could donate a toilet and a sink. Someone ordered gray and didn't like it once they saw it.

Rick managed to get Randy on the phone at the store to get his approval.

"Heck yeah, gray will be fine with me," Randy said. "And considering the price, Liz won't care either. The only thing she's set on is the shower the way she wants it. You know what I mean, those glass bricks?" Randy suggested a visual.

"I do know, and honestly, I think the gray sink and commode will be perfect with that style. Henry loves creek rocks. We can build the base and the floor with the gray rock tiles. That will be pretty. Maybe we should keep this a secret and surprise Liz."

Rick enjoyed the way he and Randy talked easily.

"Sounds good to me. I look forward to meeting you, Rick. I've decided to close our store tomorrow, in observance of Good Friday. So, we'll see you tomorrow."

"Let's go back to the Cove," Rick said to Maddie. "Our temporary home." His phone rang. Caller ID showed that the number was blocked. "I don't want to answer." He turned the screen toward Maddie.

"I wouldn't," she said.

At that moment, hers rang.

Rick picked it up off the console. "It's Nell."

"Answer it," Maddie said.

"Hello, Nell, this is Rick." He listened for a few moments. Maddie felt confused by the look on his face, so she pulled off the road to see what Nell was saying.

"Put it on speaker," she said.

"Rick, I don't know what is going on, but I'm scared," Nell was saying. "Drew is not himself. Some men showed up, and he took them down in the basement. Then, I heard loud yelling and they all left. Drew too. He didn't say a word to me. He just left with them."

"What did they look like?" Rick asked.

He listened to Nell a few more minutes, then he told her to get the

225

kids in her car and go to the Knoxville police department. "We'll meet you there," he said. "I'll call Officer Watkins. If he's on duty, you should tell him I sent you. Tell him what you just told me."

"Thanks, Rick," Nell said. "I hated to get you involved. But I didn't know who to turn to."

Maddie spoke up, telling her to stay calm as not to scare the children. She pulled back onto the road and drove out Alcoa Highway as quickly and safely as she could. When they arrived, Watkins was out front waiting, but no sign of Nell.

Rick had given a description to Watkins over the phone of the men as Nell described them. "Sorry to say, those men are with the Sevierville PD," Watkins said. "Didn't you say her husband was the new chief of police?"

"That's right. Do you have anyone on that team you can trust?" Rick asked.

"I already called, but they are not on duty because of tomorrow starting the Easter holiday. Seems they are running a light shift with so many off for the holiday. I don't know what to think of this. And Mrs. Perry has not arrived. Maybe you ought to call her back."

Maddie called Nell's cell. It went straight to voicemail. "Nell, call me immediately," she said. She left the message and shook her head. "But if she's driving, she won't answer her phone."

"I can send a car out to Sevierville, have him nose around a bit," Watkins said. "Maybe she decided to go to the SPD first."

They went inside to wait for any news. Rick called Drew's cell phone. Then, he remembered the blocked call he hadn't answered. Had it been Drew trying to get in touch? They waited and waited but no news. Bud was getting the special deputy treatment by the officers. He enjoyed being the center of attention.

"We can't just sit here all night." Maddie paced the room. "What if we send an officer to their house? Maybe they came back, stopping Nell from leaving. Or even calling."

"Write down the address, and I'll have someone drop by the neighborhood," Watkins said. "A sheriff's deputy wouldn't look so out of place."

He spoke with a Knox County deputy and gave Rick a satellite phone so they could communicate and told them to go back to the Cove. "There's no reason for you getting involved in any more danger. So far, Buck and his goons have no idea where you two are. Let's keep it that way. I can handle this. You don't need anything more to do with those fellows."

"What do you want to do, honey?" Rick asked his wife.

"I'm worried about Nell, but I agree; you don't need to be involved in case the guys are still looking for us," Maddie said. "Let's go home." She smiled. "To the Cove."

Arriving at the cabin just at sunset gave Maddie a secure feeling. At least no one knew about this place. And she was very sorry for Nell, but there was something about Drew—she couldn't quite put her finger on it, but she didn't trust him right now.

Rick lounged on the sofa in the living room. Maddie and Bud walked outside by the creek. Bud enjoyed wading in the cold water and occasionally came out to chase after a bird or a squirrel. The sun setting brought glorious colors of blue and orange into the clouds. Maddie watched as long as there was light.

Returning to the front porch, she stopped next to the front door, and she observed that the porch didn't wrap around the south end of the house. Was that due to the large rock wall backing the chimney? She looked up at the overhang of the front porch. There were bolts where chains once hung.

"Aw, perfect," she said aloud. "This is a great place for a porch swing." Bud tilted his head as though questioning her remark. He stood by the door waiting for her to open it. "You wait here while I get a towel to dry your feet." She walked to the SUV and pulled a large beach towel from under the back seat. She dried his legs and feet and opened the door.

Bud walked straight to the sofa where Rick lay sleeping. He nudged Rick, waking him. Maddie got a tablet from the kitchen and returned to the front porch. She sketched a porch swing suspended by chains from the overhang.

"This is my request to make life cozy here." She carried the tablet back inside and sat next to Rick. "Feeling better after your nap?"

"I didn't plan to fall asleep," Rick said. "I was wondering about Nell and the kids. If she'd have shown up at the Knox PD, Watkins would have called on the SAT phone."

"I've been thinking too. When Nell originally texted me to come to the house for a visit, she said they were staying a while on the mountain. At first, she didn't mention the job. Drew told me about that. And Nell looked surprised when he said it. After I'd been there one night, Drew encouraged me to change my hair. I thought it might be a good idea. So, I went the next day to a little shop I'd noticed because of the name, Holly's Hair Salon. When Drew came to get me, he said something that made me feel uncomfortable. He put his hand on my shoulder and with his face just inches from mine, he said, 'Damn, you're beautiful.'" Maddie shivered. "It was not like him. He used to be shy."

Rick listened as Maddie recalled other things Drew had said and ways he'd looked at her. She even told of the night they spent in a hotel on the trip from Kentucky. She noticed Drew watching her when she walked out of the bathroom with her pajamas on. He had taken her phone from her and told her to use the burner phone he'd picked up for her.

They talked into the night, even after retiring to the bed upstairs. "These things might not sound strange to you, but Drew never gave me a second thought," Maddie said. "He was so in love with Nell, he didn't look at another woman."

"So, when did they adopt the baby girl?" Rick asked.

"Another strange thing. Nell was not even thinking of another child. They'd talked about it when little Junior was getting along so well, but the adoption was unplanned. She learned of Rose the day before they picked her up. And to top it all off, that's when he told her he had a job offer in Tennessee."

"That definitely sounds fishy," Rick said. "You know how long people wait to adopt babies. And they take classes to be sure they qualify. I mean, just being a police officer doesn't pull any weight. A good income does, which Drew didn't have until he accepted the job here as chief of police." Rick sat up, leaning against the headboard. "And where did they get the cash for the down payment on the house on the mountain?"

"Nell had money," Maddie said. "She inherited it from a grandfather. And I remember she said she never put Drew's name on the account, and she felt guilty about it. Maybe she turned it over to him when they got here. I don't know, but there are too many lucky breaks if you asked me."

"How was it that Drew learned about Lost Cove?" Rick asked. "He showed up kind of unexpectedly, from what I heard others saying. I told him I didn't need him taking me to the courthouse for the deposition, but he came anyway. And then there's Donnelly having that crash right in the parking lot by my apartment." Rick shook his head. "Too many things don't line up, but he knew in advance, somehow." He got up and went downstairs for a bottle of water. "And another thing, Watkins says the Sevierville chief position wasn't advertised as far as the Knox County and City PD. So, how did Drew know of it all the way up in Kentucky?"

"And I can't help wondering how Buck always managed to escape...how many times?" Maddie said. "You're right; too many fishy questions for me to figure out." She turned her back, laying down to get to sleep.

She felt Rick's body slither down under the covers, and his cold legs touched hers. She held her breath, hoping he'd kiss her goodnight. But in a short time, she heard his soft snore. At least he wanted her sleeping next to him. She was encouraged by that small discussion they'd had. Just one small improvement at a time was all she needed. They were together and getting along again. That was good enough for her.

24

Early the next morning, Madison busied herself in the kitchen putting together a good breakfast. Rick came to offer his help.

Bud wanted outside now that Rick was up. He whined at the front door. "Is someone here, Bud, or are you ready to chase a rabbit?" He walked to the door and let Bud out. "Tell us if a car comes in, okay, Buddy?"

Rick and Maddie sat at the huge dining room table to eat their breakfast. "Liz has already proposed cutting this table in half," Maddie said. "She plans to talk with Henry about it."

"That's a really good answer to space. But this is a handmade table from the original construct. I'm surprised she'd go for that."

"Do I need to remind you of your limitations once the work begins?" Maddie asked.

"What on earth are you talking about? By my memory, I have a reputation of watching Henry do all the work." He brushed off her concern for him.

"Rick, you did read the part of the instructions saying no lifting, didn't you?" She picked up Dr. Simms's list and handed it to him.

"Of course, I told you, I'm going to do the brain work, not the lifting part. You can do the lifting," he said to his wife and winked. Then, he reached out for her hand. "Let's walk in the yard a while."

Rick turned toward the right, looking at the end of the porch. "So, you want a swing here? I don't think the eastern direction will show the best sunsets, but the shade will feel good in the heat of summer. I noticed no AC unit. Do you think we can survive sleeping when July and August bring on the heat?"

"I doubt the present electricity that's been run for the lights and water heater will support an AC window unit," Maddie said. "But at least a ceiling fan or two might make it bearable."

Bud barked excitedly, causing Maddie and Rick to turn around and see Henry's company truck with a trailer pulled behind, and Jess and Shirley right behind him in their motorhome.

Rick and Henry met with a brisk handshake. Rick said, "Man, you must have gotten up before the chickens. I'm so glad you could make it today." The two fellows walked to the trailer to look at the items Henry supplied.

Maddie met her folks at the motorhome, along with Bud. "Oh, I'm so happy you brought your bedroom," she said. "You might as well leave it here and stay for the summer." She hugged Jess, then Shirley.

"How did you find this place? It's beautiful!" Shirley said as she squeezed Maddie.

"It was meant to be is all I can say." Maddie didn't go into details. Bud jumped up, placing his front paws on Shirley's knees. "Down, Bud, you know not to jump on people. Aw, but I guess you've missed your grandma, haven't you?"

"I've missed you too, Bud," Shirley said. "I haven't seen you in a month!" She knelt to pet Bud.

"Where do you want this parked, Maddie?" Jess asked.

"Walk out here with me. I have an idea if you agree." She led Jess around to the back yard. "There are no underground lines, and this big tree will shade the motorhome in the afternoon. There's a septic tank around here someplace. Rick says they will have to dig it up to run the new drain lines, and he and Henry are installing a hookup so you can be on septic, too."

"Wow, that will be great. What about a water supply?"

"There's a faucet by the corner of the porch. Is your hose long enough?"

"Oh, yeah. I brought an extra-long one. This is a good spot. Looks to be level also."

"Years ago, it was a garden area," Maddie said. "You can park here whenever you'd like. But come in and see the inside the house first. This is a rare treasure." She walked with Jess back to the front yard.

Henry had pulled his truck and trailer to the side of the house. Since most of the work was in the back, it made good sense to have the supplies as close as possible.

Maddie joined Rick and Henry. "Too bad Holly and the kids couldn't come."

"Maybe she'll join us on Sunday," Henry said as he hugged Maddie. "She misses you."

"And I can't call her either, not without climbing the ridge for a signal," Maddie said. "I needed to go up there this morning, but I haven't made it yet."

Rick turned to her and said, "Don't call Nell. Henry believes Drew is involved with Buck somehow. Drew double crossed us. He is not our friend."

"That's why he was trying to keep me corralled with Nell. But Nell would never—" Maddie shook her head. "I just can't understand. I thought it was my relationship with Drew in the past making me feel hesitant to trust him. I was warned." She rested her head on Rick's shoulder.

"And when you talk to Holly, don't mention Nell and Drew," Rick said. "Henry hasn't said anything to her. She doesn't need to know any details. He checked her phone and all through the house with a de-bugger. It's clean. So, no one learned by listening to your phone calls when you have spoken to Holly." Rick pulled his wife close, holding her for a few moments. "We will be back to normal soon."

Henry's brother, Ross, pulled into the front of the house with a small backhoe on a trailer.

"Guess it's time to get to work. The gang's all here," Henry laughed. He guided Ross as he backed the trailer up beside Henry's truck.

Rick helped Jess back the motorhome to the shade of the old chestnut tree at the opposite side of the work zone. When they returned to the front yard, still another vehicle drove up.

Liz and her husband walked to the front of the house. Maddie met them with Shirley in tow.

"Everybody, this is Liz and Randy, the owners of this fine cabin in the Cove," Maddie said. She continued introductions, "My dad, Jess, and mom, Shirley...That's Henry and his brother, Ross, and of course, my husband, Rick."

The men shook hands and walked to the back yard. Ross unloaded the backhoe, following them. They'd agreed to begin with uncovering the septic tank. Henry held two shovels. Randy took one and started feeling around for what he remembered was the lid location. In just a few minutes, he hit metal.

"There it is," Randy said, and he and Henry started digging. In just a couple of minutes, they exposed the underground tank. Henry looked it over and declared it was plenty large enough, saving them a trip into town and lots of hours burying a second one.

Meanwhile, in the house, Shirley, Liz, and Maddie prepared gallons of tea, lemonade, and put bottles of water in the laundry tub, filling it with ice. That way, the guys could easily get water without traipsing through the house. A cooler of ice sat on the floor by the large dining table. Shirley brought stacks of paper cups and paper towels. Next to the cooler filled with ice sat a smaller Styrofoam chest. Maddie was curious when Jess brought it in, so she slipped the lid off, releasing the aroma of the delicious smell of barbecue chicken.

"Do I smell lunch?" Liz asked. She stood next to Maddie.

"Yes, Jess and Shirley's handy work. They are accustomed to feeding everyone." Maddie placed the lid back on, keeping in the warmth. "I'm glad Randy was able to join us."

"He's all for your plan and volunteered to help," Liz said, linking arms with Maddie. "He knows I've wanted to do more out here. This was the best chance; he and I can't do the work we need. This is as good a deal for us as it is for you and Rick."

"You can't imagine how excited I am," Liz whispered.

"Oh, I think I can," Maddie grinned. "Our house in Cold Creek began as a three-room shack from the 1700s. You ought to see it now."

"You'll have to tell me about it," Liz said.

The men were gathered in the large empty space. Henry made chalk marks on the floor signifying where each detail needed attention: holes in the floor for drains, water lines coming in, and finally, the walk-in shower. Liz was most excited about that feature.

"Henry, can we leave the window in the shower?" Liz looked hopeful.

"Yes, ma'am, we can," he said. "In fact, we can enlarge it if you want." He smiled.

"That could be nice, if the window can still open."

"Not a problem." With chalk, Henry added width to the already tall window. "I'll show you examples I've done in past years."

Maddie suggested the ladies leave the work to the men and start gathering samples of creek rocks. She couldn't wait to tell Liz about the shower floor. They joined Shirley on the front porch, where she sat in a new rocking chair.

"Liz, I hope you wouldn't mind me keeping this rocking chair here for when I visit. And it has a matching porch swing in the motorhome."

Liz squealed in excitement. "Oh, I love it. And we used to have a porch swing. That's so wonderful. Who do I thank for this?"

"You can hug Jess for the swing," Shirley said. "He got busy and finished the one he started for our house. And I suggested we get the rocker at Cracker Barrel." She stood up and hugged Liz. "You have been a big help to our Maddie. There's no need for thanks. We appreciate you."

"We kind of friended each other. It was meant to be," Liz said. "You want to help us look for flat rocks from the creek?"

"No, you girls go on," Shirley said. "I'll keep the chair company."

Maddie and Liz walked to the creek, followed by Bud. No one went near the creek without his company.

In the meantime, Rick heard the SAT phone ringing and ran downstairs to answer. It was Officer Bryce Watkins.

"Hello, Rick," he said. "I haven't forgotten you. But these friends of yours have avoided me no matter how I try getting in touch with them. I've learned that job Drew fell into was a payoff by that Buck fellow. And it goes higher than that, I'm afraid."

Rick sighed, "I suspected as much, but I can't figure how Buck has so much reach and power."

"I'm still digging. There's a couple pieces missing, but for now, I just want to tell you to stay put. You and Maddie don't contact either of them. I can't find any wrongdoing involving Nell, but the law in Louisville is looking for a kidnapped baby. Didn't Maddie mention the couple had just adopted a baby girl?"

"Yes, and her parents supposedly were killed," Rick said. "This is just too surreal. I know some of my memories are scrambled, but they were such good people. Maddie would never have been friends with people capable of such deceptive measures."

"Now, don't worry," the officer said. "I'm sure the arrangements, bad as they are, have had nothing to do with Nell. Your wife's friend is no doubt caught up in her husband's scheme without her knowledge. I wouldn't mention this to Maddie if I were you."

"No, she's been through enough. Just keep me in the loop."

Rick disconnected the call. He joined Ross and Jess out back where the backhoe was busy digging the ditch for the waterline.

The girls were surprised at the number of flat rocks they were retrieving from the creek. They made small piles on the bank so that when the shower floor was ready, the backhoe would move the rock piles to the house. They had an assortment of colors. Since the toilet and sink were gray, Liz was happy finding the many grays and charcoals to mix in with the browns.

By the time the work was well underway, Shirley had to insist that the fellows take a break and eat lunch. The cooler holding warm barbecue chicken found the temporary worktable, and a feast began. Maddie and Liz walked back to the cabin. Bud chose to lay on the front porch for a nap. In no time, the tender chicken was all gone, and the work resumed.

The day seemed to fly by, but the crew worked well together, and Rick was pleased with the progress. He built a fire off the back porch, and Shirley brought a dishpan filled with baked potatoes wrapped in foil. Then, Rick fired up the grill for steaks. Ross carried six lawn chairs from his truck, and Jess brought Shirley's rocker from the front porch. Randy and Henry brought the cooler with beer and soft drinks out of the kitchen.

"Dinner under the stars; my ancestors would be so happy," Liz said as she handed out beers for whomever wanted them.

Rick declined and took a Coke for him and a 7UP for Maddie.

She looked at him with questioning eyes. "You remembered."

He sat next to her and nodded with a smile. "I did."

Maddie felt a twinge in her gut. Every little thing Rick remembered gave her hope. He reached for her hand and squeezed it tenderly.

25

Early the next morning, the sound of a jigsaw awoke Maddie and Rick. They sprang from the bed with bright light shining through their window.

"You overslept," Rick teased Maddie.

"Me?" she argued. "Where's Bud?" They both hurriedly dressed and went to check out the sound grating on their nerves. Henry was cutting the hole in the floor to set the toilet.

"'Bout time you came alive," he said. "I let Bud out hours ago." Henry laughed and continued cutting the circle out of the floor.

Maddie pulled Rick's hand, insisting he eat breakfast. She reminded him he had pills to take and not on an empty stomach.

The day progressed to the point that the room now looked like a bathroom. All waterlines were connected, and the drain lines were in place. Ross had the shower blocks laid, but they needed to set in the caulking before the rock floor is placed. He asked Maddie and Liz to show him where their chosen samples were. The three walked to the creek and Ross was impressed with what they'd removed from the water.

"I'll get the backhoe and move them to the house," Ross said.

The remainder of the afternoon was spent picking through the rocks for color and size. Ross showed the girls how he'd shape them with a cutting tool to assemble them like a puzzle. The three worked with the rocks until Rick came to tell them dinner was ready.

Another evening around the fire was a welcome end to the busy day. One by one, they set out for their assigned sleeping areas. Shirley and Jess's motorhome slept two extra, which were claimed by Henry and Ross. Liz and Randy stayed in the twin beds. Earlier, Henry and Randy carried the bunk beds to the third bedroom and reassembled them. All they needed were sheets, but that could wait.

Rick and Maddie remained by the fire for a while. Bud started growling, so Rick shined a bright flashlight toward the hill above the house. Not spotting anything, he wrote it off as a possum or raccoon.

"Come on, sweetie, let's go to bed and let the critters prowl peacefully," Rick said and gathered his wife into his arms, giving her an encouraging hug. "This is quite an adventure you've put together for me. I can't think of anywhere I'd rather be than here, with our friends, and falling back in love with you." He embraced her, and for the first time, they kissed like they had when they first met.

Maddie breathed deeply, burying her face in Rick's chest. "I have cried so many tears and lay awake many nights thinking, what if you never get your memory back? This is the best encouragement you've given me. I've prayed for you, and I believe my prayers are getting answered,"

"Don't ever give up on me, Maddie. I need you; I know that much. That's enough for me. If I can't remember something, we will relive it. Making new memories is all we have to do for the rest of our lives." Rick kissed her again and led her to the room at the top of the stairs.

Maddie's dreams that night were alive. And she slept on cloud nine.

Sunday morning, Shirley and Jess made a breakfast of sausage, bacon, and biscuits 'n gravy, while Henry and Ross set the hardware for the shower in the tiled wall. Then, they carried boxes of the shaped rocks to the bathroom. Rick stayed on the outside of the tile wall to hand the flat stones to

Ross. Randy and Henry finished up the outside work covering all the lines and the septic tank. Maddie was the last to come down to the kitchen. Shirley offered to cook her eggs to eat with the remaining bacon.

"Biscuit and bacon will be enough," Maddie said. "You just enjoy your Sunday however you'd like without waiting on me. I should be waiting on you." She hugged the only mother she'd ever known. "Do you know how very much I appreciate you?"

"Yes, honey, you've showed me often enough," Shirley said. "You're a wonderful daughter. I couldn't have asked for anything different." She wiped a single tear from her cheek.

The two walked outside and found Jess hanging the porch swing. "Momma, where did you put the cushion you brought for the swing?" Jess asked, tightening the final bolt on the chain.

"In the overhead bin above the table in the motorhome," Shirley answered.

"I'll go and get it," Maddie said. She jumped off the porch and ran toward the motorhome. Just a couple of minutes later, she returned with a lovely, flowered, long cushion for the swing. "Who's first to try it?"

"Liz, you should have the honor," Shirley said.

Liz turned and sat back onto the swing. It moved as she sat, and she held the chain to steady herself. "Say, the chain feels good to my hand. Is it covered with something?"

"Yes, it's especially coated with a soft plastic for comfort," Jess said. "Remember how the old chains used to pinch you sometimes? No, you are probably too young to remember these old porch swings." Jess thought about what he'd said. His face glowed a shade of bright red.

"No, Jess, I'm not that young," Liz said. "I remember my grandmother had an old swing here. It fell after years of neglect, but I do remember the narrow chain links, and my fingers often caught in them, and it hurt." She laughed and gave Jess a hug. "Thank you for doing this, all of you." She turned to Shirley and hugged her also. "I want you to feel free to come here anytime you'd like. I miss my family. And if I can adopt you guys, that will give me so much pleasure."

239

Shirley sat on the swing and pulled Liz down beside her. "Consider you my second daughter. We'd love filling the absence of your family."

Jess laughed, "Time for me to hunt something else to do and let you girls enjoy your mushy stuff." He walked away.

Maddie and Liz went to check out the shower floor to see how it was shaping up. Shirley remained on the swing with Bud at her feet, sleeping in the warmth of the sun.

"Maddie, do you know how to wash the stones when they dry?" Ross asked. "It's just like with tile, only these are not exactly level, but they are smooth. So, if you run across any sharp places you might need to sand it a little. Can you do that tomorrow?" He showed her which sponge to use.

"Yes, I have cleaned up the grout on tile," Maddie said enthusiastically. "I can't wait to see the colors. It looks pretty even with the wet grout on it. This is gorgeous, Ross. You did a great job." She hugged his neck, causing him to blush.

Liz giggled, "I was going to hug you, Ross, but I see you're allergic to them." She winked instead. "I really love the whole bathroom!"

Rick and Ross picked up all the tools, carrying them down to the truck. Henry came up to inspect the final clean up. He said, "Liz, I talked with Randy about the rewiring. I'll check into the codes for this area and get what I need. I'll be happy coming back to bring you all into the twenty-first century. The best thing you can do for this house now is add a few ceiling fans with light fixtures for air circulation and better lighting."

Liz was surprised that Randy already made plans with Henry. Maybe her husband will join her out here more now. She could only hope.

Randy went home Sunday evening so that he could open the store on Monday morning. Liz remained to clean the grout off the rock floor in her custom shower. Henry and Ross also left Sunday evening. That left Jess, Shirley, and Liz.

Monday morning, Maddie got up early to ready herself for work. Shirley and Liz were already in the kitchen. Shirley made coffee in a large blue and white enamel pot Liz had found in the attic. She showed Liz how to use a paper towel in the bottom of the coffee grounds to keep it out of the finished coffee. The entire house began smelling of soothing coffee aroma.

Rick made his way down to the table awaiting the coffee. Maddie sat beside him.

"Henry and Jess are both leery of Drew's participation," Rick said. "I can't believe Drew is involved, but the signs all point to him. Everything, so I don't want them knowing where we are—just in case." Then, he wrapped both arms around Madison. "We're going to be fine right here. I told Randy what's going on and he promised we are welcome here for as long as necessary."

Rick suggested Maddie not contact Nell just yet.

"I worry about Nell," Maddie admitted. "She has the two babies to deal with and him away so much with his job as chief of police. She's new here, without any friends. It's really hard on her. She seemed so frail; she's different somehow. I think she might be overwhelmed." Maddie felt stress and blamed herself.

"She's tougher than you give her credit. Because you're a law enforcement officer and you like shooting bad guys, maybe you aren't as girly as she is."

Maddie pulled from his hold and pushed him away from her. "I'm not girly like Nell?" she huffed.

"You're strong, like a guy...a sexy kind of strong, but you know what I mean." Rick batted his eyes, knowing she couldn't resist his emerald charm. "You didn't turn my head by dropping a hankie in front of me. That's the kind of gal Nell is. You won me over by outshooting, outrunning, and out-thinking me. That's sexy!"

"And how would you know that?" She was teasing now.

"Because I remember why I fell for you. You were the most beautiful woman I'd ever been fortunate

to spend time with. We clicked, like two of a kind, like we were meant for each other. I remember the first time you kissed me, down in the silver mine. You had me at a disadvantage. You had your way with me. I remember exactly how you seduced me."

"That's not true and you know it," Maddie said. "What really happened was I said you weren't my kiss—You remember...you remember that?" She stood up so quickly her chair tuned over. She threw her arms around Rick's neck hugging him tightly. Then, she dropped to her knees in front of him.

Rick pulled her into his embrace, holding her for a time. Then, he stood up, pulling her with him. "We're going to be fine."

Shirley and Liz ran to them, and they had a big four-way hug.

Just then, Jess came in the back door. "Did someone die?" he asked, and then walked into the kitchen for a cup of coffee. He carried it to the table and sat down. "What's new this morning?"

Shirley wiped her eyes on here worn apron. "Rick's memory is coming back. We were rejoicing."

"Let's fix our plates at the stove," Maddie said, and she carried hers and one for Rick. He followed her, taking his plate.

"I'll get this; you don't wait on me anymore. I'm okay."

The others carried a plate for the hardy breakfast. And when all were seated, Jess bowed his head, catching Shirley's hand.

"Our Heavenly Father, we ask that you nourish our bodies with this food. Forgive our friends and most of our foes. Thank you for returning Rick to our fold. In Jesus's name we pray. Amen."

Amens echoed all around the table.

26

Sunset approaching, a long Monday came to an end. Maddie arrived home, finding Bud and Rick lounging on the porch. Rick stretched out in the comfort of the new porch swing, and Bud curled up underneath it. She shut the door of the SUV, quietly hoping not to wake them.

She took out her phone and quickly snapped a couple pictures. Bud must have heard the camera sound, low as it was. He raised his head looking at her and then sprang from the porch without waking Rick.

Maddie knelt next to him when he ran to her. "Hey, boy, did you miss me today? I missed you."

"And your husband missed you," Rick said as he sat up and held out his hand toward her. "Come sit with me. I have something to tell you."

She sat next to him on the swing. He put his left arm around her.

"Welcome home, my dear," Rick said.

"That's what you have to tell me?" Maddie said. She glanced up at his face.

"Well, that, and about the satellite cell call I got today."

"Oh, you mean Officer Watkins?"

"Yes. He says Michelle wants us to come for dinner one night. She is excited about Bryce meeting us. What do you think?"

"That sounds great, when?" Maddie asked.

"Will you be off Wednesday? Maybe we can go early enough to see the store before we follow her to the apartment. And Watkins is off Wednesday, also," Rick explained.

They remained on the porch swing for a while as Maddie told him some of the funny things happening in the park today.

"I guess we better go eat before supper gets too cold," Rick said. He stood, pulling her with him.

"You cooked?" The astonished look on Maddie's face made him laugh.

"Yes, and I think you'll be surprised," he said.

The long dining table was set with two plates, glasses, and silverware. Rick escorted his lady to her chair, and then proceeded bringing a casserole bowl of pasta and tomato sauce and set it in front of her. He returned to the small refrigerator for an open bottle of wine.

"I'm impressed," Maddie said. She smiled at how organized Rick was.

"Aw, wait." He walked to the oven of the fireplace. "It was kind of cool in here today, so I built a small fire and baked bread." When he set it on the plates, a waft of buttery garlic filled the air.

"Shirley's homemade Italian bread? How did you—"

"She had it in the motorhome," Rick said. "Before they left, she set it out to thaw, and I baked it. Jess brought the wine for us to celebrate. We didn't open it over the weekend due to the number of people here. Now, there's just the two of us." Rick sat in the chair opposite his wife. "I love you, Maddie. I always have, even though I didn't remember for a while. The feeling was always in my heart."

"I love you too, honey, and I always will," she said. She offered a toast. "To us, always."

Wednesday brought rain, but Rick and Maddie prepared early, planning a couple of side trips before they'd end up at the bookstore.

Michelle and Claudia had several customers when they entered, so they acted like other customers and looked at the selection of books. Madison was thrilled when she located a table setup with paperback books titled, M. McKenzie, *Law Enforcement Like a Girl.*

Claudia joined them at the table. She said, "It's great to reconnect with you, Madison. We are doing better here in the community closer to the university. And did you notice the coffee bar? Michelle is really proud of that."

Finally, Michelle got loose from the demanding customer, apparently buying a stockpile of Cliff Notes. "I'm sorry, Maddie, I couldn't afford to lose that sale," Michelle said and hugged her old friend from back in the day, when her store was in Atlanta. "You look wonderful. It was a dream come true when Bryce told me he'd run across Rick. I just couldn't wait to see both of you." She gently hugged Rick, too.

"I'm not breakable, Michelle," Rick said. He pulled her into a stronger embrace. "We're happy seeing you again, too. Small world, isn't it? Finding you through your boyfriend."

"My fiancé, you mean?" She flashed a nice diamond ring on her left hand. "Bryce popped the question last weekend!"

"Congratulations!" Maddie and Rick said simultaneously.

"Thank you, I love him so much," Michelle said. "Of course I'd attract the law!" She picked up a book. "He told you about these?"

"Yes, and I'm absolutely baffled," Maddie said. "I hadn't heard of them. I want to buy every volume."

"I can do better than that," she said and pulled Maddie toward the back room. "I had this printed for you and only you." She lifted a sizable hardback-covered book from a desk. "This is a collection of all the stories, in order as I published them. It's my thank you gift to you for the way you helped me." And she added, "You too, Rick."

Just as Claudia was leaving for the day, Bryce came in the front door. "You're coming to the house to eat with us, aren't you?" he asked.

"I can't; I had a previous engagement, and I'm really sorry it isn't anything I can cancel. Maybe next time you all get together."

"Good night, Claudia!" Maddie called out. "I'm so glad we saw you again. We won't be strangers in the future, I promise!"

"You better not be," Claudia said and locked the door behind her and left.

"Why is Bud locked inside your SUV? He's welcome in here," Bryce confronted Rick.

"We weren't sure, so I thought we'd ask first," Rick explained.

"Let me close out the register. Bryce and I will slip out the back," Michelle said. "Meet you around front, after I set the alarm."

Maddie and Rick followed Bryce and Michelle to the north side of the interstate into a well-maintained gated community. They drove to the top of a wooded ridge among high-dollar homes and condo complexes until they could see nothing but a final row of multi-level two- and three-story units. Inside the condo unit reflected Michelle's personal touches of art and her colorful nature. She was an extremely talented decorator.

"I love your interior design," Maddie expressed as she examined the many lovely forest and wildflower paintings. "You painted these, I can tell."

Michelle nodded with pride. "I went from watercolor notecards to canvas."

"These need to be displayed in a gallery." Maddie pulled Rick over to look at one she recognized. She said, "This is the Hidden Valley. And that's the lady slipper orchid that blooms in the valley of North Georgia."

"These are remarkable, Michelle," Rick said. "Why not put them in your bookstore?"

Michelle shrugged her shoulders, saying, "I love them right where they are."

"And so do I," Bryce said, hugging the artist he loved.

Bryce pulled a couple of beers from the fridge. He and Rick walked onto the back deck, off the kitchen. "How's this for a view?"

Rick shook his head slowly. "Now, that's a view! My gosh, you can see all the way to the Smokies. Is that Mount Le Conte?"

Bryce nodded. "Michelle accuses me of falling for her condo and not her." He laughed.

"Stop telling our secrets, Bryce," Michelle said, and Maddie joined

CABIN IN THE COVE

them, carrying glasses of wine. "Do you know how many men I had to drag up here before I snagged one I wanted to share my view with?"

The dinner and the company were a welcome release for Rick and Maddie. They'd been under so much pressure the last couple of months. The outside deck called to them for a while.

Bryce's phone rang, but he silenced it. And then it rang again, so he looked closer at the caller ID. "I should take this," he said and got up, walking into the house. In just a minute, he rushed back out. "Come in here and look at the breaking news on TV. That was my sergeant on the phone."

He'd already tuned into the local channel. A video played while writing at the bottom of the screen scrolled, *One dead, two injured in Knox Co. Courthouse, shooter fled into the downtown area...*

A captain of the Knoxville PD was speaking on the TV, "The Knoxville S.W.A.T responded to calls of shots fired in the Knox Co. Courthouse this afternoon. Knoxville's City Police Department was on the scene clearing the lower floor of the building. The shooting was on the second floor in the District Attorney's area. One person is dead and believed to have been the shooter. Two civilians were injured and have been transported to the hospital. Possibly a second shooter fled the scene. We are asking that everyone in the immediate area of the courthouse to shelter in place and also in the downtown streets within two blocks of the courthouse. The subject is considered armed and dangerous. Sevierville's acting chief of police, Drew Perry, who was also at the scene, will give a press conference tonight at 8:00. Tune in for updates and further details."

Michelle turned to Bryce and asked, "Does that mean you have to go in?"

"Not unless I get a call from dispatch. Don't worry, Chellie, they have plenty of help."

Rick commented, "Since we need to cross one of the bridges, I guess we should wait here."

"You'll want to wait anyway to hear what your friend, Drew, has to do with this, won't you?" Michelle asked.

"Yeah, if you don't mind." Rick looked to Maddie.

"We sure can't turn it on at the cabin," Maddie said. She shrugged her shoulders.

"Let's go back on the deck to watch the stars until 8:00," Bryce said, walking to the back door.

Drew and Maddie followed, and Michelle came in a couple of minutes.

"I bet you get a good view of the fireworks from here on the Fourth," Maddie said.

"We get to see them from all around the area, but the best view is from Calhoun's on the River, or from one of the many party boats." Michelle sat on one of the tall chairs.

"Naturally," Maddie agreed.

Rick and Bryce settled into a conversation of what Drew possibly could be doing there. Michelle led Maddie through the condo to look at her many artworks she decorated the walls with.

Soon enough, the 8 o'clock news was back on. So, they all sat on the sofa or loveseat in the living room and listened.

Drew introduced himself as the acting chief of police of Sevierville. He began by thanking the reporters for their patience. And then, he referred to a note in his hand. He said, "As of now, we have three dead, including one of our own from the Sevierville Police Department. Officer James Sydney, or Syd, as known by his fellow workers, has been on the Sevierville police force for just over a year. He was 28 years old and single. District Attorney Robert 'Bob' Rice was taken to UT's hospital and is undergoing surgery for wounds to the head and chest. He's in grave condition. Assistant DA, Bruce Smith, is hospitalized but in stable condition."

Drew looked away from his notes and continued, "As many of you know, I am the new acting chief of police due to the ill health of Sevierville's beloved Chief Martin Holt, who remains in Vanderbilt University Hospital. I was recruited by the FBI while employed in Louisville, Kentucky's detective division. My job was investigating a former FBI agent suspected of controlling a dangerous crime ring operating up and down the East Coast from

New York to Miami. I managed to get informants into the ring, and over the past three years, I learned of a long list of district attorneys, and a state attorney in D.C., who are an intricate part of the crime ring. Instead of their rightful job of getting the law enforced, they were getting criminals off and released to continue their crimes. I was in the DA's office to arrest our very own Bob Rice. We don't know how word got out, but his own crime-related buddies came to kill him. Officer James Sydney was with me to serve the warrant. Eight different arrests were made simultaneously all over the East. None resulted in injuries as we had here today. Buck, a former FBI agent, was here personally to carry out the execution. He also shot Officer Sydney. But I was able to get him before he fled. My prayers are with the officer's parents for their loss of an only son."

Drew looked to the reporters and asked, "I'm sure you have questions? If I can answer them, I'll certainly try."

"Will you remain with Sevierville PD or go with the FBI?" a reporter in the group shouted out.

"Thank you for asking," Drew said. "We'll have to wait for the next election to get that answer. I moved my family here to reclaim Tennessee as our home." He paused, then continued, "Thank you all. There's an ongoing investigation searching out other members of the ring, but we feel the heads of the snake have been chopped."

Maddie looked at Rick. She said, "Do you buy that?"

"It sounds just crazy enough to make sense," he admitted. "However, I have many questions. What do you feel, Bryce?"

Bryce's phone rang. "It's my sergeant again," he said, then answered, "Bryce here." He listened for a few seconds. "Okay, I'll be there." He turned to Rick to say, "Sarge isn't believing it either. I'm meeting our governor's jet in one hour at the FBO behind the Tyson McGee Airport."

Rick and Maddie loaded Bud into the SUV and said goodbye to Michelle and Bryce. On their way back to the Cove, the two questioned everything they'd already wondered about Drew Perry.

"He was our friend, so maybe we should give him the benefit of the doubt," Maddie suggested.

"Or maybe you should call Nell to get her reaction," Rick said.

"You mean now?" Maddie pulled to the side of the road.

"Why not? He won't be there for a long time. She's alone, free to talk."

Maddie called Nell's cell, and she answered on the first ring.

"Thank goodness, I didn't think you'd ever call me back," Nell said.

"Did you call me?" Maddie asked.

"I've left at least a dozen messages on your cell."

"I haven't gotten them." She scrolled through her recent calls. "Not even today, and I don't have a signal at work." She caught herself before she said any more. She switched the call to speaker.

"I need help," Nell said. "I want to get these babies out of here before Drew comes home tonight. I heard the broadcast, and I just don't know what to believe. I'm frightened of Drew."

Maddie looked at Rick with question in her eyes.

"Do you have a vehicle, Nell?" Rick asked.

"I do, and it's packed already. Where can I meet you?"

Rick set up a time and place to meet Nell. She followed them to the cabin.

27

After putting the babies to bed, Maddie, Nell, and Rick sat in the living room of the cabin to talk. Nell reminded Maddie that she'd told her she was suspicious of Drew's work hours while they were in Kentucky. But Rick spoke up to defend Drew in that respect.

"If he truly was working under cover for the FBI, he would not have regular hours."

"I guess not." Nell lowered her head. "But the thing I question most is the adoption. We decided not to have another baby because of the trouble I had after giving birth to our son. Drew was adamant about me not becoming pregnant. So, we discussed adoption and even went to classes to learn some of the possibilities. We never got called, and I pretty much gave up. Then, just about four weeks ago, he came home from work all excited and said he'd found us a baby girl. He said it was a little underhanded, because the parents were separated, and the dad was still in Ukraine. The mother was in the Louisville hospital. I assumed she'd just given birth. But he said, no, she'd been hurt in an accident. We were chosen to take care of the baby while the mom recovered. But she didn't recover; she died.

"And her husband was also killed. He was a soldier. It didn't make much sense, but after keeping Rose for ten days, I didn't want her going to a stranger. The poor child had been through a rough time when she was first born. And now she'd lost both her parents. I didn't want her put in the foster system. I went before a judge and begged him to let me continue keeping her until the legal papers could get prepared. Luckily, he said yes. We had the papers within a week. That's when Drew told me we needed to relocate to Tennessee for his job. He didn't tell me about the chief of police position till after we came here. We had the papers checked before leaving Kentucky, and we were told everything was in order."

"Nell, he could be telling you the truth," Rick said. "I've known of some fluke dealings that never made a bit of sense. I stopped questioning them." He got up from the sofa. "I need to get my beauty sleep. You gals can continue talking if you want. I'm going to bed."

Maddie heard Rick go out the back door and wondered where he was going. She walked to Nell's room, the one with the twin beds. They'd made a bed for Rose out of her car carrier. She was still so small for her age that she fit snug but slept comfortably. Nell would put her in bed with her if she woke up.

Maddie changed into a pair of shorty pajamas and returned to her room just as Rick came back inside. "Where did you go?" she asked him.

"I checked Nell's car for a tracker," Rick said. "Just happened to think that if he thought she'd leave, he'd put one in it to find her. And I don't want him finding us."

"Smart thinking."

The next morning, Maddie drove to see her captain at the ranger's office. "Did you hear the news last night?" she asked him.

"I did, and I immediately thought of you," Captain Ford said.

"We were in Knoxville with friends when we heard. In fact, the officer we were with had to meet the governor's jet at the airport last night as we left," Maddie explained. "Of course, we haven't heard anything this morning."

"Oh, so you didn't know? The DA didn't make it. He died while in surgery," Captain Ford told her.

"Aw, that's another one on Buck's head. Drew says he shot both the DA and the officer, Sydney. But what I can't get out of my mind is how this Buck guy keeps escaping jail. He's become a real Houdini. But I guess he won't do any more killing or escaping. Drew shot him."

"I heard through the grapevine that the DA had two different calipers of bullets in him. In his head was a .38, and a .44 Mag in his chest."

"Who told you that?" Maddie asked.

"I know someone in the morgue. And that's all you need to know," Ford laughed.

"Nothing surprises me with this case."

"Actually, I was surprised you came in today. I told my nephew he'd be on his own today. I think he rather liked the idea." Captain Ford stood up and said, "If you want to go back home, that wouldn't be a problem."

"I was going to ask you, because on our way home, I called Nell, Drew's wife," Maddie said. "She has been trying to get in touch with me. She didn't know where we were. So, she and her two babies are at the cabin with us. We had her follow us to the cabin and swore her to secrecy. She says she's gotten suspicious and is now afraid of Drew. So, he has no idea where she is right now. So, if he calls here, let us know on the SAT phone."

"He'll go to that officer I met at Rick's apartment," Ford said. "He watched when Bryce was talking so chummy with Rick. He's a smart and observing fellow. So, if he's crooked, he'll find out how to reach you all. Didn't you tell me that Nell has no family here?" Captain Ford walked outside with Maddie to her SUV. "If you need any help, use the SAT phone, and I'll be there ASAP. Did I tell you I was a SEAL? Retired, of course, but I'm no stranger to fighting."

"Wow, no," Maddie said. "A SEAL, huh? Well, that explains a lot of things I've observed." Maddie offered her handshake. "Thank you for your service, Captain Ford." She saluted him. "Drop by the cabin sometime. I'd love hearing some stories." She got in her SUV to go home. "Oh, one more thing. Has Liz been in the Cove today?"

"I haven't seen her," Ford said. "But if I do, I'll tell her to stop by."

"Thank you. I want her to meet Nell. They'd get along nicely." Maddie waved goodbye and drove back to Rich Mountain.

When she arrived at the cabin, she saw Liz and Randy parked in front. Several chairs had been brought out to the porch. But she didn't see anyone or Bud either. She stuck her head in the house and called out to Rick. Then, she walked to the backyard to find everyone sitting around the fire pit. Little Junior was roasting a marshmallow over a tiny blaze, just big enough to slightly brown his marshmallow. Liz was holding Rose, and Randy was wiping a cradle with a wet cloth.

"What's happening, folks?" Maddie realized they had not heard her drive up.

"Hey, you're back," Nell said. She ran to hug Maddie. "Randy and Liz stopped by to check on Rick, and they were surprised he has a new woman and two kids." Nell laughed.

"He's fast, isn't he, Randy?" Maddie played along. "Where'd you get that cradle?"

"It was in the attic," Randy said. "The minute we met Rose, we knew what she needed. So, I'm bringing it into the twenty-first century for her. I'm cleaning it with Minwax."

"Say, that's nice! Did you sleep in it, Liz?"

"As a matter of fact, I did, and so did my dad and my aunts and uncles." Liz acted very proud of the antique cradle.

"Obviously, you met Nell. Where'd you get the marshmallows?"

"In the motorhome; Shirley brought them," Liz said. "She told me she had them, but we never got them out over the weekend. As soon as little DJ saw the firepit, he asked where the marshmallows were. So, I helped myself."

"Captain Ford gave me the day off," Maddie said. "I'm about to be out of a job, if his nephew does well by himself today."

Rick walked over and hugged his wife. "I guess you heard the DA didn't make it? Randy told me."

"Yeah, and Captain Ford has connections that told him the DA had two different calipers of slugs in him," Maddie said.

"Really?" The surprise on Rick's face spoke volumes. "The .40 to his head...What went through his heart?"

"How would you know those were the places he was wounded?" Maddie asked.

"Bryce commented last night that if Buck shot him, it would be through the head. And I know Drew well enough that he goes for center mass, and that would be closest to his heart." Rick looked into Nell's shocked eyes. "I didn't intend on you hearing that."

"So, you're saying my husband shot the DA also?" Nell's mouth quivered.

Liz rushed over and picked up little DJ to distance him from the conversation. Randy joined her as they distracted him.

"I'm sorry, Nell," Rick said. "We talk too blunt for you and the children. I really didn't think." He walked away.

"He's right, Nell," Maddie said. "It's different with us. We are used to discussing everything. I'm sorry you heard that, but unfortunately, it was either Drew or the officer who died. And normally, a .45 is not an official service weapon. I promise we won't talk anymore about this. Please forgive us." Maddie led Nell into the cabin. "You look tired. While we have Liz here to entertain DJ and Rose, why don't you take a nap?"

"I'd like that, Maddie, and I don't think DJ paid any attention," Nell said. "It hadn't crossed my mind that Drew was capable of this type of behavior. He has not been himself, you know?"

"Yes, I agree, but we have no idea what he's been through. He'd never hurt you and the kids. I do know that much."

Maddie watched Nell go upstairs. Then, she went back outside. Liz walked DJ, and Randy carried Rose down to the creek. So, Maddie returned out back and walked to Rick. "It's okay; she's distraught and I suggested she take a nap," she said. "Liz and Randy are playing with the kids and Bud down by the creek. Come here, babe. Nell understands. She was caught off guard. She doesn't look at the situation like we do." Maddie threw her arms around Rick's neck. "I guess you were right. I'm not the girly type like Nell. Does that disappoint you?"

Rick rested his forehead against hers. "Not at all. I like my strong woman. The fact that you and I can talk shop and target practice together means a lot more to me than tiptoeing over what I say in front of you. I love you, Madison, with all my being. I wouldn't want you any other way."

The day went smoothly after all, and by the time Liz and Randy decided they'd better get home, both DJ and Rose were sound asleep in the motorhome. Maddie said that would be a fun place for them, and she was right. Since Jess and Shirley wouldn't be back for a few days, she thought it might be more comfortable for Nell and the kids. Nell agreed and put their things inside for the night. At least she didn't have to worry about DJ falling down the large staircase in the cabin.

Just before sunset, Captain Ford pulled into the yard. Bud raced to meet him. Ford said he'd had a call from Drew on his office phone. Drew was checking out the numbers from Buck's phone. "I played dumb and didn't give him any information at all."

"Yeah," Rick said. "He got in touch with Officer Bryce Watkins also. He knows Nell came to us. She had nowhere else to go, but he doesn't know where we are. Bryce convinced him to give her some time and he'd get a message to us if Drew pushes harder. I'm going to get in touch with him in a few days. I think he'll talk to me. But we appreciate you keeping our secret."

"Maddie, you were a big help with my nephew," Ford said. "He's feeling good with the position. Oh, and I nearly forgot to tell you. I was able to locate that boy's father. The illegal? Yeah, he's back in the states now, and I've put in a request for the Forestry to sponsor him. He's going to the training at Tremont. I might even get him to work with me in the Cove, eventually."

"That's great. Have you talked to his wife and son?" Maddie asked.

"No, but I thought I'd let Liz do that."

"She was here all day. You just missed them both. You have a number for Liz, don't you?'

"Yes," the captain said. He pulled an envelope from his shirt pocket. "And I have this for you." Ford handed her the envelope. "You are always welcome to give me a hand in the Cove, and you better stop in and visit when you are there."

"Oh, I will. I promise. And I'll bring Bud to see you."

Maddie and Bud walked back to the house after Bud escorted the captain's truck out to the road.

Nell came in the back door. "I should fix something for the kids and get them fed," she said. "They will go to bed early this evening. The country life is wearing them out!"

"Will they eat homemade chicken noodle soup? I put some on in the crockpot this morning. It's simmered on low all day. I checked it a little while ago. It's perfectly tender. We have fresh applesauce in jars that Shirley brought. I know they'll eat applesauce. We adults can have salad if we want. There's a fridge full of vegetables in the motorhome."

"I'd be good with just the soup," Nell said

"Me too," Maddie said. "Especially with that loaf of crusty bread that Liz brought. Her neighbor bakes fresh bread every morning. And it's so good!"

Rick came in the door with DJ swinging from his leg and Rose in his arms. Maddie stared at him till tears welled up in her eyes.

"Now, there's something I thought I'd never see," Nell said. She took Rose from him and laughed. "Rick, kids look good on you."

He reached for DJ and lifted him up to his shoulders. "You mean like this?"

DJ held on with both hands tightly in Rick's hair. "Down, put baby down," DJ spoke in a giggling tone.

"Be careful, Rick. I'm pretty sure DJ weighs more than you're supposed to lift," Maddie said. She reached for the little boy.

"Yes, he's over 27 pounds by now!" Nell said. She pulled DJ's hands loose so Maddie could take him. "You ready to eat, DJ? Maddie made your favorite chicken noodle soup."

"Zoup," Rose said. "Zoup."

After feeding them, Nell took the kids up to the shower. "I might as well shower with them; I'm going to be wet anyway," she called down the stairs.

The SAT phone rang, so Rick answered it. He listened for a few minutes. He turned to Maddie and asked, "Do you think she's ready to talk with Drew?"

Maddie ran up the stairs and caught Nell before she got in the shower. "Do you want to talk to Drew?" she asked. "He's having Officer Watkins call on the SAT phone."

Nell sat on the floor next to the shower. "Does he know where we are?" she asked.

"No," Maddie answered. "I'll take over here if you want to go downstairs."

Nell got up and slowly walked to the door. "Do you think I should?"

"Do you still love him?" Maddie asked

Nell nodded but couldn't speak. She turned and ran down the stairs.

The kids went right to bed in the motorhome before the sun was fully down. Maddie and Nell sat outside on the chairs. They talked until Rick came back with Bud. He'd been in the creek and was soaking wet.

"I just put him in the shower and rinsed him off," Rick said. "He must have discovered the minnows. He was soaked to the skin and smelled like fish."

"Do you have the leash on him?" Maddie asked, looking at Bud in the dark. "Otherwise, he's going to wallow in that fresh dirt."

"Yeah, I've got him tied to me. I can put him in the motorhome with DJ."

"I think not, Rick," Nell cut in. "Remember, whatever you do now will come back to haunt you when you and Maddie have one." She pretended to threaten him. "You heard what Drew said. Do you believe him?"

"I think I do, Nell," Rick said. "Drew has never been violent. He only did what he feels was the right way to end this. He knew about my dealings with Buck. I think he wanted to help me as much as his family by getting you back into Tennessee. He sounds very convincing to me. How do you feel?"

"I want to believe him. It's just that I've never seen him so quiet and determined to get something done. He scared me. If he'd only told me what he was doing, I could have accepted it. I don't say I like it. But Drew is a good man. I love him with everything I have. I wouldn't know what to do without him."

"Then, you need to let him know," Maddie said. "Do you want to go back to your house? I'll keep the kids."

"Yeah, that will be a great test to see if Maddie can handle children," Rick said. "After all, we can always give yours back to you." He stood up from the bench he sat on and wrapped his arms around Maddie. "Don't you think she'll be a good mom? I mean, look how well she raised Bud."

Nell laughed, "That's just a little bit different than raising a child."

"How's it different?" Rick winked at Nell. "Maddie has Bud trained better than any child ever could be."

Nell took about five minutes to get her things together and headed out in the dark to return to Drew.

"Okay, I have the route programed into the GPS in your car," Rick said. "Follow every turn she tells you, and you'll be there in about an hour. Call Drew as soon as you have a cell signal." He hugged Nell, and so did Maddie.

"Be careful."

Maddie and Rick walked to the motorhome. "She'll be okay," Maddie said. "She's a good driver, and I know she'll recognize where she is when she gets to Townsend."

"I wouldn't have let her leave if I was the least bit worried about her."

Rick opened the door. "Are you going to sleep in here with them?"

"Yeah, they like it," Maddie said. "It's like a playhouse to DJ. Are you going to sleep in the house?"

"No, I'm staying with you," Rick said and pulled her close, kissing her like it was the very first time. "You might even enjoy the camping idea. Someday, we'll have to leave this lovely cabin. Maybe we should get a motorhome and tour the United States."

"I would love that, Rick," Maddie said. She held tightly to him for another kiss. "We better do it before we get a house full of kids."

The next morning, Maddie woke to the sound of a car horn. She looked out the window of the motorhome. It was Nell and Drew. She didn't wake the kids. She slipped outside, closing the door quietly.

Rick and Bud were already in the front yard when she rounded the corner of the cabin.

"I guess this means you two have made up," Maddie said and walked to Nell's side. "Come in, and let's fix some breakfast. Your children are still sleeping."

Drew exited the car and came to Maddie. He said, "You are one of the strongest women I've ever met. I want you to know I was also trying to protect you. You're the hardest-headed woman I've met, too. But I love you, Madison. Never doubt that." He embraced her with a bear-like hug.

Rick and Drew walked around to the backyard to listen for the kids to wake while Maddie and Nell made an old country breakfast.

Rick sat on the edge of the porch while Drew looked at the fire-pit.

"Drew, I gotta ask you, what caliper you were shooting?" Rick said.

"Figured you would. Mine is a .357 Mag. Buck had a .44 S&W, and the other shooter a .380 Auto. The lab is doing an investigation, as they should."

"Good to hear." Rick stood, looking straight into Drew's eyes. "Buck had a .357 Mag through the heart. Good shooting. Who contacted you

CABIN IN THE COVE

originally for the assignment?"

"You know I can't reveal that information," Drew said, evading the question. "I made some friends in Kentucky. You shouldn't be surprised; I'd think you of all people would want this mess to end. I haven't forgotten the things you told me about your days working under Buck. Maybe you forgot. Maybe your deposition wasn't the way he remembered it. But Buck wanted you and Maddie dead."

"Don't get me wrong, I'm glad it's over," Rick said. "I only hope you didn't cross any lines in the process. That's how Buck fell into the lap of crime. I don't want that for you. And I don't want any more hiding for Maddie and me."

Rick walked toward the motorhome. When he opened the door, DJ flew down the steps and leapt into his daddy's arms. Rick went inside to pick up Rose, who began crying, seeing her brother missing. Together the men carried the kids into the cabin.

"I smell breakfast," Drew said.

"Biscuits and gravy, with sausage and hash brown potatoes," Rick announced "Did you fry up a dozen eggs? Rose and DJ are hungry!"

"You know we did!" Maddie chuckled.

Drew and Rick got a good taste of old-time cooking on the kitchen fireplace. They all sat around the big family table, talking, eating, and thanking God for their good fortune.

Maddie broke the news that she and Rick were through chasing bad guys and enforcing the law. They'd become gypsies, traveling in a camper, hopefully fulfilling their dreams of beautiful children.

The cabin in the Cove would forever be solid ground to come back to. When they told Randy and Liz of their plan, Randy promised he'd provide a campground for anyone wanting to get in touch with the old ways.

Michelle and Bryce planned a fall wedding on the cabin property. Shirley and Jess stayed in Cold Creek, close to the restaurant, but their motorhome became a permanent fixture as their private Airbnb in the Cove.

261

Drew stepped into Captain Ford's shoes when Ford retired from the rangers. The cloud of suspicion was never really far from Rick's mind. He and Drew might some day in the distant future resolve the issues between them. For now, their wives maintained a sisterly relationship, keeping friendship close to the heart.

THE END

About the Author

Bev Freeman, born in Virginia, lived in the Appalachian Mountains until her teens. Her family relocated to Florida in 1963. Missing the mountains and changing seasons birthed a love for writing, allowing her an escape for at least a short stay. In 1993, Bev and her son followed her parents back to the Appalachian region. Writing became her passion once more. In 1996, she married a local, God-fearing man, and life is beautiful in East Tennessee. She has three spirited grandsons living close by. Bev's role as caregiver for her 91-year-old mother ended in February 2023, affording her time for completion of book four—*Cabin in the Cove*, a continuation of *The Madison McKenzie Files*.

www.ingramcontent.com/pod-product-compliance
Lightning Source LLC
Chambersburg PA
CBHW031940010726
47493CB00007B/2014